Wayward Fortune

Jeffrey Clayhold

For Deborah

Part One

1

"T HIS SCIENCE FICTION STORY is starting out just the way it should," thought Jorgan Rome, "Inside the head of its brooding protagonist." Soon, he realized, the action would pick up and the interiority would disappear forever. But for now it seemed just about right. He brooded a few moments more. He rolled over in his bunk. As he looked out the porthole he saw that the star field was as beautiful as ever. It looked just like a sheet of black velvet, backlit, with light leaking through tiny pin holes.

Jorgan Rome almost missed the first sign of the trouble to come. He was ready to turn away from the porthole when he saw a couple of thalden appear out of nowhere and attached themselves to the port and starboard navigation centers. "They won't be coming for me," he thought, "but this will complicate things." As it turned out, he was wrong about that.

He had signed on as an assistant chef aboard the Vandin-fala, a sleepy cruiser servicing the Barthan sector. His job, feeding day-trippers and pensioners, allowed him to travel throughout the sector without drawing attention. His duties were preparing the lunch buffet and keeping the kitchen provisioned. It left him enough time for his own projects as the Vandinfala traveled the galaxy.

Jorgan Rome nearly fell out of his bunk when the cruiser hove suddenly to starboard. He was alone in his cabin and that was good. "Just blend in and I'll be OK," he thought. "We'll ride this out, deal with their formalities, and be underway again. If only I'm not too late!" Then he saw the ship appear in his window as the cruiser continued to turn. His heart sank. This would be no ordinary customs inspection. The ship that he saw from his window was long and narrow, a Mantar class vessel flying the royal standard. "Just keep your head down, Mr. Assistant Chef!" he told himself.

The Vandinfala lurched again as it was forcibly docked to the Mantar warship. Jorgan Rome did what everyone aboard the Vandinfala was doing, hiding the valuables and keeping out of sight.

"Jorgan Rome to the Reception Room! Jorgan Rome to the Reception Room!" Great, he thought, we're entertaining them now! He made his way down the gangways to the Reception Room.

Enormous windows, eight meters tall, paneled the walls on three sides of the great Reception Room. The Mantar warship was docked at an angle to the Vandinfala. It dominated the view out of the windows from the lower left to the upper right. From every porthole of the warship, faces peered out from across the space between the ships and into the Reception Room.

Entering through the main archway, he found a scene of mayhem. All the ship's officers were manacled and hanging from the walls. Several hundred passengers were flat out on the floor, asleep, in suspension, or maybe worse. Standing in the middle of the great room was Calcha herself! The would-be Empress was here in person! Her robots blocked the exits. A pair of robots scanned Jorgan Rome for weapons and then stepped away.

The first words that Calcha said were "So you are Jorgan Rome?"

Jorgan Rome nodded.

Jorgan Rome observed the arrangement of Calcha's escort detail. Two robots in front, two robots in the rear, and one robot on each side. Humans were relegated to the periphery. That was interesting.

Calcha took her own time to study Jorgan Rome. "Why you look like…you look like the kind of person I don't appreciate very much."

The robots in her retinue thought that was funny. The lights on their faces flashed randomly and brightly for a few moments. Jorgan Rome didn't respond. He observed one of Calcha's human attendants pick up a Reception Room chair and bring it in her direction. A flash of disdain from Calcha was enough. Two robots turned to block his path. He set the chair down as if he had intended to put it just where it was.

Finally, Jorgan Rome said, "I work in the galley. How may I help you?"

Calcha raised her eyebrows and made a small "o" with her mouth, a look of exaggerated disbelief. "I think you're a space adventurer," she said.

Jorgan Rome said nothing and kept his face blank. Some might have taken him for slow-of-mind. Out of the corner of his eye he noticed a faint glistening, just a small spot, on the ceiling of the Reception Room. The ceiling was ornately painted and bejeweled, but this shimmering little patch was new. Jorgan Rome avoided looking at it because he didn't want anyone to follow his gaze. He was certain that only he had noticed it.

Calcha continued. "I think we might have to arrange a final space adventure for you," she said. "One that all of us here will be able to watch," said Calcha, indicating the windows of the Reception Room.

Jorgan Rome understood now why all those faces were pressed into the portholes of the Mantar warship. They knew what was coming. They wanted to see for themselves. For Jorgan Rome, the threat of summary execution was his cue. It was his moment to disable the nearest pair of robots and bound out of the Reception Room. But he didn't move. The crew of the Vandinfala had been manacled to the wall but he, Jorgan Rome, had been left unrestrained. It meant that Calcha had some other hold over him. Jorgan Rome relaxed his shoulders, let his arms fall lower to his sides, and stood taller.

Calcha nodded at a robot standing next to her. The robot stepped forward and, in a voice too loud for the room, said, "Jorgan Rome, you destroyed a military base in the Bimlan Autonomous Region."

"I had to do it," admitted Jorgan Rome. And it was true— from his perspective. The base had been established to lend secret support to the Vegans in their war against the Ovolac-tans. Once the Vegans had the upper hand, Calcha would simply declare the Velar Fricative and it would all be over in Bimlan. So Jorgan Rome intervened. He had made it appear as if a small meteor strike on the outer dome had damaged a coolant line. Flash-frozen coolant caused a crack in the inner dome. The base was wrecked without casualties. A military engineer was blamed. Nobody even knew that Jorgan Rome had been anywhere nearby. Nobody knew or cared who Jorgan Rome even was. So how could Calcha possibly know what he had done?

"I want to be very clear," said a hoarse and broken voice. Everyone turned. The captain of the Vandinfala, chained to the wall, was speaking. "This person…this individual…had no permission to…" A robot moved with blinding speed over to the wall and struck the captain hard on the head. The captain slumped and went quiet. Calcha nodded her acknowledgment. She prodded the robot at her side to continue.

"Jorgan Rome," boomed the robot, "You fomented a coup on Ralwentalus."

"I wouldn't call it a 'coup,'" said Jorgan Rome without affect. "But I did replace their governing council. It was necessary." It had also been done secretly. Nobody should have known that Jorgan Rome played any role in the events on Ralwentalus.

Calcha looked Jorgan Rome up and down. "There is no way that this is going to end well for you," she said.

On his far left, Jorgan Rome noticed the galley chef, chained to the wall and staring daggers at him. In his peripheral vision, Jorgan Rome saw that the small glistening spot on the ceiling had spread over much of the room. Jorgan Rome only noticed what was on the ceiling because he knew to look for it. Ahead of him, Jorgan Rome observed that the human attendant, recovered from his humiliation over the chair, was settling in to enjoy Jorgan Rome's predicament.

"Jorgan Rome," boomed the robot, "You diverted an expeditionary force on a secret…" The robot stopped. Calcha wasn't paying attention. She was in a private conference with another, smaller, robot in her retinue. Calcha nodded. The small robot left the room. "I'm sorry," said Calcha. "Please continue."

"That's OK," said Jorgan Rome. "I countermanded their orders and sent the expeditionary force where they were needed." A murmur went through the room. The robot raised a hand for silence. Jorgan Rome continued, "The expeditionary force arrived in time. They saved hundreds of thousands of lives. They deserve medals."

"They didn't get medals," said Calcha. "That's not what happened. Perhaps you would like to rescue them? I have to tell you that you are too late."

Jorgan Rome made no visible reaction. He noticed something happening within the glistening areas on the ceiling. It was something he was partly expecting. Little white crystals were beginning to form under the shiny surface. Those little white crystals were explosive.

Calcha switched languages. She began to speak fluent, if accented, Naveeran. Naveeran was a holy language, a dead language, a language that only Jorgan Rome spoke natively. It was the language of his home planet, gone in an instant, but glorious in its time. It had been a realm of hope and of learning. With a hundred schools of philosophy and ruled by the wise and kind Khadar, Jorgan Rome grew up knowing that his very own planet was a model of civilization and good living for the rest of the galaxy. Or at least it had been until the day when the planet was burnt and all life was extinguished. Their civilization, language, all the philosophies, and a billion lives were lost in a flash. Only by a fluke had Jorgan Rome lived. He told only a very few people of his origins. So far as the galaxy was concerned, there had been no survivors from Naveer. Everyone knew that Calcha had spent years on Naveer as a prisoner or hostage, depending on who told the story. What Calcha said in Jorgan Rome's language was, "I have your daughter."

Jorgan Rome started. Calcha smiled. "So, it's true," she said, reverting to her own language. "You are Jorgan Rome from Naveer. You are Jorgan Rome, the very last disciple of the Ammun Ghobar!" A murmur went around the room again. The robot called for silence. "So sad," said Calcha. "But it does mean that there is something that you can do for me." The small robot entered the room again. He was followed by a pair of larger robots who escorted Jorgan Rome's daughter, Raia, into the room. The robots each held her by an arm and they walked her just a little too fast for her comfort.

Raia was twelve and she was his adopted daughter. Jorgan Rome and his sidekick, Cholley, had found her locked in the cargo hold of an empty freighter that was hurtling into a gas giant planet. She would have perished. They all would have, if Cholley hadn't pulled that maneuver which was the single bravest thing that Jorgan Rome ever witnessed.

Raia was naturally at home on a spaceship. When Jorgan Rome worked the kitchen, Raia spent mornings in the Vandinfala's engine room or at the navigation controls. Jorgan Rome had hoped that Calcha didn't know about Raia. Somehow, Calcha seemed to know everything.

"Are you prepared now to take this business more seriously?" asked Calcha. Jorgan Rome said nothing. Calcha continued, "Let's recap. This isn't going to end well for you. But if you are helpful, a couple of things can change. Like, who has to witness your final space adventure. Or who has to accompany you."

Raia began to say something but Jorgan Rome shook his head. Over their heads, Jorgan Rome saw more of the little whitish crystals forming. Now there were patches of pale green, too. Raia had noticed them. Jorgan Rome was sure of it. He looked over at Raia and blinked his eyes slowly once. She understood.

"So now we have established what you have done, who you are, and the terms of your cooperation," said Calcha.

"It's time to tell you what I want. I'll need to know about your accomplices. But really all I want from you is the Naveeran Karamand."

Jorgan Rome was stunned. He stared at Calcha. The Naveeran Karamand! All she wanted was the most precious item in the Galaxy, the holiest relic of a dead planet. But what could she do with it? Nothing! It required intensive study just to possess the karamand safely. Using it, even just once, could come at a terrible cost. And nobody alive knew how to use it. Back in the days on his home planet, the karamand had been an icon of the distant past, knowledge of its usage thought to be lost forever. But Jorgan Rome knew better. He had once seen it used by the man who would become his mentor, the Ammun Ghobar. And the Ammun was never the same afterwards. The Ammun once had an easy smile, a warm heart, and a gentle laugh, everyone said. After using the karamand, the Ammun's laughter was never heard again. The karamand was said to change everyone.

The karamand hung from a chain around Jorgan Rome's neck. He did not understand how Calcha could have known that.

"I can offer something in return if that's helpful," said Calcha. She was toying with him. Calcha turned to look behind her. She beckoned a robot forward. The robot a carried glass bowl and set it down on a chair in front of them. The glass bowl held a squirming gelatinous substance. So that's how Calcha knew about Jorgan Rome, the exploits, Raia, the karamand—everything! Somehow she had recovered a piece of Cholley after their adventure with the traitorous Neerlan envoy! Cholley was a gelatinoid. He could ooze undetected into a room or out of a trap. Cholley had saved Jorgan Rome on many occasions. When the Neerlan envoy sealed his escape hatch, a part of Cholley was severed and must have been taken to Calcha!

"So, where is this sidekick of yours?" asked Calcha.

Jorgan Rome shrugged his shoulders. He realized that neither Calcha nor any of her retinue had any experience of full-sized, adult gelatinoids. They seemed unaware of how great was the danger amassing above their heads.

For a few moments nobody spoke. Until Calcha smiled and prodded Jorgan Rome, "The karamand?" Jorgan Rome reached into his shirt. As he did, weapons appeared everywhere. There were at least a dozen bzzapmasters aimed at his head. Jorgan Rome withdrew his empty hand, slowly moved his arms down to his sides with palms open and forward. Calcha gestured for the weapons to be lowered. Jorgan Rome retrieved the karamand. But he wasn't about to bring it to her. Someone would have to come take it. Jorgan Rome held the karamand aloft in his right palm. One of the humans in Calcha's entourage, the one who had earlier offered the chair, decided that delivering the karamand was something that he could do. He marched forward. Approaching Jorgan Rome, the man reached up, but when he touched the karamand he gasped. His eyes bulged. He froze. Paralysis was one of the things that the karamand could do to a person unversed in its proper handling.

The weapons appeared again but there wasn't time. The entire room came under sudden attack from a large gelatinoid, primed and angry, on the ceiling. The gelatinoid threw explosive tendrils like lightning around the room and every tendril found its target. If the target was a robot, the tendril slithered around under its neck until a bolt of bioelectric charge dropped the robot to the ground. If the target was human, they were given a dose of acid and surface toxins that was enough to make them forget any other concerns.

They fell to the ground, too. In less than half a minute, the chaos was complete. Only Jorgan Rome, Raia, and Calcha were left standing. The floor was littered with incapacitated robots and writhing humans. One of them knocked against the paralyzed man with the karamand, toppling him to the ground. The karamand fell and rolled. The single most precious relic of a dead civilization rolled away from Jorgan Rome in the mayhem. It rolled toward Raia. She bent down to pick it up.

"Raia! No!" yelled Jorgan Rome. She glanced at him before plucking the karamand from the floor. "I can do this, Daddy," she said. As she crouched over the karamand, she began speaking a language that neither Jorgan Rome nor anyone else on that ship could understand. Jorgan Rome could barely hear her over the din. And then everything went white. It became so bright that Jorgan Rome had to close his eyes. When he opened them again he saw that he was with Raia and Cholley in an open grass field—the Vandinfala was gone!

"Where are we?" asked Jorgan Rome.

"Earth," said Raia, without expression.

Earth! Raia, who had never once in her life been to Earth, or even near it, had somehow used the karamand to transport halfway across the galaxy to Earth!

"Earth," said Jorgan Rome. "OK, Earth." He thought for a moment. "I guess we're safe here. On Earth." He looked at Raia.

Raia didn't respond. She said nothing. She registered nothing.

Jorgan Rome continued, "But nothing is happening here. We're safe, sure, but safe is not where we need to be. From here it would take four months to get back. We'll be too late!"

"I'm not agreeing with you," said Cholley. "While everyone was screaming and you two were fiddling with that karamand, I reconnected with the other piece of me. I know just a little bit now about Calcha's plans. It all starts on Earth!"

"Well, OK," said Jorgan Rome. "I guess that means we have a head start!" said Jorgan Rome. "Maybe we can get the Dar Telku to help us!"

"Cholley needs an apple!" cried Cholley. There was no response from Raia, or Jorgan Rome, who was deep in thought. "Cholley needs an apple!" he cried again.

Jorgan Rome pulled an apple from his pocket and lobbed it toward Cholley. Cholley splashed up around the apple. The apple dissolved in less than a second, leaving only the seeds. As usual, Cholley expelled the seeds. The seeds flew in random directions and one stuck to Jorgan Rome's cheek. Raia smiled.

2

CHOLLEY THOUGHT FOR a moment. "Well, that was inciting," he said. "What…?" said Jorgan Rome. "That incident, on the ship."

"How do you mean?" asked Jorgan Rome.

"We're on our way, right?"

"Well, yes."

"So I'm ready for my arc. Let's go!"

"I don't know," said Jorgan Rome. "Aren't you being a bit idiocentric? I mean, what if you're not a protagonist here? What if neither of us is?"

"I don't like where you're going with this," said Cholley.

"We should face the possibility. We might be side characters."

Cholley was silent for a moment. "I'm not buying it," he said.

"It's unlikely," agreed Jorgan Rome, "But possible. And that incident? What if the real inciting incident happened long ago? What if the causal shift…what if it happened to somebody else?"

Cholley thought for a moment. "We'll just have to wait and see."

Jorgan Rome nodded.

"What happens next?" asked Cholley.

"You know the drill, old friend. Antagonists and allies. We'll encounter some of each."

"I know," said Cholley. "But if Tom Bombadil shows up, I'm out of here."

Raia had been silent during the conversation. Jorgan Rome turned to her. He studied her face.

"Daddy, I'm OK!" protested Raia. She held out the karamand for her father to take back.

"No, you hold on to that," said Jorgan Rome, handing over the single most precious relic of a lost civilization to a twelve-year-old girl. "I think we'll all be better off with the karamand in your keeping."

Raia said, "My sister and I used to play with one, you know, before..."

Before. Before getting trapped in that cargo hold. Before Cholley saved them all. Before Jorgan Rome adopted her as his daughter. Before she joined Jorgan Rome and Cholley on all those adventures. But what really struck Jorgan Rome was learning that Raia had a sister. And there was another karamand somewhere in this galaxy.

Jorgan Rome needed to meditate so he cleared a space and sat. Cholley and Raia went off to reconnoiter the surroundings and perhaps find some food. After a half an hour, they returned and Jorgan Rome roused himself.

"We saw some flags, Daddy!" said Raia.

"What flags, Raia?" asked Jorgan Rome.

"They're square and red. They have three diagonal slits in them."

"We've got to leave this area," said Jorgan Rome. "That's not good."

They hurried towards a forested area nearby. They were deep in the woods when Jorgan Rome suddenly signaled for Cholley and Raia to stop and stay quiet. Listening for a moment, he then silently but urgently gestured for them to crouch low and hide themselves. Three men in uniforms, some kind of patrol, approached. The patrol paused to look around. Their uniforms were black with one red sleeve. The red sleeve had three slits in the upper arm. Bandannas obscured their faces. The patrol moved on.

"Just what I thought!" said Jorgan Rome.

"Who are these knuckleheads?" asked Cholley.

"They're not knuckleheads," said Jorgan Rome. "I'm pretty sure they can be dangerous. They're followers of the Ammun Mettell. I don't know how they came to Earth, but I have an idea." Jorgan Rome sat on a stump in a clearing of the forest. "The Mettellites are from Naveer. They were the so-called, 'hundred-and-first' school of philosophy. They were nothing like the older, established schools. The Mettellites claimed to be nihilists and scoffed at external laws. Their only belief, as they said, in the 'Law of the Self.' The Ammun Mettell commanded complete devotion from his followers."

"That makes no sense," said Cholley. "How can a bunch of self-interested people just give themselves over to another guy, Ammun or not?"

"Well, according to them—and this is ironic—it was all part of the Law of the Self. Their claim was that if the only applicable law is what comes from you, then a promise, an oath, can never be broken. The Ammun Mettell was clever. He made sure to extract an oath of obedience as a condition of joining. But the Mettellites played it both ways when it was convenient for them. They were careful to follow the protocols of a School of Philosophy only for the legitimacy it conferred. You see, it was just an expedient for them. They grew rapidly. Without rules, they were tough. A certain kind of young man was drawn to them, almost magnetically. In less than a year, it seemed that everyone had a colleague, a friend, or family member who went over to the Mettellites. Even my cousin Sam joined."

"The one you looked up to? You mean your cousin, Bob?" asked Cholley. "Only you called him Sam."

"That's right," said Jorgan Rome. "It was a dangerous organization for Sam to join."

"Ooh," muttered Cholley.

Jorgan Rome continued. "Here was the problem. Naveer was a peaceful planet. It was said of Naveer that it had no laws but ten thousand customs. With the Khadar, the Hundred Schools, and the citizenry in agreement, it seemed like everything, all aspects of life, went smoothly. The Mettellites threatened all of that. They used raw power to take over small businesses, citizens councils, and then bigger businesses."

Cholley asked, "But what did the Khadar do about it?"

"Nothing, at first. Later, quite a lot, but in his way, a way that no one knew about. As for me, I was a teenager then and very jealous of Sam. I'd see him in that uniform, and I wanted one, too. I wanted to be just like him, but Sam wouldn't let me join. So one day, as he left home in uniform, I followed him. I followed him to the Mettellite Assembly Hall. The Assembly Hall was enormous. It had barricades and Mettellite guards. No ordinary citizen ever entered the Assembly Hall. Even then, before my formal studies, I was adept at jumping walls and avoiding detection so getting inside wasn't difficult for me. I found a ventilation shaft that led to the center of the building. From way up high and in the back, I actually witnessed the Last Meeting of the Mettellites."

"What was it like?" asked Raia.

"To a teenager like me, hiding behind a pillar, I'll tell you this. It was frightening," answered Jorgan Rome. "They had drums, they had flashing lights, they had precision marching everywhere. The Ammun Mettell knew how to work a crowd to his advantage. It was menacing. It felt to me like they were on the edge of violence, every single one of them."

"Now there's one thing you need to understand about the customs we had then. On Naveer, there was a lot of communication among the different Schools of Philosophy. It was an old tradition that an Ammun of any School could address the assembly of any other School. The Ammun Mettell had made cunning use of that protocol when it suited him. That night, I saw that the Ammun Ghobar had arrived to address the Mettellites. He looked so shabby, compared to the Mettellites, in his faded blue robe. The Mettellite crowd didn't try to conceal their contempt. Even the Ammun Mettell was rude, saying things along the lines of 'What can you say to us, old man? Look at us! We are the future!' Even to me, as a teenager, it was shocking."

"The Ammun Ghobar was calm. 'It's true that I don't have much to offer,' he said. 'I don't think you will even understand what it is that I have to say.' He pulled a small object from his cloak. It was the Naveeran Karamand! Then he spoke in a language I had never heard before, and never since—until yesterday," said Jorgan Rome, looking at Raia. "The Mettellites all vanished. They were gone. Every single Mettellite on Naveer disappeared in that moment. They have never been heard from again. At least, not until now."

"So there I was in the enormous, and now empty, Mettellite Assembly Hall, still hiding, especially hiding now, from the Ammun Ghobar. I knew how not to be seen, but he knew I was there behind that ventilation panel. He looked right at me before he turned and left."

"No one knew what had happened to the Mettellites. No one but me, that is. There were rumors only, that the Ammun Ghobar had done something, that he worked at the request of the Khadar, but nothing was known for sure. I knew one thing for sure, though. I wanted to join up with the Ammun Ghobar! The Mettellites were a tough bunch, I thought, but he was tougher! I wanted to be part of that. He wouldn't have me, though."

"Why not?" asked Raia.

"Because he knew my motivation was wrong. I went to see him but his disciples turned me away. I took to secretly following him through the city but he always knew I was there. He told me to leave him alone. Then, to get rid of me I think, he gave me a problem to solve. And I had only two weeks to solve it. I think he thought it would be impossible for me. I was to bring him, within those two weeks, the 'Karakanth Pasrund.'"

"What's that, Daddy?"

"Well, that's another story. The point is, I managed to find it in the nick of time, so I was able to join with the Ammun Ghobar after all." Then Jorgan Rome chuckled. He said, "I do remember thinking it would be an adventure quest, but the Karakanth Pasrund turned out to be a one-thousand-year-old religious poem! I spent ten days without sleep in the library!"

"So I became a disciple of the Ammun Ghobar, but it cost me, though. I lost all contact with my family. They burned with rage at losing Sam. They blamed the Ammun Ghobar. They blamed me after I began my studies with the Ammun." Jorgan Rome paused, lost in thought.

"So now the Mettellites are on Earth," said Cholley.

"Apparently so," said Jorgan Rome.

"I'm pretty sure these knuckleheads figure into Calcha's plans," said Cholley. "I'm thinking that I heard the name, 'Ammun Mettell,' when that little part of me was with Calcha."

Suddenly the Mettellite patrol reappeared in the clearing. There were three of them, one guarding the entrance to the clearing. The nearest one said brusquely, "All of you. Stand up. Put your hands in the air."

Cholley giggled. "Didn't I say they were knuckleheads?" Suddenly all the Mettellite weapons were pointed at him. The Mettellite said, "You think that's funny? You're only a microsecond away from being vaporized." Turning to Jorgan Rome, he asked, "Who are you?"

"We are visitors here," Jorgan Rome said plainly. "We have no food and no shelter. Will you help us?" Jorgan Rome stole a glance at Cholley and glimpsed the beginnings of rotation. Cholley was beginning to circulate inside.

"No," answered the Mettellite. "How did you get here? How did you get past the perimeter defense?"

"Well, that's a long story," said Jorgan Rome and suddenly all the weapons were pointing at him. Normally, the weapons would not have presented Jorgan Rome with any difficulty, but Raia was here. And then there was the problem of Cholley, who was circulating a little faster each moment.

"Well that's just fine," said the Mettellite who seemed to be leading the interrogation, "because we have all the time we need to hear it." No you don't, thought Jorgan Rome. With Cholley spinning like that, you've got less than a minute.

"May we sit down?" asked Jorgan Rome.

"No," said the Mettellite interrogator, who had obviously never seen a full-fledged gelatinoid attack, or he wouldn't be standing so close to Cholley. When Cholley flung himself out from a circulating flow state, the attack was especially grim. There wasn't much time left to save the lives of the Mettellite patrol.

Jorgan Rome played a hunch. Turning to the Mettellite at the entrance to the clearing. "It's you, Sam, isn't it?"

3

THE METTELLITE AT THE HEAD of the clearing stepped forward, removing the bandanna from his face. It was Sam! "Lower your weapons," he said. The interrogator kept his weapon leveled at Jorgan Rome. "This one likes to shoot things. Lower your weapon!" Cholley was still spinning.

"How are you, Sam?" asked Jorgan Rome.

"Not well," said Sam. "Who are your friends?"

"Sam, this is my daughter, Raia. And this is my good friend, Cholley. Old Cholley, who has saved my life on many occasions."

"That makes him a friend of mine, too," said Sam. Cholley stopped rotating. Jorgan Rome breathed easier. "So what happened, Sam? How did you end up on Earth, of all places?"

"The last thing I wanted. You know, I joined up with the Ammun Mettell because I wanted to run things. Now, I'm on Earth. I run a forest patrol."

"What happened?"

"Who knows. One minute we are all in the Great Assembly Hall, and then we wake up in a dark holding pen.

We were put there somehow, by some magic, by the Ammun Ghobar." Sam spat on the ground. "Curse that name forever!"

No one spoke for a few moments. Jorgan Rome wasn't about to mention his own connection to the Ammun Ghobar. Jorgan Rome observed Sam closely. There was no sign that Sam knew. "We ended up in exile, all of us," continued Sam. "On Gurfann."

Jorgan Rome made a face.

"Been to Gurfann, have you then?" asked Sam.

Jorgan Rome shook his head.

"Well, don't go there," said Sam. "It was bad enough that some of us had telescopes. They were pining for the homeworld, I guess. That's how we saw it happen. We actually saw our own planet die."

"Solar flare," muttered Jorgan Rome.

"No. A mass ejection event," said Sam. "Fried the place. And we watched." Sam looked at his cousin. "I thought you were dead, Jorgan Rome!"

"I was...I was away," said Jorgan Rome. How could Jorgan Rome tell Sam why he was away or where he had been at that time?

"We escaped it. Looks like you did, too. We even escaped from Gurfann in all the confusion. Not that it matters very much. Look where we ended up—on this backwater in the middle of galactic nowhere, marching around a forest."

"Maybe I can help," said Jorgan Rome.

"What can you do to help, little cousin?" asked Sam.

"Maybe not so much. Maybe a lot," said Jorgan Rome, who was now looking at the other members of the Mettellite patrol. "Introduce your colleagues to me, Sam."

"This is Mathori, he's our scout," said Sam, indicating the Mettellite who hadn't spoken yet. Mathori and Jorgan Rome shook hands. "And this fellow here, who was giving you all the trouble, is Ketchett." Ketchett reluctantly shook hands with Jorgan Rome. Jorgan Rome sat down on a rock. He said, "I can try to convince all of you that you're free. Nobody has any power over you, Sam. Not even the Ammun." Ketchett reached for his weapon. Sam gestured for him to stand down.

"Not sure about that" said Sam after a pause. "A Mettellite promise, like I made to the Ammun, has the force of law."

"But don't your Central Principles include a Rule of Voluntary Associativity?"

"How could you know that?" asked Sam. "Yes, sure, that's what allows us to organize, despite the Law of the Self. What are you getting at?"

"Just this. If anyone, even the Ammun Mettell, is in a non-voluntary situation, such as forced exile, then your promise to the Ammun has no reciprocity. By Mettellite custom, it becomes invalid. You are free, Sam."

Sam grinned. Then he turned serious. "That's all just words, little cousin," he said.

"That's all it ever was," said Jorgan Rome.

Sam studied Jorgan Rome, taking the measure of his cousin.

Jorgan Rome continued, "Maybe it's time for you, for all of you, to get off this planet," said Jorgan Rome, "Sam, you have the whole rest of your life in front of you."

Sam winced. A wave of despondency flashed across his face. "The rest of my life…," he said. Then he brightened. "You're right, of course you are." He sat down next to Jorgan Rome. "I won't stay on this planet," he said, as if to convince himself by hearing it said out loud. Turning to his fellow Mettellites, he asked, "Are you coming with me?" Mathori and Ketchett shook their heads. They would not be coming.

"But are you going to try to stop me?" asked Sam. Mathori shook his head while Ketchett thought about it for a moment. Ketchett shook his head. "What about you, little cousin?"

"I have a hunch that I have some things to do here first. But we'll catch up, OK?"

Sam nodded. "One more thing. These Mettellites," he said, "stay away from them."

"You always used to tell me that," said Jorgan Rome.

"I'm still telling you that," said Sam.

4

"That ventilates the keep," said Jorgan Rome, pulling aside some bushes. He and Raia and Cholley had scrambled halfway down a steep gorge because of what Jorgan Rome expected to find. Sure enough, behind the bushes, all grown over was a rusted, thin metal grate, two meters by two meters. its single remaining hinge threatening to give way at any moment. Cholley flowed through the holes. Jorgan Rome pulled on the grate and watched it plummet a hundred meters to the creek below. He looked up to the castle thirty meters above. There was no response. None of the Mettellites had noticed. Jorgan Rome and Raia clambered inside where Cholley was waiting. At no time did Jorgan Rome need to explain what he had been searching for or why. Cholley and Raia understood the protocols of space adventuring. When you need secret access, or a place to hide, look for a ventilation shaft. Ventilation shafts are the space adventurer's best friend.

"Didn't we promise, like in the last chapter, not to do this thing that we're doing right now?" asked Cholley.

Jorgan Rome shook his head. Raia said, "No."

"So we just walk in on them? Is there no better plan?" Jorgan Rome didn't say anything. He didn't need to. Cholley already knew the answer. There was no better plan or even much of a plan at all. "And why a castle?" asked Cholley.

"No idea," said Jorgan Rome. "Lots of these things on Earth. It was probably derelict and they just moved in."

The ground became smoother, no longer rock and sand as it began to slope upward. A prepared walkway. The air was dryer but stale. "No one comes down here very often," observed Jorgan Rome, "We can use light." He switched on a flashlight. Cholley extended a bioluminescent feeler. They saw that the floor was littered with body parts. All of them from robots. An arm here, a pair of feet there. An entire torso. Rounding a corner, they came across the bodies of six robots. None of them had heads.

"Looks like a robot slaughter," said Cholley.

Jorgan Rome bent down. "These are very old robots. They're not from this century. But they're all the same model." He stood up and thought for a moment. "They sure made them differently back then."

"Different protocol, too, with the old robots," said Cholley. "First thing when you switched them on, they told you their name. Then they would inform you that they were a robot."

Jorgan Rome continued to look around. He nudged a robot torso. "This is peculiar. These robot parts haven't been here very long. One or two years, tops."

Turning another corner, the passage widened into a small room. Opposite them was a fully intact but dormant robot, of the same make as the other robot parts. The robot was shackled to the wall. Next to the robot along the wall were empty sets of shackles. Jorgan Rome went up to the robot. He inspected it closely. Raia and Cholley came forward. Without warning, the robot's face lit up. Raia and Cholley jumped back. Jorgan Rome didn't move. The robot scanned its head from left to right. It made eye contact with Jorgan Rome. The robot spoke with a synthesized female voice. "I am Teera. I am a robot."

"See! Called it!" said Cholley.

"I heard you talking," said Teera.

Jorgan Rome smiled for a moment. Then he asked the robot, "Why are you here?"

"I think it's obvious," said Teera, indicating the manacles. "A better question is why are you here?"

"We're going to…talk…with the people up there," said Jorgan Rome.

"Are you good friends with them?" asked Teera, who continued without letting Jorgan Rome respond, "I didn't think so, or you wouldn't be sneaking in through the gutter."

"Ventilation shaft."

"I'm sure that's an important distinction," said Teera. "But you seem neither swift nor wise. I'm not sure I like your chances."

Jorgan Rome shrugged. "This way?" he asked, indicating one of two exits from the keep.

"Are you going to cut me loose?"

"Yes," said Cholley. "See, I know about these things," he said to Raia, "If we release her, she'll remember us years from now, which is good if we have to face her someday in combat in, like, a big arena."

"I'm not sure," said Teera. "Crowd approval. It can sway your head." Raia smiled. Cholley burned through the manacles. Teera stepped free and said, "I'll show you the way."

Jorgan Rome said, "Are you…"

"Coming with you? Yes. The worst that can happen is I end up back here. As for you, well, that's another matter."

"What we need is a vertical ventilation shaft," said Jorgan Rome.

Teera led them through a labyrinth of underground passageways. No one spoke. She stopped at the bottom of a thirty meter high ventilation shaft. "This is the only way up to the main chambers, unless you want to go knocking at their front door," said Teera.

Jorgan Rome said, "No, this will do," as he looked at the glass-smooth walls of the shaft. Most observers would have said that there were no handholds at all, but Jorgan Rome studied and found his line. "Everyone stay safe," he said, "I'll be back." He proceeded up the shaft. In a couple of places, he bounced from wall to wall as he ascended. In less than a five minutes, he was at the top and leaning over the railing up there. He waved down to Raia, Cholley, and Teera far below. Jorgan Rome hated to leave them there, but there were some things that only Jorgan Rome could do and, besides, he knew they would be safe. He saw the three of them having a discussion at the bottom of the shaft. Then something strange happened. Teera grabbed Cholley and threw him against a wall of the shaft. Cholley dissolved the wall of shaft and made—a handhold! Teera extended a robotic tendril into the handhold as she threw Cholley against the opposite wall to make another handhold. Working as a team, they steadily climbed the shaft. Soon they clambered over the railing and were next to Jorgan Rome. Raia stayed below, but only for a moment. She pulled the Naveeran Karamand from her pocket and vanished. She appeared again at the top of the shaft with Jorgan Rome, Cholley, and Teera.

"We decided to come with you, Daddy." said Raia.

Jorgan Rome laughed. "OK, I deserve it. I won't take my team for granted." Jorgan Rome put his hands, palms flat, on a heavy wood door—the only door—nearby. "There are maybe a dozen Mettellites behind this door," he said, glancing at Raia. Raia pulled the Naveeran Karamand from her pocket and muttered words in different language. "Now I sense an empty room," said Jorgan Rome. "Where did they go?"

"They are down in the tunnels," said Raia.

"Good work," said Jorgan Rome as they entered the room. It was a long narrow room, nearly a hallway, with a single door at the far end. Reaching the door, Jorgan Rome announced, "There are over thirty Mettellites in the next room. They are heavily armed." He looked at Raia.

Raia shook her head. "I can't help," she said. "Too many for me. I don't know where to put them."

"OK," said Jorgan Rome. "We'll have to do this the old-fashioned way. But I'll need help. I can only take care of about half that number by myself. Remember, no killing, just render them harmless."

"Party pooper!" said Teera.

"I'll go in first. Then, Teera, you distract the Mettellites between me and the door. Cholley, you know what to do, but only take out their weapons, OK? Raia you should stay here until the coast is clear. Then bring that bucket over there, full of water, to Cholley. He'll need it." Jorgan Rome went to the door and Cholley began spinning inside. Jorgan Rome opened the door and went in. There was no sound, no reaction from the armed Mettellites. They didn't see him, until it was too late for them. Teera entered, with lights blazing and intense subsonic sound. Any Mettellite who looked up at her was instantly hypnotized. Some went into seizures. Jorgan Rome moved quickly to disable and disarm all the Mettellites at the back of the room. Cholley, spinning rapidly, entered, then exploded. Highly corrosive pieces of Cholley

seemed to go everywhere, but landed only on the exit ter-
minals of the Mettellite weapons. The Mettellite weapons
instantly destroyed. In a matter of seconds, the Mettellites
were dazed or asleep, disabled and disarmed. "Raia, the coast
is clear!" yelled Jorgan Rome. Everyone was safe, except for
the Mettellites and Cholley, who slowly reassembled himself.
Cholley was not well. He was green and very, very slow.

"What's wrong with my little jellypot?" asked Teera.

"That's metal poisoning from the weapon muzzles. He's
very sick," answered Jorgan Rome. "Raia, he needs water."

Raia poured water on Cholley. A great rush of steam
rose from Cholley as he shook violently and then stiffened.
Cholley became as hard as stone. "He'll need to work through
this. It will take some time," said Jorgan Rome. "Raia, please
stay with Cholley. Give him an apple when he asks for it.
He'll be OK." To Teera, he said, "Now we've got an appoint-
ment with the Ammun Mettell. I'm certain that he is behind
this door. There are maybe a couple of hundred Mettellites
in the room with him."

"A couple hundred?"

"They're not armed. I'm guessing that this room is the
meeting hall. There won't be any weapons."

"You're guessing? Isn't it dangerous for the two of us just
to walk into a room with hundreds of Mettellites, armed or
not?"

"In principle, we're just going to talk with them, but it
could be very dangerous if the Ammun Mettell knows who
I really am. I'm certain that no follower of the Ammun Ghobar could ever expect to get away unscathed if the Mettellites
knew his identity. So we have to keep a secret."

Teera replied, "I'm a robot. I can only speak the truth. I
cannot lie."

Jorgan Rome shot her a glance.

"Only kidding!" said Teera.

Jorgan Rome opened the door and went in. The door opened onto the stage of a large auditorium. Mettellites of all sorts filled the seats of the auditorium, even though no meeting was in progress, no action on the stage. They sat in small groups, talking. Some slept. On the stage, a group of Mettellites was gathered together. One by one, the Mettellites in the group on the stage looked up and noticed Jorgan Rome. Something about Jorgan Rome's bearing commanded respect, so, one-by-one, the Mettellites looked again at the ground and stepped away. They were clearing a path for Jorgan Rome to approach. Finally, Jorgan Rome saw what it was that they were congregating about: a small, folding, card table full of plans and maps and a man seated behind it. So, thought Jorgan Rome, the throne of the Ammun Mettell is reduced to a a folding chair and a folding table! There was no mistaking the Ammun Mettell. His quick motions and powerful focus set him apart. His red and black cloak was tailor-made. His menace and intelligence were obvious and made him the most dangerous man in any assembly. The room went silent and the Ammun Mettell looked up at Jorgan Rome.

"I know who you are," said the Ammun Mettell.

5

A LL EYES WERE ON Jorgan Rome. He paused. He took a breath. "Then that will shorten our discussion," said Jorgan Rome to the Ammun Mettell.

"Oh, considerably," replied the Ammun Mettell, who then looked down at the table, returning his attention to the maps and plans. As an afterthought, the Ammun Mettell raised one finger and said calmly, "Detain him."

Several Mettellites surrounded Jorgan Rome and held his arms. Jorgan Rome said, "I have a proposition for you."

The Ammun Mettell took a breath. He placed his palms flat on the table top and looked up. "You penetrated our perimeter defense, then our fortress defense, then you passed by our outer and inner sentries to arrive here in front of me. I didn't imagine that you did all that on a lark. Of course you have a proposition."

"That's right," said Jorgan Rome. "What I'm..." The Ammun Mettell held up a hand for silence. The Ammun Mettell said, "I don't know how you managed these latest escapades, but they will not continue." With a flick of the wrist, he sent the command to all the assembled Mettellites to rise.

Cholley bounded into the room. "Is it mealtime yet?" he said. Then Cholley stiffened upon seeing Jorgan Rome held by the Mettellites. Jorgan Rome raised an eyebrow and shook his head. Cholley took the hint and did nothing.

Just then, Raia appeared. "Cholley's better, Daddy! He ate an apple!" she said. The Ammun Mettell noticed Raia. He stood from his chair, knocking it over backwards. He started to speak but then held his words. He was thinking. The Ammun Mettell pirouetted around in a half circle, now with his back to the assembly. After a minute he turned around and addressed Jorgan Rome. Speaking slowly, the Ammun Mettell said, "I challenge you to Parlat Pantel!"

Parlat Pantel! Jorgan Rome smiled. He said simply, "Surely the Ammun Mettell is aware that custom and protocol forbid me to take up this challenge. I am not an Ammun."

"Yes, you just made it altogether obvious that your training is less than complete," replied the Ammun Mettell. "When the Ammun Marchar died just before the Convocation of the Schools, it fell to his senior disciple to represent their school. The Khadar declared at that moment that senior disciples act in full capacity as an Ammun, when there is no other, for inter-school matters. The challenge is binding. Circumstances have made you the senior disciple of..." The Ammun Mettell paused for just a moment, to focus the attention of everyone in the room "...the senior disciple of...the Ammun Ghobar!"

The room erupted. "Silence!" commanded the Ammun Mettell. "Challenge is proffered." Jorgan Rome stared at the Ammun Mettell. It was all so clever. The Ammun Mettell had adroitly transformed an unfocused, lazy assembly into a lynch mob with just two words. Now there was no escape, except by way of the Parlat Pantel.

"I accept," said Jorgan Rome. "But I require prepara-tion."

"Five hours!" replied the Ammun Mettell. To the Mettel-lites holding Jorgan Rome he said, "During that time, show our guests every hospitality." The Ammun Mettell returned to his maps and plans. Jorgan Rome, Teera, Cholley, and Raia were led away.

They were taken to a large room with sofas, chairs, desks, and tapestries on the wall. There was a table full of food. The Mettellite guards left the room, but they locked the door behind them. Once they were alone, Teera said, "So, this Parlat Pantel, is that some kind of battle to the death? You know I have no stomach for any sort of Ammun-on-Ammun violence!"

"No," said Jorgan Rome. "It's no battle to the death, but it might as well be. It's more sophisticated than that, but every bit as dangerous."

"So how does it go, this 'Parlat Pantel?'" asked Cholley.

Jorgan Rome thought for a moment, then said, "It's a very old tradition. It has to do, sort of, with the annual celebration of the Khadar's birthday. The celebrations would last about a week. There were parades; every town had a parade. Families exchanged gifts. There were elegant dinners, speeches. New buildings were dedicated to the Khadar. Tributes came in from every province. The highlight of the week, however, was always the Debates. Of the hundred schools of philosophy, two of them were selected to present a public debate. Perhaps a hundred thousand people, wearing their very best clothes, would attend. The stadium was adorned with banners and flowers in the colors of the two opposing schools. The Khadar himself would sit in the first row. The debaters were always students, the most promising students, and the debates were formal and highly choreo-graphed. For months afterwards, it seemed, the newspapers and citizens of Naveer would be rehashing the arguments and points of the Debate."

"So that's a Parlat Pantel?" asked Cholley.

"No," said Jorgan Rome. "The Parlat Pantel was an il-legal event, held privately later that night. If there was a grievance between the two schools, then, unknown to the public, there might be a Parlat Pantel challenge behind the public debate. At the Parlat Pantel, the two Ammuns would debate and the stakes were very high. The Ammun who was defeated would lose everything. His school of philosophy was dissolved. His followers were taken into the winning school."

"Oh, I get it," said Teera. "It's debating for pink slips."

Jorgan Rome shot her a glance but said nothing. "The public debates were often a set up. The schools tried out their weakest arguments, or set traps for the opposing Ammun. The public had no idea about what was really going on during the Debates."

"I don't get it," said Cholley. "I mean, suppose you win this Parlat Pantel thing. What do we get out of it?"

"Several hundred Mettellites working directly with us against Calcha," answered Jorgan Rome.

"Oh," said Cholley. "What if you lose?"

Teera answered, "They're going to try to fit a gelatinoid into a red and black uniform, that's what!"

"Teera's right," said Jorgan Rome. "We all become Met-tellites at that point."

"Sounds like you better win," said Raia.

"I still don't get it," said Cholley.

"The challenge is very clear," said Jorgan Rome.

"No," said Cholley. "I can't figure it. Why challenge you? He could have had us all wasted, no problem."

"I guess he wants me to work for him," said Jorgan Rome.

Teera didn't agree. "I don't know how to break this to you, but I'm pretty sure he hates your guts," she said. "He changed his whole plan when he saw our darling Raia come into the room."

"Raia!" exclaimed Jorgan Rome. "Why Raia?" Speaking to Raia, he asked, "Raia, have you ever met this man before, the Ammun Mettell?"

"No, never," answered Raia.

"But when he saw you..." Jorgan Rome figured it out. "I'm guessing that he has seen her use the karamand. That's what he wants!"

"Why doesn't he just take it from us?" asked Cholley.

"Because he can't use it! He wants us—Raia—working for him and using the karamand at his command!"

"Wow!" said Cholley. "That Ammun Mettell sure is clever!"

"And you're planning to debate this guy?" asked Teera.

"Daddy! You've got to win!" said Raia.

"I'll do what I can," said Jorgan Rome, as he pulled out a small box from behind his belt buckle. "This," he said to Teera, "is very precious. It's memory. It is a complete cultural record of Naveer up to the month before it was destroyed. It very likely contains records of several Parlat Pantels. I need you to use your circuitry to analyze this memory. Find out how the Ammun Mettell competes in a Parlat Pantel."

"Okey dokey," said Teera as she placed the memory into a slot in her abdomen. She appeared to shut down as her circuitry absorbed the contents of the memory.

Jorgan Rome took a place in the middle of the room and began to meditate. Cholley jumped onto the table and began to dissolve every piece of fruit he could find. Raia ate a piece of cake.

Teera came alive again. "Oh. That's not good," she said.

"What's not good?" asked Cholley.

"This Ammun Mettell. He never loses!" said Teera.

One hour later, Cholley had oozed out over the table, having doubled in size after eating every piece of fruit. Teera was whirring and clicking as she analyzed past debates. Jorgan Rome awoke. "I'm finished," he announced.

"I agree," said Teera.

"No!" said Raia. "He always says that when he's done meditating."

"Teera! could you please advise me what you have learned about debating the Ammun Mettell?" asked Jorgan Rome.

"You shouldn't debate him. That's obvious, but it's a little late for that."

"What should I do?" asked Jorgan Rome.

"There is some strategy that might delay the inevitable. Think of the debate as a pursuit race. The first person to make a move is at a disadvantage. It's easier to score by destroying an assertion than by making one."

"OK, what else?"

"Never engage the Ammun Mettell on his home turf. That would be any subject bearing on the self, moral obligation, or political organization."

"Libertarian topics," observed Jorgan Rome. "Sort of unavoidable in Golden Age science fiction."

"Whatever. Just never go there."

"OK, got it. What else?"

"His weakest responses are to a particular three-pronged rhetoric that..." Teera was interrupted by a loud knock on the door. It swung open and a Mettellite wheeled a cart into the room.

"Presenting the Manjen-Sorel for inspection!" said the Mettellite. On the cart were three helmets, all covered with flaky metallic scales. Each helmet had a pair of antennae and a pair of oversized goggles.

"Those look like helmets with antennas on them!" muttered Cholley. "I'm not wearing one of those."

"They're not for you, Cholley. They're for the judges," explained Jorgan Rome.

"So you're trusting the judgment of people who think it's OK to go around wearing fish-head helmets? Just bring me a Mettellite suit now and get this over with!" said Cholley.

"The Manjen-Sorel make the judges impartial. They override prejudice, personal history, and individual desire. Without them there is no Parlat Pantel," said Jorgan Rome. To the Mettellite, he said, "Do you assure me, as a Mettellite Promise, that these helmets function correctly?" The Mettellite said that they did. "Then there is no need for inspection," said Jorgan Rome, waving the cart away.

Three hours later, it was time for the Parlat Pantel. The audience was full of Mettellites. Jorgan Rome's small party of three followers was placed in a box in the balcony. The stage was barren. Its only furnishing was a stone plinth at dead center. Jorgan Rome walked onto the stage from the right. He was, for the first time in his life, dressed as the Ammun of his school. He wore a sky blue robe with gold trim, just like the Ammun Ghobar before him. The Ammun Mettell, appearing on the left, was all in black with one red sleeve. Each of two opposing Ammuns wore laurel leaves in their hair. The Ammuns approached the plinth, stepping in unison to the beat of an offstage drum. Meeting at center stage, they acknowledged each other with the barest of nods, then removed their laurels and placed them on the plinth.

Accompanied by the drum, the Ammuns each took four steps away from center stage.

"This is fun!" whispered Raia. Raia, Teera, and Cholley observed everything from their balcony seats on the right side, Jorgan Rome's side.

"No, Dear, it's not," whispered Teera.

Three judges, carrying helmets entered from a center door backstage. Cholley noticed that two of the judges were overweight. "They like their fish food," he muttered.

"Look who's talking!" whispered Teera.

The judges took seats in the front row. As the judges donned their helmets, three brilliant white gas torches ignited high above the plinth.

"What's that?" whispered Cholley.

"White is neutral," answered Teera. "If a torch turns blue, it means that a judge has awarded the argument to Jorgan Rome. Red torches are bad torches."

The Ammun Mettell spoke, "As the challenger, I now ask the Ammun Jorgan Rome to state the theme of this Parlat Pantel."

"I choose to discuss the Nature of the Self," said Jorgan Rome. The audience gasped. The Ammun Mettell shook his head. "You are a fool, Jorgan Rome."

Jorgan Rome spoke calmly. "The concept of the self is a mis-conception. Perhaps the most invidious of all misconceptions, for the harm that it does and for the imbalance it imparts." There it was: the central statement of the Parlat Pantel, the first statement uttered by the challenged Ammun.

"Do you believe that yourself?" asked the Ammun Mettell, to the great amusement of the Mettellite audience.

"My understanding is that japes of that sort are out of place in a Parlat Pantel," remonstrated Jorgan Rome.

"Forgive me," said the Ammun Mettell, "the distinguished Ammun Jorgan Rome is correctly aggrieved. It's just that I couldn't help myself," he said with a smirk.

"The perceived self," explained Jorgan Rome, "is nothing more than a succession of cognitive actions, one after the other, nothing more than a sequence of synaptic events in the hypothalamus. Having no material existence of its own, it cannot be said to exist other than as metaphor." The torches were unchanged, bright and white.

The Ammun Mettell took on the demeanor of a weary instructor. "It is simple. The Self is self-defining." Jorgan Rome opened his mouth to object but the Ammun Mettell motioned for silence. "That is neither jape nor tautology but the truth. Perhaps your School is unschooled in the nature of emergent phenomena. The reality of the Self arises from your mythologically fundamental interactions of neurons and atoms and whatnot, including that hypothalamus of yours." A torch changed color and burned bright red. The Ammun Mettell continued, "The Self is no less real for being, in principle, derivable because the near impossibility of that derivation provides the Self with its own behaviors that are not practically deducible. Essentially, we may say that if it quacks like a Self, then it is a Self."

Two more torches changed color. Now all three torches were red. The Ammun Mettell's face betrayed a hint of a smirk when a kettle drum offstage announced that he had scored. Bumm-Bummm! went the drum as the Ammun Mettell took one step towards center stage, one step closer to the plinth, one step closer to claiming both of the laurels resting on it.

"Uh oh," said Cholley, "the roly-poly fish heads don't like Jorgan Rome very much."

"It's like the Ammun Mettell knew just what to say to bring those other two judges to his side," remarked Teera.

The torches became white again in preparation for another round. Jorgan Rome was ready. "Let's see what happens," he said, "if we accept your behavioral taxonomy of self versus non-self. Our own brains have many simultaneous, disparate processes whose behaviors obviate the idea of a single self. Persons who suffer schizophrenia will hear voices, other consciousnesses, that behave—and this is your criterion—as separate selves." One torch turned blue.

The Ammun Mettell smiled. He said, "Perhaps there are disparate processes in your brain, Ammun Jorgan Rome. It wouldn't surprise me. It is, however, a little surprising that someone of your School would conflate the brain with the self. As for your example of schizophrenia, it proves nothing other than that schizophrenia is a condition to be cured." Two torches turned red.

"That was fast!" said Teera. "No point yet but he changed those two torches in record time...Wait!...Something is going on!"

"What?" said Cholley.

"Not clear," said Teera, "but I'm scanning."

The successes of the Ammun Mettell compelled Jorgan Rome to find a new approach. He thought for a moment and then said, "The concept of the self as promoted by your School is not consistent with nature. All things have a beginning, but never a sudden one. There is growth, transformation, a necessary 'becoming.' The Self which is instantly its own Self would have no precedence in nature. If we were to posit a Self, then as it became its own Self, it must necessarily have passed through half-Self, perhaps quarter-Self, even non-Self—a state you deny." One torch changed from red to white, flickered blue, then stayed white. The torches were evenly divided.

"OK, I have it!" said Teera. "That Ammun Mettell is clever! He's communicating with eta waves! No one uses eta waves anymore. It's only because I'm over two hundred years old that I even have eta wave detectors."

Raia said, "Teera! You really are over two…"

"Just a minute, Dear…yes, definitely eta waves."

"Is that cheating?" asked Cholley. "Can you jam the signal?"

"Oh, silly!" said Teera. "Eta waves have topological protection. You can't jam them. You have to overwhelm them or stop them at their source."

The Ammun Mettell continued, "Certainly the Self is unlike all else. Of course, without any doubt, our concept of the Self is unlike other things in mere nature. You have just now discovered why the Self is at the center of philosophical discourse in our School." The white torch returned to its earlier red color.

Jorgan Rome refused to concede the point. "Nothing can 'rotate' about the Self, for it is surely constrained by its obligations. You, yourself, any self cannot abandon the helpless. Picture a small boat with no motor, marooned in the middle of a large lake. Picture that you have a tugboat. What do you do with the stranded boat? What choice do you really have?" "You have no choice." Jorgan Rome paused for effect. "The argument is clear, you must pull it across!"

A judge must have agreed with Jorgan Rome because one torch turned from red to blue. Jorgan Rome was ahead by one torch for the next point, but he remained a full step further from the plinth than the Ammun Mettell. A trumpet sounded to mark the break. The Parlat Pantel was half over. The Ammun Mettell retired to his side of the stage. He was soon surrounded by a dozen grinning Mettellites. Jorgan Rome retired alone to his side of the stage. A few minutes later, Raia, Cholley, and Teera found Jorgan Rome wandering blankly around the backstage area.

"Just keep comin' at 'em, Champ!" said Cholley. "Never rest! Show 'em what you're made of, Tiger! Do it for da Cholley!"

Jorgan Rome just looked at him. He turned to Teera. "What have you got?"

"Maybe something. Maybe nothing. I think he's receiving communications. By eta waves," said Teera.

Jorgan Rome raised his eyebrows. "Is he...", Jorgan Rome started to say, but he reconsidered. "Can you locate the transmitter?"

"Probably," said Teera.

"Do what you can," said Jorgan Rome. The trumpet announced the resumption of the Parlat Pantel.

The Ammun Mettell began, "Once we posit the existence of a Self, which we must do, or I wouldn't be standing here..." The Ammun Mettell grinned as he pointed to where he stood on the stage, closer to the plinth than Jorgan Rome. "...we must next ask what properties that Self possesses. It is more than tautology to suggest that the Self owns itself. Owning itself means that it owns its labor and the products of its labor." One torch turned red as the Ammun Mettell continued, "How dare you, Jorgan Rome, require some particular action of your hypothetical tugboat captain, for that would be theft! Your luckless sailors should really have had stranding insurance, or failing that, are free to negotiate with the tugboat owner at market rates."

The final blue torch went red. The kettle drum sounded. The Ammun Mettell took one more step towards victory.

Teera said, "I found it. The source of the eta waves is a secret room two floors below the stage. The problem is that I can't go down there without being seen."

"I could go," offered Raia, pulling the karamand from her pocket.

"No," said, Teera. "We're being watched up in this balcony. They would notice when you disappeared from your seat."

"We need a plan in a hurry!" said Cholley. "Because this debate isn't going to last much longer."

Jorgan Rome appeared a little flustered. "Que possède-je? What do I own? That's hardly a basis for a philosophy: 'Where's my stuff? It's over there. In a box. You can't have it!' Your philosophy of ownership reminds me of a toddler protecting his pile of toys!" Nothing changed. All torches burned white. Teera shook her head. Raia looked down at her lap. Teera turned to stare at Cholley. "What?" he asked. "You can separate into parts, can't you?" asked Teera.

"Yeah, but I don't like where this is going. Small parts of me are kinda stupid, you know? Not exactly reliable."

"OK, from you, that's saying a lot," said Teera, "but it's our best plan. Little sub-Cholley finds the eta wave transmitter and disables it. He uses this to take it out," she said, holding a small transmitter in her hand. "That's all he needs to do."

Teera and Raia watched Cholley until he took the transmitter and reluctantly separated a small portion of himself. Raia held the karamand low and away from view as she muttered a few words. The transmitter and sub-Cholley were gone.

Jorgan Rome was becoming desperate. "The Self is not property nor can it be discussed in terms of property rights for the simple reason that you cannot put a fence around it, as it were, to define it distinctly from other Selves. Even if we accept your emergent conception of the Self, then it necessarily defines itself only in relation to other Selves. We must study others to answer the question: Who am I?" A single torch changed to blue and it was enough to revive Jorgan Rome's hopes.

"That's your moral assertion, an assertion for which we have no use in our School," said the Ammun Mettell, "as rigorous philosophy must always proceed from carefully stated axioms." The torch went back to white and then to red. Another torch turned red.

Teera brought up a video link to the transmitter carried by little sub-Cholley. The images showed a small room with stone walls and carpet on the floor. The video image began to spin, jerking around and rotating clockwise. Then it reversed, tumbling and jumping in the other direction. "What's going on?" asked Teera.

"Little sub-Cholley is rolling on the carpet," said Cholley.

"Why is he doing that?" asked Teera.

"Because it's fun," answered Cholley.

"Oh, dear!" said Teera.

The Ammun Mettell scored another point and little sub-Cholley, two floors below was frightened by the sound of the kettle drum. He scurried under a table, which was fortunate because the eta wave transmitter that he was looking for happened to be under that very table.

"Oh, very good," said Teera.

"It then follows from the centrality of Self that…that…," The Ammun Mettell appeared to stumble. "Forgive me, I lost my train of thought," he said.

Jorgan Rome waited for a couple of minutes for the Ammun Mettell to recover. When the Ammun Mettell remained silent, Jorgan Rome continued, "It is a known fact that a person kept in solitary confinement will go insane. His or her Self is not, I repeat, not, robust against isolation from other Selves, thus proving that a Self in isolation is, in fact, non-Self. Property rights cannot pertain to something that cannot be defined or isolated." One torch turned blue.

"That's...not...right!" said the Ammun Mettell with effort, which, to the judges, must have sounded like an assertion in lieu of argument. Two more torches turned blue. The kettle drum accompanied Jorgan Rome as he took his first step toward center stage.

Having lost a point, it was the Ammun Mettell's turn to offer a new proposition. He took his time. Finally, he said, "The nature of necessary political organization which arises from the central Self is particular."

"And...?" asked Jorgan Rome.

"That's it," said the Ammun Mettell. In quick succession, three torches turned blue, the kettle drum sounded, and Jorgan Rome, puzzled, found himself one step closer to the plinth.

The Ammun Mettell regained confidence. He smirked just a little as he offered up his next argument. "The Self is axiomatic."

Jorgan Rome pounced. "Invalid," he declared. "claiming the central proposition as an axiom is disallowed." The Ammun Mettell looked unsurprised as the judges, one-by-one, agreed with Jorgan Rome. Jorgan Rome had scored the final point. He stood next to the plinth with two sets of laurels on it.

Jorgan Rome reached out for the laurels. The Ammun Mettell kept a brave face but flinched as Jorgan Rome took up his laurels. Then Jorgan Rome addressed the audience and judges. In a clear voice he said, "I cannot presume to claim the laurels of the great Ammun Mettell. They, with all of his work and the School he created are rightfully his to keep, if only for the price of a simple promise."

The Ammun Mettell stared at Jorgan Rome, swallowed, and then asked, with a slight quaver in his voice, "What promise?"

"A promise of friendship, of cooperation until, working together, we have eliminated Calcha as a threat to the galaxy," said Jorgan Rome.

"I make you that promise," said the Ammun Mettell.

"My heart is glad," said Jorgan Rome. "Please take your laurels."

The Ammun Mettell stepped up to retrieve his own laurels. He looked again at Jorgan Rome. "But you are a fool, Jorgan Rome!" he said. "The promise you asked for, it extends only until Calcha is gone. After that, I might decide to find you next."

"We'll cross that bridge when we come to it. If we come to it at all," said Jorgan Rome. "Until then, we're good friends."

"Agreed," said the Ammun Mettell, who shoved his laurels into a pocket of his robe and walked away. Jorgan Rome watched the Ammun Mettell leave. When Jorgan Rome turned around, he found Raia, Teera, and Cholley waiting for him. Jorgan Rome smiled broadly and declared, "Well, that wasn't so bad after all!" Neither Raia, nor Teera, nor Cholley said anything. Jorgan Rome said, "OK, I had a bit of a rocky start, but I, but we managed to pull it off at the end," to continued silence from Raia, Cholley, and Teera.

"What I mean to say is 'Thank you,'" said Jorgan Rome, "For taking care of that transmitter. With a level playing field, things worked out for us."

"Here's the issue. We didn't have any luck with the transmitter," said Teera. "We found it. We sent a subCholley to disable it, but we couldn't do it. The transmitter was all sealed up. When a couple of Mettellite sentries entered the room, we had to pull the subCholley out of there. We never even touched that transmitter."

"But…"

"But nothing," said Teera. "The Ammun Mettell began to lose because that's what he decided to do. He threw the match."

"Why would he do that?" asked Jorgan Rome.

"Who knows?" said Teera.

Part Two

6

AFTER A DAY OR TWO Jorgan Rome understood that it was time to pay a visit to the Dar Telku and so he asked Raia and Cholley to accompany him.

"How will we get there?" asked Cholley.

"We're walking," said Jorgan Rome.

"It's a big planet, you know," said Cholley.

Jorgan Rome looked over at his old friend with surprise. "Well, I had thought you would know by now. In science fiction, once you land on a strange planet, everything is in walking distance. That's how it works."

"Oh," said Cholley as they set out on the trail early in the morning.

"Besides," said Jorgan Rome, "walking provides an excellent opportunity for narrative."

"Who is this Dar Telku, anyway?" asked Raia.

"Thank you, Raia," said Jorgan Rome. "What you should understand is that the Telkans have all been traders, going back over hundreds of years. 'Born a Telkan, born a trader,' is what they say about themselves. Which made the Dar Telku's rebellion all the more unlikely."

"So he's not a trader, OK," said Raia.

"She." said Jorgan Rome and Raia perked up. "Not for many years. Which was unthinkable."

Jorgan Rome continued, "The Telkans are based in the Sutarfeni sector."

"Sutarfeni!" exclaimed Cholley with a shudder. "Not going back there!"

"You don't need to!" said Jorgan Rome. To Raia he explained, "It's a globular cluster, barely bound to our galaxy. Coming all the way to Earth was the culmination of her rebellion. But it was a rebellion that started long ago, when she was your age, Raia."

Raia didn't say anything but Jorgan Rome noticed that she was paying close attention.

"What happened was, she started reading the legends of the Allozetts, the mythical people who—according to the legends—ruled the galaxy long before us." said Jorgan Rome, and Raia turned away, disgusted. "And she fell in love with them."

"With the Allozetts?", asked Cholley.

"No, the legends. Well, maybe with the Allozetts, too, but she became obsessed with the legends. Which is normal, I guess, for a girl of that age." Except for Raia apparently, thought Jorgan Rome. "So the Dar Telku read them over and over and over again. She convinced herself, even as a young girl, that the Allozetts must actually have existed!"

"That's crazy!" said Cholley.

"Well, listen further," said Jorgan Rome. "By reading them so many times, she noticed things that other people had missed. Take for example, the Legend of the Vanishing Caravan."

"OK, That one's my favorite!" said Cholley.

"It is a good one. If you remember, in that story, a mysterious caravan visits a planet."

"Yes, I remember!" said Cholley.

"After a while, a few individuals are allowed to visit the caravan. Then the caravan vanishes without a trace!"

"Everyone was pretty upset," said Cholley.

"In the story, they're completely stunned!" said Jorgan Rome. "Then, a quarter of a century later, the captain of the caravan is spotted again. They capture him and put him on trial."

"It's very exciting," said Cholley.

"On the day of the trial, in front of the court, before the whole planet, the Chief Prosecutor announces that she refuses to prosecute the prisoner. It's another big shock, so she tells her story."

"Ooh, a story within a story…very confusing," said Cholley.

"She herself had been one of the women kidnapped on the caravan! But it was never a real kidnapping at all. It had been a ruse. As a young woman, she was forced into a life she didn't want so she and others like her teamed up to create the Vanishing Caravan."

"Good story! I remember that they let the prisoner go at the end."

"Right, and he boarded a ship that vanished without a trace!"

"Perfect!" said Cholley. "What do you think, Raia?"

Raia made a face but didn't say anything. When Jorgan Rome and Cholley both turned to her, she finally said, "Maybe it's not my kind of story, OK?"

"Well, it meant so much to the Dar Telku when she was young, that she noticed something odd about it: The story only makes sense if the Allozetts somehow expected that they could see every ship in the galaxy. For us, these days, it's pretty easy to hide somewhere out in space…"

"We've done it!" said Cholley.

"Of course," said Jorgan Rome. "Any number of times. But we wouldn't have been able to hide from the Allozetts!"

"If they existed! They're not real." declared Cholley as Raia kicked a rock from the trail.

"That's what everyone thought. Remember the legend of Thyramus and Pisbee?"

"Love story! Yuck! Not my favorite!" said Cholley.

"Thyramus tries to pluck an orchid to bring to Pisbee and he falls down a gorge. Pisbee appears as a holographic image and guides his progress up the gorge wall, giving him courage when he needs it most."

"Yuck! Yuck! Yuck!" said Cholley.

"Except, if you read the story carefully…"

"Never!" said Cholley.

"If you read the story carefully, there's almost half a galaxy between them. There are several clues in the text, but the main one is that Thyramus was posted with his regiment! So if you take the legend seriously, as the Dar Telku did, then the Allozetts must have had some amazing communication technology," explained Jorgan Rome. "So the Dar Telku became obsessed with finding the remnants of their communications network."

"She imagined that the Allozetts might have used giant mirrors of ionized, interstellar gas. Not very efficient, perhaps, but on a vast scale they would be remarkable. Over centuries, without maintenance, diffusion and convection of the gas would take them out of shape, but they might still have focusing power for very, very long wavelengths."

"By this time, the Dar Telku had left school. She had joined the family business. But on trade missions, she would secretly deposit long-wavelength beacons at sites associated with the legends. Then she spent the next several years listening for echoes."

"She eventually detected weak echoes—coming from Earth. She stopped trading altogether and came here. She set herself to work, tuning up the mirrors, refashioning them and making a network. The Telkans removed her portrait from the Counting Room and divided her shares. Fifty years later, she finally has her galaxy-wide network. In the end, it's helped her in the market, too. 'Born a Telkan...' I guess."

"So the legends of the Allozetts...?" asked Cholley.

"Apparently really happened."

They walked along quietly for the next five minutes. Finally, Raia muttered, "She shouldn't mess with other people's stuff."

"But those mirrors have been derelict for centuries," said Jorgan Rome.

Cholley asked, "So what happened to the Allozetts?"

"Nobody knows. But if you read the legends closely, in what is probably chronological order, you'll notice fewer people in the later stories. The earliest ones are on planets teeming with people. The last ones are about far-flung outposts, or single families in space. The Allozetts seem to have thinned out and gone away."

"Without a war, without a crisis..." said Cholley.

"Right. I've heard rumors that the Dar Telku believes they might still exist out there somewhere."

"Now I know she's crazy!" said Cholley.

"Careful!" said Jorgan Rome. "We're almost there." A long, low building came into sight. The building itself was understated, at least on the outside, but was festooned all over with antennas, dishes, lasers, mirrors, and miles of cable. Approaching the building, Jorgan Rome warned that the meeting could be delicate. "The Dar Telku might know many things. It's almost certain that she'll know who we are. But she'll have no idea that we're on Earth and she doesn't like surprises."

They arrived at the entrance. The door swung open. A young man appeared and said, "Jorgan Rome! The Dar Telku will see you now."

Inside, they found that the building was much larger than it appeared from the outside. Stairs descended deep into a marble-floored atrium that was two stories high. When they reached the ground floor, the young man disappeared behind a door and the stairs retracted. They were trapped. Eighteen large spiderbots skittered down stone pillars and aimed beam weapons at Jorgan Rome.

Raia clutched the karamand. Cholley began to rotate. Jorgan Rome quickly shook his head and Cholley and Raia relaxed. "We need to talk to the Dar Telku," he said.

The Dar Telku entered. "That's right, you do need to talk to me," she said, clutching a cup of tea. "Forgive me, I'd like to finish this before it cools. I'd offer some but, well, it's very rare. And you're not invited, are you?" She sat on the only chair in the atrium.

She continued, "I will know why you have come. At the moment you are targeted by eighteen lethal weapons."

Jorgan Rome replied simply, "I count twenty, if we include your phased-array ultrasonic panels hidden in the ceiling."

The Dar Telku pursed her lips for a moment but said nothing.

Jorgan Rome said, "Your weapons will only slow us down. And make a mess of this very nice room."

The Dar Telku thought for a moment. Then the spiderbots skittered away.

"And the hidden weapons?" asked Jorgan Rome.

"Deactivated," said the Dar Telku. "Please come with me."

They passed into a much more comfortable room, with ornate woodwork, plush carpets and billowy sofas. The Dar Telku indicated where each was to be seated, with Jorgan Rome next to her on the largest sofa. Then, faster than anyone would think possible, she slipped a bracelet on Jorgan Rome's arm.

"That, I'm afraid, is a paralysis bracelet. You can speak, of course, but you will remain immobilized here until you tell me what I need to know."

Jorgan Rome offered quick glances of reassurance to Raia and Cholley.

"Now tell me please why you have caused this uproar. Why have you come to Earth?"

"But nobody knows I'm here," said Jorgan Rome.

The Dar Telku choked, sending a great spurt of tea over her clothes, the sofa, and the carpet. "Nobody knows! Everyone knows!" Then, staring incredulously at her visitor, "You are a fool, Jorgan Rome!"

"Lots of people tell me that," said Jorgan Rome.

"With good reason! Didn't I say that was expensive tea? Look what you've done!" Then, muttering, "Nobody knows you're here! Nobody knows you're here!" she turned to an assistant and asked, "Please show our esteemed guest the current stream of chatter devoted to his ostensibly-unknown presence on this planet."

"That will overload capacity."

"Then filter it somehow," commanded the Dar Telku. The room changed. The walls revealed themselves as floor-to-ceiling computer screens, filled with the tiniest of text moving very rapidly. "All of that," said the Dar Telku, "Is central galactic communication about you and your presence on Earth."

"That's only a small part of it," said her assistant.

"So you really must tell me what you are doing here!" said the Dar Telku.

"I'm trying to stop a war."

"Stop a war, or start a war?" snorted the Dar Telku. "There's something very suspicious about you, something suspicious indeed! Violent destruction follows you everywhere but you, you are untouched!" She paced around. "Very suspicious!"

She stared at Jorgan Rome for a full minute before continuing. "You had a simple task. Just a few years ago, wasn't it, that you were to escort the Kaltar prisoners to justice?"

"You know about that?" asked Jorgan Rome.

"Of course I know about that!" shouted the Dar Telku. "Do not underestimate me…never…ever! Do that again, and I'll activate the pain injectors on that paralysis bracelet. Now tell me what happened to the Kaltar prisoners!"

Jorgan Rome said nothing.

"I'll tell you what happened! They all escaped! Everyone of them! Poof! Gone!" She moved in close, "So how is that possible, Mr. Jorgan Rome?" With no response from Jorgan Rome, she muttered, "They murdered half a planet, you know!"

Cholley had had enough. "It was a setup!"

"Silence!" ordered the Dar Telku. "I'm speaking to your owner!"

Cholley exploded. A jet of corrosive, gelatinous fluid burst upwards to the ceiling. Pieces of ceramic tile fell to the floor all around.

"I'm not crazy. Who's the crazy one here?" said the Dar Telku. Picking up shards from the floor, she added, "I'm charging for this."

"Kaltar was a setup," said Jorgan Rome. "Those weren't criminals at all."

"Not your decision to make!" snapped the Dar Telku.

"No, they were victims. They were—are—the very last surviving Shanden people, mind-transferred by the Triad into bodies of the captives."

"The ship was a time bomb!" yelled Cholley, still angry.

"By escorting them, we didn't know that we were doing the Triad's work, until almost too late," explained Jorgan Rome.

"Hmmph," said the Dar Telku. "That's of no matter, the Triad no longer exists."

Jorgan Rome raised his eyebrows, and the Dar Telku turned to him, "You took out the Triad?" Jorgan Rome nodded, "Cholley and I did. It was necessary."

"I seem to have underestimated you, Jorgan Rome. And your friend."

Nobody said anything for several minutes. The story of the Kaltar Prisoners with its happy ending—the Shanden secretly resettled—dispelled some tension in the room, but only slightly and only for a moment. Jorgan Rome knew that the Dar Telku was building towards another confrontation. About the thing that bothered her most.

Turning suddenly to Jorgan Rome, the Dar Telku demanded, "How did you survive the destruction of your planet?"

"I was away," said Jorgan Rome, simply.

"Away? Really! How many other people were 'away' when it happened? How many other survivors were there? Tell me!"

"None," admitted Jorgan Rome, "Or so I thought, until this week, when I found the Mettellites here."

"But they had long before been exiled to Gurfann, so of course they survived," sniffed the Dar Telku. "No mystery there. They don't count. What I want to know is how many people, other than Mr. Jorgan Rome here, left the planet one day before its destruction!"

"I imagine I would be the only one," admitted Jorgan Rome

"Exactly!" exclaimed the Dar Telku. "It's very suspicious! Were you often away from Naveer in those days?"

"No. It was my very first time off-planet. I was on a mission."

"A mission! Very mysterious—not to mention, very suspicious! Who sent you on this…mission?"

"The Ammun Ghobar. It was planned that I would meet up with him at Hurum."

"Is that so?" snorted the Dar Telku. "Is that so? Did you 'meet up' with him at Hurum?"

"You know the answer to that."

"I do. And it's very suspicious! You have always brought destruction, Mr. Jorgan Rome…and then just stepped out of the way! Am I right?"

Jorgan Rome maintained his composure. Cholley nearly boiled over once more.

The Dar Telku continued, nearly screaming, "And now you want to bring your destruction to my world, to everything I have built!" She gestured brusquely to her assistant who brought up an image of three warships on the wall screen before them.

"These vessels are on a direct path to Earth!" noted the assistant.

"These ships are meant for you, Mr. Jorgan Rome! You are bringing them right to my door! Thank you! Thank you! And you, of course, will step away, just…step away…from the ashes of my entire life's work!"

Jorgan Rome stood up, removed the paralysis bracelet from his arm and placed it on an end table. He walked over to the wall showing the incoming ships. The Dar Telku's jaw dropped as she looked from the bracelet, to Jorgan Rome, and back again. Jorgan Rome, at the wall, asked the assistant to back-calculate the trajectory of incoming military vessels. Where did they come from? And when did they launch?

With some astounding graphics that will look just super in the movie, the screen showed the past trajectory of the incoming ships. "It appears they launched three weeks ago from Pongal Starport."

"Which means they have nothing to do with us," said Jorgan Rome. The Dar Telku narrowed her eyes. "We've only been on Earth for four days," said Jorgan Rome. "Five days ago, we were in the Barthan sector on a ship called the Vandinfala. These inbound ships were already on their way to Earth while we were on the other side of the galaxy."

"Well, well," said the Dar Telku finally, putting down her tea. "You have a karamand. Probably the Naveeran karamand." She thought for a moment. "And apparently, you know how to use it. Use it with exquisite skill."

Jorgan Rome said nothing.

"This changes things," announced the Dar Telku. Turning to her assistant, she asked, "Would you mind terribly making up some tea for our guests. And perhaps some fruit for our gelatinoid friend." After they were served, quietly sipping tea and noisily dissolving apples, the Dar Telku turned to Jorgan Rome. "I'm still quite agitated about these ships. If they're not after you, then what purpose do they have?

Are they coming to work with your Mettellite friends in that castle?"

"No," said Jorgan Rome, "I don't think they're on the same side."

"Then they're coming to eliminate him. And us. And everything I've created."

"Isn't that an exaggeration?" asked Jorgan Rome. "There can be no planet-wide attack. Or any attack, really. With only three ships, Earth Defense Forces will make short work of them. This must be a formal visit, nothing more."

"You are a fool, Jorgan Rome!"

"Perhaps, but what are you trying to say?"

The Dar Telku stood up, walked over to the wall screen, and motioned the others to follow. "Zoom and enhance on the lead ship," she asked. "Show the command bridge."

"Is that possible?" asked Cholley.

"Only for the Dar Telku," said Jorgan Rome.

The image panned and magnified. They were looking into the windows of the ship. They saw the command bridge. With more magnification, they could see ship's commander. The ship's commander was a robot, made of cold, gray metal.

"Oh," said Jorgan Rome.

"That's Counter-Admiral Tokar!" said the Dar Telku.

"Yes, I know," said Jorgan Rome.

"Is that all you can say? The Counter-Admiral has bestowed his graces on many planets. By which I mean that he leaves nothing alive. Complete annihilation!"

"Yes, I know," said Jorgan Rome, deeply disturbed. Nobody said anything for a long time, so Cholley stepped up to ask when the ships would arrive at Earth.

"We're computing sixteen days," said the Dar Telku's assistant.

"That means we have just over two weeks," said Jorgan Rome. "We need to engage Earth Defense Forces right away! Two weeks should be enough to prepare a defense against three ships, Counter-Admiral or no Counter-Admiral!" Turning to Raia, he said, "Please stay here with the Dar Telku and learn what you can. Cholley and I need to leave right now."

After Jorgan Rome and Cholley left, the Dar Telku went to the table where Jorgan Rome had put the paralysis bracelet. She studied the bracelet for a moment, then put it on her own arm and promptly fell face-first into a sofa. Paralyzed. "Help me!" she said.

Raia came over and removed the paralysis bracelet. "May I keep it?" she asked, then wore it like a bangle. Then she walked back over to her own chair.

"Well...that's good, then," said the Dar Telku.

7

DURING THE WALK OVER to Earth Defense Command, Jorgan Rome summarized the situation. "The Counter-Admiral's ships are far enough away that Earth Defense Forces might not even know they're coming. That's our primary task, to apprise them of the threat. Later, if we can help them to engage more effectively with Tokar, so much the better."

Coming to the top of a rise, they looked out and saw the Earth Defense Command headquarters looming in the distance.

"There it is," said Jorgan Rome, "the Enneacontakaihenagon, the famous ninety-one-sided building. The culmination of centuries of polygonal one-upmanship among Earth's militaries. The largest building on the planet."

"Is this the part of the science fiction story when we rue the folly of mankind?" asked Cholley.

"Yes, it is," said Jorgan Rome.

"So many species, lost forever," muttered Cholley.

"So sad," said Jorgan Rome. "I sometimes wonder about the guy who shot the last womp rat. What was he thinking?"

The Ennea…whatever… was still an hour's walk away
Even from that great distance, Jorgan Rome became uneasy.
"Something's wrong," he said.

What was wrong became apparent when they approached
the building. There was no vehicle or pedestrian traffic anywhere. The main entrance door was open and unguarded.
Not a soul stirred in the great lobby.

"Strange," said Cholley.

"Follow me," said Jorgan Rome who never got lost, even
in an empty maze of this vast scale. They walked through
corridor after corridor, past empty offices, an empty cafeteria,
an empty auditorium, through deserted atria, up countless
flights of stairs towards the highest and center-most part of
the building.

Entering a new corridor on the highest floor, Jorgan
Rome paused. "We're getting somewhere," he said. A siren
sounded. Cholley flung a tendril and took it out of action.
When they were halfway down a long corridor, heavy steel
doors dropped from the ceiling at each end, sealing them
in. Jorgan Rome didn't even break stride as Cholley poured
forward under the barrier , dissolving the mechanism and
raising it up. "Just around this corner, I believe," said Jorgan
Rome.

Around the corner was a large office door with a sign that
said "Director." They entered without bothering to knock.
The outer office was empty. They heard rustling sounds
coming from the inner office. Somebody was at the desk
in the inner office but with their chair turned around facing
away.

The chair turned around. And there was Ketvick! Ketvick, the Traitorous Neerlan Envoy! Ketvick, the diplomat
who had sold out his own people, putting them irrevocably
in Calcha's power. Ketvick, who had scuttled out an escape

hatch, cutting Cholley in two with a sliding door. Ketvick, who must have offered up the little piece of Cholley to Cal-cha and so revealed Jorgan Rome's identity and tactics.

Ketvick recognized them of course. Fixing his attention on Cholley, he said, "It's a surprise to see you again. Perhaps not a pleasant surprise, but there it is. I certainly offer my congratulations on your reunion…Separations, I know, can be so difficult, which makes it gratifying to see the family together again as it were, well, perhaps 'family' isn't the right word but you're certainly one bit of glop again."

"It was your fault that I was cut in two in the first place!"

"Well, no…perhaps there was some shared blame there. You were quite menacing. I know that I felt menaced."

Jorgan Rome interrupted, "We can settle this later. Right now, we need to find the director of Earth Defense Forces."

Ketvick made a tight-lipped smile and a palms-up gesture.

"You?" asked Jorgan Rome. "How is that possible?"

Ketvick replied, "I guess a certain diligence is required. You do need to keep the resume up to date, work the net-work, and—now this is most important—always ask ques-tions during the interview."

Cholley burbled with irritation.

Ketvick said, "Now you'll have to excuse me."

When neither Cholley nor Jorgan Rome moved from their chairs, Ketvick sighed, "Such a workload I have. You may have noticed our acute staffing crisis as you came in. It's been such a burden on me."

Cholley and Jorgan Rome were unmoved.

"But perhaps I can manage to find a few minutes for dear friends. Imagining, of course that our friendship, dear or less dear, has survived these troubled times."

"We need ships," said Jorgan Rome

"Of course you do. Of course you do. What kind of ships are we talking about?"

"Multiple ships. Armed. Small crew. Capable of quick-maneuver, low-orbit defense."

"Oh, dear, dear, dear. Let's inquire, shall we?" said Ketvick, pressing a button on his desk console. When there was no reply, he made a hapless face that said "See what I mean!"

"Where are the ships?" asked Jorgan Rome.

"The ships? Many are out on loan to the Ghari. Then, of course, there's maintenance. The previous director seems—-here I don't wish to speak ill of my predecessor but it needs to be said—seems to have neglected maintenance. So the rest of the fleet is off for much-needed maintenance, I'm afraid."

"All of them?"

"Well, the ones that haven't been scrapped. But, yes."

"This is unacceptable," said Jorgan Rome.

Ketvick turned to Cholley. "I understand why he does it, being a self-righteous type and all, but what's in it for you?"

"He promised me an insula," said Cholley.

"And what was there for you," said Jorgan Rome with uncharacteristic anger, "that let you betray your people so utterly?"

"'Betray!' I prefer 'facilitate,'" said Ketvick. "Keep it positive and we all move forward together." Then, leaning back in his chair, Ketvick continued, "Besides, don't you think you're painting us with an overly broad cultural brush? Just because we're Neerlan, you expect us to stick together?" He smiled broadly and made an expansive gesture to suggest that he had scored a conversation-ending riposte. Ignoring Jorgan Rome and Cholley, he made a show of returning his attention to the papers on his desk. Hoping they would leave.

Jorgan Rome and Cholley stayed where they were.

"Look," said Ketvick, "I have an illustration here. You should see it. I asked my assistant to prepare it," he said as he looked through the stack of papers, "back when I had an assistant before this unfortunate round of layoffs…Here it is! It should be a photograph of a duck sitting on a chair…no, dear, dear, it seems to be just a sketch and not a very good one at all…perhaps it's difficult to photograph a duck on a chair…or maybe there's some animus here on the part of the assistant who no doubt saw the layoffs coming…this will affect my recommendation letter…but there it is. A sitting duck. That's you. If you stay on this planet. Which I'm not recommending."

Rummaging further, Ketvick extracted a service photo of Counter-Admiral Tokar. "And this represents Counter-Admiral Tokar." Then Ketvick took up the sketch of the duck again and tore it into little pieces, scattering them at Jorgan Rome and Cholley. "There, I think that makes some kind of a point or other that we can all understand. So why don't you take that little trinket of yours that I've heard so much about and pop off to somewhere else?"

"We're not going anywhere!"

"You are a fool, Jorgan Rome!" said Ketvick.

Jorgan Rome stood up abruptly. Charging toward the desk, he demanded, "Where's the general in charge?"

A wave of panic crossed Ketvick's face. He jumped back quickly and pulled a lever. Then he fell down a hole that opened behind the desk. Faster than you can blink, Ketvick was deep down the escape hatch. Jorgan Rome and Cholley heard banging as he caromed from side to side down the metal duct.

"That probably hurts," muttered Cholley.

After the banging stopped, there was true silence in the room and everywhere in the building. The largest building on the planet, center of its defense, was now empty of sound and devoid of activity. Deep in its core, Jorgan Rome and Cholley felt keenly their vulnerability to the imminent attack by an unstoppable Counter-Admiral.

Looking out the window, they caught a glimpse of Ket-vick rising up and away on some kind of flying tricycle, hunched forward over the control bar urging it to flee faster, ever faster away.

"That looks really stupid," said Cholley.

"He always gets away," said Jorgan Rome.

8

I T WAS AFTER MIDNIGHT when Jorgan Rome, along with Cholley, arrived in a grim mood back at the Mettellite compound. The Mettellite second-in-command, a young fellow named Barteng, was still on duty.

"Welcome back, Commander!" said Barteng with a half smile, "Good news from your wanderings, I hope."

Jorgan Rome stopped where he was and looked Barteng in the eye until Barteng looked away. "Send me Teera, now," was all that Jorgan Rome said.

Teera appeared within minutes. That Barteng, thought Jorgan Rome, he's arrogant but he's efficient. Barteng offered them the use of a small conference room. After closing the door, Jorgan Rome told Teera about the Counter-Admiral. He told her of the encounter with Ketvick at Earth Defense Command. He told her there were no ships.

"Can we retrieve the Earth ships from the Ghari?" asked Jorgan Rome.

"Unlikely," said Teera. "At present, the Ghari are engaged in border skirmishes, quite intense, for which they are under-equipped. What's more, Ghari are fantastically corrupt and the ships have likely passed into other hands since the transfer. Further, you have no recognized standing to request the ships. Finally, they're simply too far away to help in time. No, those ships will not be available."

"Ketvick did his work," muttered Jorgan Rome. "What about private ships from Earth? How many can we commandeer?"

"Again, you have no authority to commandeer ships. You'll be prosecuted."

"What if I don't care?"

"I've just checked my data sources. You won't find any space-capable ships in private hands. That's all regulated on this planet."

Jorgan Rome sat down. He exhaled. He looked at Teera. "What can I do?"

"You can leave," said Teera.

Jorgan Rome shook his head.

"Or, you could improvise something," said Teera.

Jorgan Rome gave a weary smile. "What have we got?" he asked.

"Not much," admitted Teera.

"Well, what about the ship the Mettellites arrived in?"

"A transport ship. Likely just some variety of barge. Even if it could fly, you'd be a sitting duck."

"I've been told that's what I already am," said Jorgan Rome, settling deeper into his chair.

"The Mettellites have a workshop," said Teera.

"A workshop?"

"It's supposed to be a secret," said Teera, "but it's hard to conceal things from a robot."

"OK, we'll defeat Tokar with wrenches and screwdrivers," said Jorgan Rome.

Which is just the sort of thing you've always done, thought Teera, as Jorgan Rome fell asleep in his chair.

It was midmorning when Jorgan Rome awoke. Teera was still at his side. Jorgan Rome stood up, shook the sleep from his head, straightened his clothing and said to Teera, "Come with me."

Entering a large common area, Jorgan Rome stopped the first Mettellite he encountered. "Please bring me Barteng," said Jorgan Rome. Barteng appeared a few minutes later, obviously roused from sleep but doing his best not to show it.

"Let's see the workshop," said Jorgan Rome, registering the surprise on Barteng's face.

A moment passed before Barteng found his smugness. "That…that will not be possible," he announced. Gaining steam, he continued, "The workshop, such as it might be—if it existed at all, in fact—would be inaccessible. If there were to be a workshop of any sort."

"Wrong answer," said Jorgan Rome.

"I'm afraid that's the only answer I've got, Commander," said Barteng, now fully in control of his smirk.

"I shouldn't need to remind you," said Jorgan Rome calmly, "that by Mettellite tradition, by traditions that long predate your school, even, that you are working for me now. With me. That means not against me. Until the forces of Calcha's Empire are defeated, until she and her imperial schemes are thwarted forever, until…"

"Umm, Commander?"

"until the Empire no longer threatens the galaxy with war, until…"

"Umm, Commander?"

Jorgan Rome pivoted around to address the unknown young man who kept interrupting. "Who are you?" asked Jorgan Rome.

"I'm from the legal department?"

"Yes?"

"Commander, it's just that another science fiction enterprise has asserted rights to the terms 'Empire' and 'Imperial.' Oh, dear, I shouldn't say 'enterprise!' Slip of the lip! With regard to 'Empire' and 'Imperial,' however, while we certainly feel that we have a strong case, it's been decided to avoid unnecessary challenges going forward."

"What am I supposed to say?"

"'Realm.'"

"'Realm?'"

"'Realm.' The adjective form would be 'Realmish' but we're looking for marketing input on that."

Jorgan Rome turned away. He focused his whole attention on Barteng, leaving the young man from the legal department to slink away toward the nearest exit. "Where is the Ammun Mettell?" asked Jorgan Rome.

"Busy," said Barteng.

Jorgan Rome stepped closer and took a breath.

"But I'll take you to him," said Barteng, "if you'll spare me the speech."

They found the Ammun Mettell in the central courtyard of the castle, seated at a stone table in bright sunlight. He had a crate of oranges on the ground at his side. As they approached, he took up an orange in his left hand, a knife in his right hand, and they saw the orange fall apart in mere seconds into skinless, pithless wedges.

"Oranges?" asked Jorgan Rome.

"One of the few recompenses of life as an exile on this planet," said the Ammun Mettell. "Bitter oranges with raw cane sugar. Perhaps vanilla." The Ammun Mettell took up another orange.

"I'll try to remember that you like oranges," said Jorgan Rome.

"No. These aren't for me. These are for my…loyal crew. The least of rewards become the most sought after." He cut another three oranges before looking up at Jorgan Rome. "I'm imagining that you wish to see the workshop."

"With your permission," said Jorgan Rome.

"Under two conditions," said the Ammun Mettell. "The first is that you maintain a safe distance from the beam line."

Jorgan Rome opened his mouth to speak, but the Ammun Mettell continued, "and the second is that you do not inquire about the operation or purpose of the beam line."

"Accepted," said Jorgan Rome.

The workshop, thirty meters below ground, was accessed by a secret elevator whose control panel Barteng tried to conceal. At the bottom, the elevator doors opened on a vast space. The far end of the single room was more than 100 meters distant. The right wall was a floor-to-ceiling stack of lead bricks, behind which the beam line was surely located. The entire room was well-lit, full of activity and immaculately ordered. This workshop was clearly at the center of the Mettellites' purpose on Earth. As Jorgan Rome, Teera, and Barteng exited the elevator, it seemed as if every Mettellite in the place stopped to stare. Barteng faced them, raised his arms and made dismissive "back-to-work-nothing-to-see" gestures with his hands. Which mostly worked, except that the Mettellites still stared when the group passed near. By now, Jorgan Rome had grown accustomed to strange reactions from people on this planet and so took it in stride. Until he noticed that it wasn't him they were interested in. They were staring at Teera.

"Are you recording this?" asked Jorgan Rome in a whisper.

"Of course," said Teera.

They walked past all sorts of activity, from industrial-scale manufacturing to high-tech laboratory setups. They saw metal casting in in one corner and oversize eta wave resonators in another. In one area, three Mettellites were doing intricate metal work with open, hand-held hyper-plasma torches. They waved the torches rapidly and fearlessly through thick metal plates.

"That's dangerous," said Jorgan Rome.

"They are experts," said Barteng.

The tour went on and on. The more they saw, the quieter Jorgan Rome became. Teera noticed Jorgan Rome's pensiveness. She came to his side and whispered, "Have you seen anything we can use?" Jorgan Rome shook his head. "Have you?" he asked, not expecting an answer. Teera said nothing. They had only walked a few steps further when Jorgan Rome abruptly interrupted the tour. Addressing Barteng, he said "I want to see the ship you arrived in."

"That's not here," said Barteng with a half-smile. "That's in the big room."

A pair of large bay doors at the back of the workshop opened onto what was indeed a very big room. A very big junk room it was, piled high with laboratory and industrial detritus, as disordered as the main workshop was ordered. The room must once have been the landing pad for the Mettellite ship, now with a roof and earthen cover for camouflage. The Mettellites never intended to use that ship again. Its skeletal remains were in the center of the room.

"And this is our ship," said Barteng, making no attempt to hide his satisfaction at scoring one on Jorgan Rome. But what Barteng didn't notice, and Teera did, was that Jorgan Rome was in his element in this room. His eyes darted about. "And what are those over there?" asked Jorgan Rome. "Is that a stack of thalden?"

"Oh...yes...right...guess we're not supposed to have those, but...well...things happen," muttered Barteng.

Everyone knew that collecting thalden was highly illegal. They belonged to the Port Master. When your ship arrived at a planet, the Port Master dispatched a pair of thalden to guide it in—and collect the ship's navigation history. Fleeing the planet with the thalden still attached was something that only pirates did.

"We can use those," said Jorgan Rome.

"You're a...!"

"...a fool?"

"Uh...no. That's not...what I was going to say," said Barteng.

"Yes it was," said Jorgan Rome.

"It's just that a civilian thalden isn't going to work on a military vessel! The protocols are different for military thalden. There's encryption!"

"Nevertheless, please ask your technical people to have three of these made operational."

"Sure, whatever."

"And spacesuits? Is that a pile of spacesuits over there?"

"Oh, those," said Barteng, "They're just the emergency suits from the ship."

"Will they still hold pressure?" asked Jorgan Rome.

"Maybe," said Barteng.

"Have them checked," said Jorgan Rome, walking deeper into the room. He didn't get far before a young Mettellite burst in to interrupt.

"Commander Jorgan Rome! Commander Jorgan Rome!"

"Yes?" said Jorgan Rome.

"Commander, you have a message on the underspace telephone!"

"Wait...'underspace telephone'...is that like..."

"Subspace radio? No. It has distinguishing features."

"I'll take it here," said Jorgan Rome, who then heard the voice of the Dar Telku. "Dar Telku here. There's something coming in. You need to see this. Immediately,"

"I'm on my way. Jorgan Rome out," said Jorgan Rome, leaving Barteng to puzzle over the nature of the woman who could crisply order Jorgan Rome about. "I imagine we're almost done here," said Jorgan Rome.

"I hope so," said Barteng.

"Wait. What are those?" asked Jorgan Rome, indicating a box of what appeared to be styrofoam balls.

"Oh, those." said Barteng.

Jorgan Rome waited. Finally, Barteng said, "A couple of years ago, I had to decorate for the Harvest festival. I guess I stuck them here when it was over."

"Pack them up and come with me," said Jorgan Rome.

Barteng grimaced but did as he was told. In the main room, Jorgan Rome noticed a work area he had overlooked before. A Mettellite was working a drill press, making holes in metal sheets. Lots of them. Pointlessly, it seemed. "What's going on here?" asked Jorgan Rome.

"Don't engage with him," advised Barteng.

"I am your drill thrall," said the Mettellite at the drill press. "But I'm taking night classes. I hope to become a milling machine thrall."

"Told you," said Barteng.

Jorgan Rome shook his head and continued toward the elevator. Halfway there, he saw a laboratory table covered with a drop cloth. Lifting the cloth, he saw the severed head of a robot, covered with burn marks, attached to plastic tubes and clip-on wires. The robot must have been the same model as Teera. Jorgan Rome dropped the cloth quickly and hoped that Teera hadn't seen it, but of course she had.

"Let's get out of here," said Teera

9

T HE GROUP LEFT IMMEDIATELY for the short journey to the Dar Telku's compound. Joining Jorgan Rome was Cholley, of course, but also Teera, who wanted distance between her and the Mettellite workshop. Taking the rear was Barteng, sullenly lugging the box of styrofoam balls. Barteng was acutely aware of being the only member of the party with baggage. Jorgan Rome, ever astute, knew exactly how Barteng felt. Jorgan Rome might have offered to help, but didn't.

"And who is this?" asked a wary Dar Telku in the reception area.

"My name is Teera. I am a robot."

The Dar Telku shot an incredulous glance at Jorgan Rome, asking, Really? Is this serious?

"That joke is getting old," said Cholley.

"So are we all," said Teera.

"I meant, who is this?" asked the Dar Telku, indicating Barteng in his Mettellite uniform with obvious disdain.

"He works for me," said Jorgan Rome.

"I should have expected that, I guess. Let Jorgan Rome in and he invites all his friends." The Dar Telku opened the

77

door to the plush room with computer screens for walls and motioned the group to follow. Jorgan Rome, Teera, and Cholley entered, followed by Barteng who muttered to himself, "My name is Barteng."

"Hi, Daddy!" said Raia jumping up from the sofa.

"I brought something for you," said Jorgan Rome to Raia. Turning to Barteng he said, "those are for my daughter."

Barteng winced with a little cry of anguish, realizing that he of all people, the Mettellite second-in-command, had been duped into carrying a box of styrofoam balls for a child. He dropped the box on the floor and took himself away, furious, to a far corner of the room.

"That's lovely! She's certainly a proper young lady!" said the Dar Telku. "You can leave her with me anytime! She's so intelligent! Did you know that she was able to tell me stories of the Allozetts? Stories that I—even I—had never heard before! A remarkable young lady!"

"I've always thought so," said Jorgan Rome, "In fact…"

"What is this?" cried Barteng. Everyone turned to see Barteng standing agog before the screen showing Counter-Admiral Tokar on the bridge of his incoming ship. Crew members could be seen moving around but Tokar remained motionless.

"That is probably our doom," said the Dar Telku.

Jorgan Rome went over to the image of Tokar's warship. "He hasn't moved one jot in days, has he?"

"Why should he?" noted Teera.

"How is this possible?" asked Barteng.

"Is this what you want me to see?" asked Jorgan Rome.

"No," said the Dar Telku.

The Dar Telku waved an arm at a blank wall that became yet one more display screen. The screen showed a very small spacecraft. A digital display showed that it was traveling at an astounding speed.

"This ship, or whatever it is, left the Council Planet just six hours ago. It will arrive here in less than two days. I've never seen anything so small or so fast. We're having some trouble with the dynamical phasing. But of course we can do it."

"Only you can do it," said Jorgan Rome.

"That's right," said the Dar Telku.

"How…?" stammered Barteng.

"The ship, or the imaging?" asked Cholley.

"Both," said Barteng.

"I have a suspicion that someone in this room already knows what we're looking at," said the Dar Telku. "Can you enlighten us, Mr. Jorgan Rome?"

"Excuse me for a moment," said Jorgan Rome, who went over to confer privately with Raia. While everyone watched, he gestured to the box of styrofoam balls, then to the screen showing the Counter-Admiral. Raia nodded. Jorgan Rome returned to the group. "That's a friend of mine," said Jorgan Rome.

"Of course it is! Of course it is!" exclaimed the Dar Telku. "The welcome mat is out, apparently!" Leaning in close to Jorgan Rome, she said in a stage whisper, "Please roll it up again." Then louder, "And kindly tell the rest of us what this is!"

"It's the Dersen Vala," said Jorgan Rome.

There was a silence in the room. No one could quite believe that this could be the Dersen Vala.

"The Grand Councillor? Himself?" asked Barteng.

"Yes. I work for him." More silence. "I arranged that ship for him. I know some secret shipbuilders, out near the edge of the galaxy. No one else these days has their skill. I made sure he would have a super-fast, single-person ship for urgent matters. Or for escape."

Raia walked over and leaned on the back of a sofa. "He's coming to be safe. He told me to look after you, Daddy. And if things got bad, take you to Earth. He said we'd be safe."

"Is that why we're here?" asked Jorgan Rome.

"Yes," said Raia before returning to the box of styrofoam balls.

"When did you start working for the Dersen Vala?" asked the Dar Telku.

"That would have been about eight years ago. My first assignment, if you can call it that, was just to suss out the political landscape of the Prentassar delegation upon their accession to the Council. Of course he already knew absolutely everything. It was just a test. A test that I failed utterly when I reported to his face that their governing faction had a secret reactionary cell. He ordered me to leave his office. My career was finished before it began. For some reason, though, I hung around outside the building and watched the Prentassar delegation arrive. And I saw it. Just a glimpse, really, but I saw the way their adjutant walked with an altered gait. A kind of flop of the foot—and he tried to hide the splayed fingers of his right hand. A genetically-engineered fungus had taken control of his mind. Like a flash, I was inside the building and up the ventilation shaft. I jumped down, right into the Dersen Vala's office and immobilized the adjutant. Now you have to know that the Dersen Vala never loses his cool, but he was livid then as he ordered me to leave. But I wouldn't leave. Not until I had disabled the explosive spore generator under the adjutant's jacket. Then I looked at the Dersen Vala and said, 'I'm leaving now.' And he replied, 'But I hope you'll come back.'"

"OK, so the Dersen Vala liked you," said the Dar Telku. "Still, you must have fallen from favor. Was he the one who made you work in food service on a cruise ship?"

"Actually, yes. That was his idea."

"How's that?"

"The ship, the Vandinfala, offered a 'Secret World Tour' with visits to the infamous 'walled-off' planets."

"Voris Sannar and Kemis Sannar," said the Dar Telku.

"That's right," said Jorgan Rome. "The Vandinfala was the only tourist ship allowed to visit Voris Sannar and Kemis Sannar. And, with the ruse of provisioning the ship, I was able to operate."

"If you had been caught…" said the Dar Telku.

"…he would have been executed," said Barteng, who smirked a little when everyone turned to look at him.

"As a matter of fact, I did get caught," said Jorgan Rome, "but then Cholley…well, we can talk about that later."

"I recall the scandal," said the Dar Telku. "The negotiating teams of both governments were revealed to be in Calcha's employ."

"That's right," said Jorgan Rome.

"Your work?" asked the Dar Telku.

Jorgan Rome nodded. "It was necessary."

"Such a dangerous game!" said the Dar Telku, pacing around. "If the Grand Councillor is actually conspiring against Calcha…then the Council is undermining a member state!" Shaking her head, she muttered, "It's unthinkable!" To Jorgan Rome, she said, "You know, there would be hell to pay if Calcha found out."

"That's why I arranged the ship," said Jorgan Rome. "Although it's difficult to imagine that Calcha could know of the Dersen Vala's intrigues. He compartmentalizes information like no one else."

"She found out about you and Cholley," observed Teera.

"Well, yes," said Jorgan Rome, turning to face Cholley. "But we think we know how that happened. When Ketvick—the traitorous Neerlan envoy—escaped, slicing Cholley in two pieces. The small piece was taken to Calcha."

Cholley burbled in a way that could be interpreted as a shrug. "But I don't think she learned anything useful about the Dersen Vala," he said.

Jorgan Rome excused himself. He went over to Raia, standing with her box of styrofoam balls in front of the screen showing Tokar's squadron. "How's it going?" he asked. Raia made a face. Then she plucked styrofoam ball from the box, and with the karamand in her other hand, flicked the ball at the screen. The ball vanished from the room but then appeared briefly in a corner of the screen, zipping off into space far away from the Tokar's ship. Raia scowled at missing her target. Tokar, as ever, remained un-nervingly still on the bridge of his ship.

"Try again," offered Jorgan Rome. Raia took up another styrofoam ball and sent it on its way. This time the styrofoam ball appeared dead center on the screen and then glanced off the underside of the incoming war ship. Tokar turned his head.

"Excellent!" said Jorgan Rome.

"That's ingenious," muttered Barteng. "The ball made contact inside of their defenses. No ships needed. Just a hard projectile. Or a bomb, and they're finished."

"No," said Jorgan Rome. "We're not killing anyone."

"They plan to kill people, you know. Lots of people. Everyone on the planet, I think! Perhaps that makes some difference to you?" asked the Dar Telku.

"No. Nobody dies," said Jorgan Rome simply. He turned to Raia and asked, "Now do you think you can do that with a thalden?" "Maybe," she said.

"OK, I think we're done here," said Jorgan Rome. To Barteng and the Dar Telku, he said, "I'll need help from both of you, arranging a reception for the Dersen Vala."

"There is one other thing," said the Dar Telku. "I intercepted a communication. On a frequency that only I monitor. Very strange."

"Can we hear it?"

The Dar Telku waved a hand and one more section of wall became a computer screen. A garbled voice message began, "…clee…ellum ohverghass…"

"That's the Dersen Vala!" said Jorgan Rome. "He would know that you monitor that frequency."

"And then there's this," said the Dar Telku as the recording continued, "I…am kkkhhtt…bringing the…mkhmkt…."

"The macguffin," said Barteng, "He's bringing the macguffin."

"OK, we'll deal with that, whatever it is, when he arrives," said Jorgan Rome.

A day-and-a-half later, as the sun was about to set, a small crowd had gathered near the landing site. Jorgan Rome was there with Cholley, Raia, and Teera. The Dar Telku stood with a contingent of her top technicians. She monitored the progress of the Dersen Vala's ship on a handheld device. The Ammun Mettell was represented by Barteng at the head of a small delegation of Mettellites. One of the Dar Telku's crew sidled up to Jorgan Rome and asked, "So, you've actually spoken to the Dersen Vala? What's he like?"

Jorgan Rome thought for a moment, then said, "People with that much power, you don't really want to get too close to them."

"Look!" said someone as a glint of sunlight reflected from a fast incoming ship.

The spacecraft zipped quickly along an arc to the landing area, hovered a moment above the pad, then opened out three landing legs and settled down. Then nothing happened for several minutes. The spacecraft shook from side to side. Jorgan Rome exchanged glances with Teera. Jorgan Rome dashed toward the ship but stopped when the ship's exit door opened and the Dersen Vala appeared at the top of the ramp. The Dersen Vala, eyes wide and looking surprised, arms flailing for the rail, his mouth gasping, fell forward down the ramp. He had a knife in his back.

10

JORGAN ROME RUSHED forward again. He was just about to step on the ramp when he jumped back. Jorgan Rome had sensed something. He ran around to the side of ramp where the Dersen Vala lay. It was too late. The Dersen Vala was dead.

Jorgan Rome turned around. Teera was already at his side. Teera began, "Your mentor, you must…" but Jorgan Rome cut her off. "Not the time!" he said. With the hyper-vigilance that would come upon him in times of crisis, Jorgan Rome was looking, listening, sensing, in every direction at once. Then he focused his full attention to the interior of the spaceship. "There's…" he started to say, but Teera finished his sentence, "…no one in the ship. I know."

"It's a single-person craft," said Jorgan Rome.

"Could he have…?"

"No!" said Jorgan Rome.

Teera touched his arm and gestured toward the crowd. Their collective surprise had dissipated and, losing their fear, they began to approach the spacecraft. Jorgan Rome saw that it was urgent to protect the scene but also to protect the crowd. He summoned the full strength of his character, straightened up, and bellowed, "Stay back!" They all flinched. Jorgan Rome recalibrated. More calmly, he said, "Please, we need to set a perimeter." Understanding the mollifying effect of having an action plan, Jorgan Rome extemporized, "The investigation begins immediately. I want a conference of team and technical leaders tomorrow at 8 am. And please, everyone, maintain the best operational security. We don't want any galactic chatter about this until we understand it ourselves." Indicating the Dar Telku, he asked,"Do any of your people have medical training?" She nodded. "Have them take the body of the Grand Councillor but without setting foot on the ramp." Jorgan Rome found Barteng and told him to ask the Ammun Mettell to attend the meeting in person.

A half hour later, the Dersen Vala's body had been taken away, the crowd had vanished, the Mettellites had posted a watch over the spaceship, and Jorgan Rome was tired. He looked for a place to sit down. There wasn't any so he sat on the ground. One by one, Teera, Cholley, and Raia joined him, sitting in a circle on the open ground. Raia said that it was like a campfire but with no fire. Teera offered to incinerate some brush but Jorgan Rome said "No. Let's just sit in the dark for a while."

After about ten minutes, Teera ventured some conversation. "Are you going to try to find out who did it?"

Jorgan Rome exhaled. With a wry, sad face, he said, "A mysterious murder? Killed in a locked room? Sorry, not my genre!"

"Calcha!" muttered Cholley.

There was a long pause. "No, I don't think so," said Jorgan Rome. "If Calcha were able to eliminate people…this way…" Jorgan Rome left the thought unfinished. Another quarter of an hour passed before he spoke again, "No, this is another thing entirely. Something very dark."

"Ooh…a dark side!" said Cholley. "We got a dark side!" Everyone ignored him. "Can I be a high-pressure dark-side salesman? Please? I've been practicing the patter for years!" Everyone continued to ignore him. "Feel the power of the dark side!" said Cholley.

Teera saw that Jorgan Rome was beginning to get irritated. He shot a glance at Cholley that clearly said, "Quit it!"

"Read our brochure about the dark side!" said Cholley. "Attend a free seminar on the dark side!"

Jorgan Rome snapped, "No! That's not what I meant!" More calmly, he continued, "I'm saying that this is something so dark—so big— that it won't be resolved in this book, or in any single book."

"Ooh…we get a sequel!" said Cholley.

Despite himself, Jorgan Rome had to grin, which had been Cholley's intention all along.

The next morning just before eight o'clock, several people including Jorgan Rome, the Dar Telku, the Ammun Mettell, Barteng, a communications tech from the Dar Telku's laboratory, the Mettellite security chief, and Cholley arrived at the Mettellite compound for the meeting.

"We'll be meeting in the Frank Herbert Conference Room," said Barteng.

They all took seats, leaving Jorgan Rome at the head of the table. The Ammun Matter looked distinctly uncomfortable seated among them. Jorgan Rome began the meeting crisply, "We have two broad areas of concern. I'd like first to touch on matters related to the arrival and passing of the Dersen Vala. We'll then move to updates on our upcoming rendezvous with the Counter-Admiral. Yesterday's events…"

but he didn't get very far before the guiding spirit of the Frank Herbert Conference room began to assert itself:

"Two items of business?" thought the Dar Telku's communications tech, "Or is that just a cover for something else?"

"This meeting is clever, indeed clever," thought the Mettellite security chief.

Barteng looked over at the Dar Telku and thought to himself, "She knows more, that one does, than she says."

The security chief caught the eye of the communications tech. "If he is thinking what I am thinking that he is thinking," he thought, "then this is no meeting, but a showdown!"

The communications tech thought, "I have been thinking all wrong! It's obvious that he's thinking that I'm thinking I know what he's thinking, when instead I now think that he's not thinking so much that I'm thinking he's thinking what I'm thinking, but he thinks he can outsmart me! I cannot let that happen!"

The Mettellite from the workshop stole a glance at Cholley. "That gelatinoid!" he thought, "he is the dangerous one!"

Cholley thought he was going to burp.

Finally, Jorgan Rome cried, "Enough! We're moving to a different room!"

They arose and moved into the hallway to find another meeting room. The Ammun Mettell followed behind. In the hallway was an angry Tapeerian, part of the Dar Telku's laboratory, who had not been invited to the meeting. He stood squarely in front of Jorgan Rome and stamped his hoof on the ground. "I know you are pre-occupied with finding out who killed the Grand Councillor," said the Tapeerian.

"Not really," thought Jorgan Rome, saying nothing but simply nodding.

"You humanoids say we are not clean!" hissed the Tapeerian, spitting on the floor, "because we have horns!"

"Actually," thought Jorgan Rome looking at the floor, "it's not about the horns."

"Because we have hooves, you say we are not kosher! Look to someone driven by extremities!" Then, staring into Jorgan Rome's eyes, he added, "Toes are reasons for murder!"

Jorgan Rome thanked the Tapeerian for his input and led his group down the hallway. The Dar Telku came up to him and said, "He's not so bad. You just have to let Tapeerians be Tapeerians."

"Nevertheless," said Jorgan Rome as they entered the new meeting room, "you might avoid wearing sandals."

Once everyone was seated in the new room, Jorgan Rome wasted no time. "We need to know why the Dersen Vala came here." There were nods of agreement around the table. "Was he fleeing something? Did he have something to tell us? Was he bringing something? Who did he plan to visit?"

When no one said anything, Jorgan Rome looked around the table. The Ammun Mettell, hitherto silent, said, "It would not be in the nature—or practice—of the Dersen Vala to flee. Ever."

"Understood," said Jorgan Rome, wondering how the Ammun Mettell could know that.

"Then why did he come?" asked the Dar Telku.

"He must have been bringing something," said the Mettellite security chief. "We're all set to search the ship."

"No!" said Jorgan Rome. "Forgive me, it's just a feeling, but I'd rather no one enter the ship just yet."

"We've done a complete scan. There's no one in there!" said the Mettellite security chief.

"Bear with me on this," asked Jorgan Rome, dividing the sentiment in the room between those who trusted his intuition and those with no patience for a mere gut feeling. "I'll work up a plan for that. In the meantime, is there anything we can know from communications intercepts, vessel tracking, or history?"

"We have nothing," said the Dar Telku.

"Except…" began the Dar Telku's communications tech. Everyone turned and focused attention. "Except…maybe…a life recorder."

"Life recorder?" asked the security chief.

"Everyone at the rank of councillor has one. The Grand Councillor will certainly have one. It's a recorder for continuity of business. Plans, ideas, last messages…in case something happens."

"Like they end up dead?" asked Barteng.

"Yes."

"We'll search the ship!" said the security chief.

"No, it'll most likely be on his person somewhere. We could work on finding it in the lab."

Jorgan Rome approved. "Make it…the way you just said." The business then turned to the imminent encounter with Tokar. "Do we have any updates on the possible off-planet alliances?"

"We have an update. And it's not good. Not good at all!" said the Dar Telku. "The Octonions will not associate with us!"

"What about the Sedenions?"

"Bunch of zeroes! Useless!" muttered the Mettellite security chief.

"Others?" asked Jorgan Rome.

"There are the Denarians…" said the Dar Telku, "…but I can't even talk to them! They think they know everything!"

"Let's focus on our own efforts then. What about those space suits? Do they hold pressure?"

"Yes," said Barteng. "Five of them pass testing."

"Then I'll need four volunteers to help me take out the Counter-Admiral," said Jorgan Rome.

"We'll find them among our people. And volunteer them," said Barteng.

The meeting concluded, they filed out of the room. The Dar Telku returned to her base to monitor galactic communications. Her technicians returned to the lab to search for the Dersen Vala's life recorder. Jorgan Rome and Teera stayed behind to confer. Cholley found himself following Barteng and the Ammun Mettell. Perhaps it was mere curiosity, or possibly remnant mistrustfulness that lingered from the Frank Herbert conference room, or maybe it was something he noticed that made Cholley ooze along the ceiling behind them, his body changing to match the color and texture of his surroundings. They went down the hallway then turned into another hallway that was empty of people. They entered an unused room. There, Barteng began to talk vehemently, gesturing this way and that. Cholley was unable to hear what they said. The Ammun Mettell nodded from time to time. The Ammun Mettell gave Barteng a melancholy half-smile, made a few observations, then nodded once more to conclude the discussion. When Barteng left, Cholley had to decide which of them to follow. He stayed with the Ammun Mettell. The Ammun Mettell returned to the hallway, rounded a corner and looked both directions. Then he vanished into thin air.

"Into thin air?" asked Jorgan Rome when Cholley recounted what he had seen.

"Pfft," said Cholley. "He looked around first to make sure no one was watching."

"I don't know what to make of this," said Jorgan Rome. "Teera, ideas?"

"None. Wait. Searching." After a few moments she said, "Here, I have this." It was a video from the collected records of Naveer. "I searched for discontinuous images of the Ammun Mettell on Naveer. Here is from a back alley security camera." In grainy, night-time footage of a deserted alley, a figure approached. It was the Ammun Mettell. He looked around. And then he vanished.

"What in the world?" asked Jorgan Rome.

"'What' is the question," agreed Teera.

"We need to know what's going on," said Jorgan Rome. "It's definitely time for some narrative exposition."

"Hemingway didn't do exposition," said Cholley.

"Hemingway didn't do gelatinoids, dear," said Teera. Cholley splashed with indignation. The lights on Teera's face flickered.

"What I mean," said Jorgan Rome, "is that we need some sort of plot device that will reveal who—or what—this Ammun Mettell really is."

Part Three

11

EARLY THE NEXT MORNING Jorgan Rome heard about a break-in at the Dar Telku's compound. No sooner had Jorgan Rome told Teera than they were on their way. When they arrived they found the Dar Telku outside waiting for them. She stared at them for a few moments in silence. Then she muttered, "You've heard?" and let them enter. "The whole incident is on video," said the Dar Telku, bringing them to a display screen.

The video was black-and white. and silent. It showed a empty laboratory at night. All the things you expect to see in an deserted laboratory were there: A Jacob's Ladder arcing and rising, "*BZZZ—WAPP! BZZZ—WAPP,*" an oscilloscope screen with an animated Lissajous figure, some kind of glowing chemical dripping from a retort into a conical flask, an outsized panel thick with knobs, another filled with meters whose needles were dancing in sync to a slow sinusoid. And fog, of course, rolling down from a container of dry ice.

A door opens. An intruder enters and begins rifling through drawers, looking at computer screens. He looks around. When he finally faces the direction of the camera, his identity is apparent. The intruder is Barteng.

"Recognize him?" asked the Dar Telku.

Jorgan Rome nodded.

"What type of people you consort with, that's your business. Do not, let me repeat this, do not make it my business, Mr. Jorgan Rome!"

"I'm sorry," said Jorgan Rome.

"Not good enough," said the Dar Telku. "You, yourself, are barely welcome here."

The video showed Barteng continuing to search the room. Then it showed the Dar Telku entering.

"I've turned the sound down, to spare you. He is a very rude young man," said the Dar Telku.

On the video, the Dar Telku confronts Barteng. Barteng sneers and says something. Watching the video, Jorgan Rome and Teera winced. The Dar Telku noticed and realized that they could each lip-read. On the video, the Dar Telku says something calmly and then Barteng pulls a weapon. With a half-smile, believing he had mastered the situation, and focused on the Dar Telku, he failed to notice what was apparent to anyone watching the video. Spider-bots descended the wall behind him.

The Dar Telku switched off the video.

"I'm sorry," said Jorgan Rome.

"Good," said the Dar Telku.

"Is he…?" began Teera.

"He's never been better!" said the Dar Telku, enigmatically failing to answer the question that she knew Teera was asking.

No one said anything for a few moments. Then the Dar Telku motioned them to another screen. "With that settled, this here is what I really need to show you." She waved an arm and the screen showed another video, this one in color and with sound. Barteng was seated at a table and facing the direction of the camera. He was wearing something like a hospital gown. The sides of his head were shaven clean. Offscreen the Dar Telku's voice asked, "How are you feeling?"

"Very well, ma'am, thank you," said Barteng.

"Do you have something to tell us?" asked the Dar Telku.

"Yes, ma'am," said Barteng.

"Please tell us about the Ammun Mettell," said the Dar Telku.

"OK," said Barteng.

"Stop!" commanded Jorgan Rome. "What have you done?"

"It's temporary!" snapped the Dar Telku. "A few days at most! Besides, I like him better this way."

Jorgan Rome started to say something, then decided against it.

"Now be quiet. Observe!" said the Dar Telku, pushing open a pair of doors to the video room. Barteng was still seated behind the table. He seemed pleased to see his friends.

12

BARTENG BEGAN TO TELL the story. "They had an orchard," said Barteng, "the Ammun Mettell and his family. I mean, he wasn't the Ammun Mettell then, that came later. But his parents had an orchard."

"And..." prodded the Dar Telku.

"Oh, right. The orchard." Jorgan Rome made a quizzical face but the Dar Telku ignored him. "The orchard was big but they couldn't sell anything. Then the subsidies, they stopped."

The Dar Telku waited for Barteng to continue.

"So they sent the Ammun Mettell to check into it. Well, he wasn't the Ammun Mettell then. That came later."

"It's OK to call him that, dear," said the Dar Telku.

"He went to the Central Agricultural Subsidy Office in the capital. He filled out a lot of forms but nothing happened."

"The Ammun Mettell!" marveled Jorgan Rome, "filling out subsidy forms!"

Barteng became agitated. "You don't know anything, do you? You have no clue! You have to..."

"…it's OK, dear! He's just leaving." said the Dar Telku in the most reassuring tone she could muster. Then, in a whisper to Jorgan Rome, she said, "If you don't stay quiet, I'm going to process *you*."

Jorgan Rome nodded.

"I'm calm," said Barteng, smiling again. "So the Ammun Mettell…well, he wasn't the…OK, anyway, he decided to confront the bureaucracy head-on."

Confront the Khadar's bureaucracy? thought Jorgan Rome to himself, now who doesn't have a clue? Barteng saw Jorgan Rome's face, saw the skepticism there and took offense. "It's easy for you to just…sit there and…" The Dar Telku stepped forward, telling Jorgan Rome, "That's it for you! You can watch the video later!" and hustled him out of the room. Returning, the Dar Telku invited Barteng, as sweetly as she could, to continue his story. There would be no more opinions offered. "OK," said Barteng.

The Ammun Mettell, if we can call him that, thought about returning to the Subsidy Office but it was obvious that there was nothing more to be done there. So he went instead to the Central Market. That was where products from all over the planet were distributed to the capital region. That was where his family was unable to sell anything. You had to be a vendor to get access to the market grounds, but the Ammun Mettell slipped in anyway. He walked for miles through all the buildings. He noticed and analyzed everything just like he always does. Then he went and found the market director's office. He just walked in and announced, "There are numerous inefficiencies in the operation of this market!" The market director barely had time to narrow his eyes and scowl before the Ammun Mettell commanded, "Walk with me!" To his own surprise, the market director found himself doing as he was told.

The Ammun Mettell led a brisk tour of the entire market, pointing out aisles that were too narrow for transporters to pass, incompatible storage conditions, redundant sorting systems, and a hundred other things until the director cried "Stop!" So the Ammun Mettell paused.

"As my new Assistant Market Director, you'll help fix *all* of these things. Won't you?"

The Ammun Mettell said, "I'll need to know one thing first." The Market Director smiled. He was prepared to be generous with salary. But the Ammun Mettell sensed that the time was right to find out what he really wanted. He asked why there was not a single thing from his home region on offer in the market.

The Market Director took a breath before answering. "We have no control over that. All I can say is that one of the Khadar's closest advisors is from a competing region. Perhaps that's more than I should say, but you will need to understand the constraints we have."

The Ammun Mettell nodded briefly. He neither accepted nor rejected the job offer but, in fact, his mind was elsewhere. He had just learned how decisions were made on his planet and in what close detail they emerged from the Khadar's inner circle. He left the market with new plans in mind.

A familiar voice said, "I saw you going into the market!" The Ammun Mettell looked around and saw Laddlo, from his own home region, sitting on a bench. "Very skilled and very dignified—under the fence and over the boxes...but I knew you'd be coming out the front door."

The Ammun Mettell grinned broadly. Laddlo had always had his number.

"Laddlo?" muttered Jorgan Rome, watching the video of Barteng's story.

"It is an unusual name," said Teera.

"I know," said Jorgan Rome.

Laddlo asked, "So what's next in store, Mr. Assistant Market Director?"

"Next," said the Ammun Mettell, "is the Khadar's Palace."

Laddlo raised his eyebrows in mock admiration. "Are we climbing any fences to get in?"

The Ammun Mettell noticed the word, 'we.' "No, we're going in the public entrance."

The next morning, the Ammun Mettell signed them both up for the afternoon public tour of the Khadar's Palace. The tour, for which a small group assembled under the main portico, would show an assortment of unused reception rooms, ballrooms, along with hallway after hallway adorned with copies of ancient proclamations. It would be a tour of frippery and gewgaws having nothing to do with the Khadar's real operations, so there's no telling why the Ammun Mettell wanted to take the tour, let alone take it twice. But he did.

For a half-hour the tour progressed. The guide, who mentioned that he had been leading tours for a decade, pattered on in a way that confirmed his long tenure. Almost everyone was bored. After entering each room, Laddlo exclaimed "Lovely chandelier!" which pleased the tour guide until the fourth or fifth time when he finally caught on that Laddlo wasn't serious. Everyone was bored except the Ammun Mettell. He observed closely, and there were things that puzzled him. Why, for instance, was there no security? And what was with those little hesitations? Turning a corner, the tour guide seemed to pause and take a breath before committing to his path. And so it went, from music room to historic council chamber to library to courtyard, always with the littlest hint of trepidation before entering a room or hallway. Then came a moment when the guide stepped into a corridor and scurried immediately back. There was a commotion in the corridor. A large group of people approached. One of them was the Khadar, striding rapidly with an advisor in tow. Perhaps a decision about agricultural subsidies or education policy was being made at that very moment. When the Ammun Mettell caught the Khadar's eye, he was certain that he, the Ammun Mettell, could give that advice and make those decisions.

The Ammun Mettell turned around and saw Laddlo, with a wry smile, pointing at a large vase. The Ammun Mettell found the tour guide hiding behind the vase. "Tour's over!" spluttered the guide.

"No," said the Ammun Mettell, "It's merely interrupted."

"Come back tomorrow!"

"We will," said the Ammun Mettell.

The next day's tour was much the same, but not identical. They heard the same tour patter, saw many of the same rooms, if in a slightly different order. Midway down a long corridor, the Ammun Mettell glanced down a connecting hallway and froze where he was. Laddlo came over to him, puzzled.

"That's the wrong hallway," whispered the Ammun Mettell.

Indeed, the hallway was different from the one he had seen on the previous day's tour. The day before, it had been marble-walled with gilt flashing. Today the walls were dark filigreed wood. This hallway was longer but with fewer doorways. The Ammun Mettell was not mistaken. He had a photographic memory in those days.

Watching the video, Jorgan Rome wondered aloud whether it was possible to lose photographic memory. Wouldn't he still possess it? Teera suggested that they watch more of the video.

The tour guide noticed the Ammun Mettell's consternation. "That's right," he said, "the 'Shifting Palace'," with a conspiratorial smile. Then he continued the tour. The Ammun Mettell understood in a flash. The Palace could reconfigure itself! Exactly which corridors connected to what rooms and other hallways was something that could change daily or perhaps even hourly! The labyrinth of the fortress-like Palace was dynamic! Access to the current Palace map likely would be controlled. The Ammun Mettell smiled as he formulated a plan. He would own the dynamical Palace map and, with no other obvious security in place, have access to the Khadar. His confidence in his ability to make older men listen to him was unbounded.

Standing outside on the plaza, the Ammun Mettell looked back at the palace and said under his breath, "I just need to be in there every day for about a month. That's enough."

"Not possible, unless you're some kind of councillor. Or a janitor, maybe," said Laddlo.

The Ammun Mettell raised his eyebrows.

"Oh! I guess we could do that," said Laddlo.

"'We?'"

"It's OK. I'm sort of between things right now," explained Laddlo. "I mean there's no problem, we're doing fine…my wife's family and all…and, besides, I've got some projects that I'm working on…"

The Ammun Mettell listened.

"Like I'm writing a novel. I'm having a good time with it. All my characters are named after food, you see. You'll have to bear with me on this…I mean…I've got this character, he's like my main guy, Sir Beef Wellington, and he…" Laddlo noticed the look on the Ammun Mettell's face. "I've got other things I'm working on, too!" said Laddlo quickly.

"So that's how the Ammun Mettell—and his friend—became janitors in the Khadar's Palace!" said Barteng on the video. "But you have to know something about the Ammun Mettell. He really takes to hard work. I've seen him when it comes to real work. I'll bet those two were the best janitors that Palace ever had."

"They must have made a great team," said the Dar Telku.

"I think so," said Barteng.

"So, Laddlo today, what's he doing?" asked the Dar Telku. Barteng said nothing but made such a face in response that the Dar Telku didn't pursue it.

There were special conditions attached to working as a janitor in the Palace. There were no set shifts. They had to report to work at different times each day. When they arrived, they were given maps of the rooms that needed work that day. They had firm instructions to finish their work in six hours. Laddlo and the Ammun Mettell knew, of course, that the strange time requirements marked the hours of the Palace reconfigurations. Because they worked quickly, they had time left over each day for a little exploration beyond they map they were given.

At first, the Ammun Mettell had planned to rely on his prodigious memory to map the Palace. But the number of possible reconfigurations was overwhelming and he soon lost track of where the corridors, even just the ones he had seen, might connect. Fortunately, Laddlo had hobbies beyond writing.

One day, outside the Palace, an hour before their shift was to begin, Laddlo turned to the Ammun Mettell and said, "I've been playing around with eta waves."

"Now here's the thing," said Barteng. "If anyone back then said to you that they were 'playing around with eta waves', you'd just walk away. Right? So antiquated! But the Ammun Mettell knew his old friend better than that."

"To what purpose?" asked the Ammun Mettell.

"Making the tranceivers smaller. Untraceable."

The Ammun Mettell smiled. "OK, show me what you've got." Now it was Laddlo's turn to smile because the Ammun Mettell had seen right through him. Laddlo pulled a handful of tiny gray buttons from his pocket.

"What do they do?" asked the Ammun Mettell.

"They automatically pair up with their nearest neighbors to make a network."

"A dynamic network…"

"…like the Palace itself."

"So, if we place one at each end of a corridor…"

"They will automatically report back—to us alone—the configuration of the Palace."

"Brilliant," said the Ammun Mettell.

During their shifts at the Palace, Laddlo and the Ammun Mettell became skilled at placing the eta wave repeaters in rooms and hallways where they worked. Confident that the Palace wouldn't rearrange itself during work hours, they began to explore and plant the little repeaters beyond the extent of their daily map. One of them, typically Laddlo, would act as forward scout, the other would keep an eye out for activity at their rear. Between shifts, and on days off, they studied the parts of the Palace labyrinth that their devices reported back to them.

One evening, in the middle of their shift, exploring at a considerable distance off the edge of their daily map, Laddlo peered around a corner. Something he saw must have frightened him. He backed away quickly, returning the way he had come. Turning again, into a familiar hallway, he must have seen something else that alarmed him. Looking for refuge, he opened a pair of double doors and slipped into the room behind them. When the Ammun Mettell came along and didn't see Laddlo in any of the adjacent hallways, he knew that something had happened. He also knew exactly what to do. He had a pocketful of little repeater units, all of which could pair with the units that Laddlo carried in a small pouch on his belt. They led the Ammun Mettell directly to the doors that Laddlo had gone through. Standing in front of them, he paused. What was on the other side of those doors was likely dangerous or Laddlo would have emerged by now.

"That's what you need to know about the Ammun Mettell!" said Barteng. "Going in there might well mean the end of his whole project! But he went in anyway! He never abandons his people!"

Watching the video, Jorgan Rome muttered, "That's telling." Teera understood. To Jorgan Rome, failing to rescue a colleague was inconceivable. Barteng had as much as admitted that he, at least, would consider walking away.

Opening the doors, the Ammun Mettell saw Laddlo pinned to the wall by three robots. A few people were gathered around, asking him questions but Laddlo was defiant. The Ammun Mettell had taken no more than one step into the room before a pair of robots came for him in the blink of an eye. Ever calm, the Ammun Mettell had time to reach into his pocket and activate the highly-illegal botdropper that he had fashioned for emergencies. All the robots in the room collapsed to the floor. The Ammun Mettell looked over at Laddlo and motioned with his head toward the doors. Laddlo brushed himself off, stepped over the robots, and was about to leave with the Ammun Mettell when a young woman spoke up, "Please don't go! The robots are ill-behaved and I do apologize on their behalf, but, please, we'll make it up to you."

The Ammun Mettell hesitated. Laddlo looked at him and looked at the doors.

The young woman said, "My name is Calcha."

13

T HE YOUNG LABORATORY technician stepped quietly into the room. "Umm…Commander?" Jorgan
Rome blinked himself awake. He had switched off the video
and allowed himself to fall asleep in his chair. "Yes?" he said,
turning to the lab technician standing in the doorway.

"We think we've found it."

"Excellent…where was it?" asked Jorgan Rome, strug-
gling to recall what this might be about. Teera noticed and
discreetly lent some help. "So the Dersen Vala's life recorder
was not where you expected it?" asked Teera.

"Oh! Not at all! Not at all! I mean, you'll really have
to come down to the examination room to see for your-
selves…if that's OK, Commander."

"I'll be along in just a moment. Thank you," said Jorgan
Rome. Standing up, he motioned for Teera to lead the way.
"But first I'd like to look in on the squadron," he said. Stepping into the Dar Telku's reception room, they went over to
the wall screen that showed Counter-Admiral Tokar's ships.
On the bridge of the command ship there was more activity
than before. It was crowded there now, with crew members everywhere installing equipment, doing calibrations,

performing calculations. Tokar himself was at the rear, giving instruction and, apparently, telling stories. The crew around him laughed at what must have been a punchline.

"I guess you'd laugh, too, at an Admiral's story," said Teera.

"Would I?" asked Jorgan Rome.

"No, you probably wouldn't," said Teera.

"Maybe a person will naturally just have to like the jokes told by a killer robot," said Jorgan Rome.

"I really don't like that expression," said Teera.

"But he is. That's his function, his programming, his history, you know that."

"I know that," said Teera.

"Do they know that?" asked Jorgan Rome, indicating the crew.

"Of course they do," said Teera, leaving Jorgan Rome to ruminate on the value of charm in a robot who would dispose of his own crew in an instant if it suited him.

A display in the upper right-hand corner of the wall screen showed that just over eighty-six hours remained before the arrival of Tokar's squadron. The shortness of the time left would account for the pace of activity on Tokar's ship. Jorgan Rome, for his part, had no ships, no equipment, no calibrations to do nor calculations to perform.

The examination room was in a part of the Dar Telku's compound that was several floors below ground. The room had been deeply chilled to accommodate the remains of the Dersen Vala. The lab tech put on a warm jacket and offered one from the rack to Jorgan Rome. "What about them?" asked Jorgan Rome, indicating Cholley and Raia who were already waiting at the door.

"The Dar Telku felt that it might not be appropriate for…"

"Raia has already seen much more than this. She's part of my team," said Jorgan Rome.

"Certainly, Commander."

The examination room was very cold. Cholley almost instantly developed the rubbery outer skin that was the typical gelatinoid defense against cold air. The Dersen Vala's garments and belongings were strewn about a lab bench full of microscopes and analytical equipment. The lab tech walked right past the lab bench towards the table on which the Dersen Vala's body lay under a sheet.

"You mean, the life recorder isn't there, in his stuff?" asked Cholley.

"No. It's not there," said the lab tech curtly.

"It's on his person, then?" asked Teera.

"Well…I'm not sure 'on' is best word for it," said the lab tech.

"Thank you," said the Dar Telkıı, entering the examination room. "We'll let the Chief take over now." To Jorgan Rome, she said, "Let me introduce our Chief Scientist."

The Chief stood by the table with the Dersen Vala's body. "We had given up, I'm afraid. After a nearly molecular search of his belongings we had found nothing. It was only when we mustered our, well, courage, to search his person that we came across something peculiar. There is a persistent, but limited, metabolism inside of him that has not died with the man! In the brain. In a small part of his striatum."

"You mean he's not dead?" asked Cholley.

"No, he's quite dead. But we think he may have co-opted his own striatum as a life recorder."

"That's icky," said Cholley. "And impossible."

"Let me explain. As you know, Bob, the striatum is…"

"I'm *not* Bob," said Cholley.

The Chief stopped talking altogether. He made a pained smile, his fingers tapping impatiently against his thigh.

"Just go with it," said Jorgan Rome to Cholley.

"Very well," said the Chief. "As you know, Bob, we all…"

"My name is Cholley."

"This just isn't going to work!" said the Chief, throwing up his hands.

"He's Bob," said Raia.

"Thank you," said the Chief. "As you know, Bob, the striatum is the most stimulus/response trainable part of our brains. Our friend here seems to have hijacked that capability to store a program of sorts. Normally that program would dissipate at death, but he seems to have provided it with some sort of persistent metabolic support. We don't understand that yet."

"A program? How do we access it?" asked Jorgan Rome.

"There would be a code word, we think. Did he ever provide you with a code word?"

Jorgan Rome shook his head.

"A personal detail perhaps? Did he ever share something personal with you?"

"The Dersen Vala? Never. He never shared anything with anyone. Well, except maybe once…"

"And that was…"

"We were talking about succession to the Council when he suddenly looked into the distance and said that he had loved a woman once."

The Chief looked pleased. "Did he tell you her name?"

"Yes," said Jorgan Rome, "It was…"

"Don't tell me! Tell him!" said the Chief.

"To the Dersen Vala? He's dead."

"The persistent neural circuitry will be able to process a code word, I believe," said the Chief.

They gathered around the table on which the Dersen Vala lay. The Chief gently pulled back the sheet from the Dersen Vala's face. "Now, please," he said. Jorgan Rome kneeled, leaned in close, and to the dead man's ear he said "Ruth."

For a moment nothing happened. Then suddenly the body convulsed as if from an electric shock. The Dersen Vala began to breathe. Slow, rasping, autonomous respiration set in. "Oh, my, he's alive!" shouted the lab tech from a far corner of the room to which he had scurried. "No!" shouted the Chief, from the opposite corner, "That's just the program! I think." When the Dersen Vala opened his eyes, the lab tech was out the door in a flash.

Only Jorgan Rome, Teera, and Raia remained close, but even they stepped back when the Dersen Vala began to speak. "Joorgaaan Ro…o…o…me…"

"I'm here," said Jorgan Rome, to the Dersen Vala's unseeing eyes.

"Joorgaaan Ro…o…o…me…….you…are a…fool"

Jorgan Rome swallowed a bit. Cholley asked, "He programmed his striatum to say *that?*" Then Jorgan Rome waved him to silence as the Dersen Vala continued.

"Protect Raia. Stop Calcha," were the words that came from the body of the Dersen Vala. Jorgan Rome nodded. "Raia!" croaked the Dersen Vala.

"I'm right here," said Raia. To which the Dersen Vala, or his life recorder, replied in an obscure language from long ago, "*Yubbour pubbarubbents ubbare lubbivubbing…stubbay fubbar ubbawubbay, nubbot subbafe…bubbettubber wubbith jubborgubban rubbome. Ubbin mubby shubbip…thube mubbakha mubbiffubbin…Rubbetrubbieve ubbit…ubbimperubbatubbive…kubbeep ubbit ubbawubbay frubbom thubbem.*" "I understand," said Raia.

"Ammun Mettell!" said the Dersen Vala. When no response came, the Dersen Vala said only, "No…more." He went silent but continued to breathe.

Then, without warning, the Dersen Vala rasped out the name of the Dar Telku. She stepped forward. She was surprised. She hadn't imagined that the Dersen Vala knew anything about her. "I'm here," said the Dar Telku.

"Dar Telku," said the body of the Dersen Vala. "Allozetts…exist…never contact!" Which was perhaps the only thing she could hear that would leave her even more stupefied.

The Dersen Vala went silent. The eyes closed and the breathing stopped.

"I…I think…that's it," said the Chief to a silent room. The lab tech found his way back to the examination table. After a long pause, the Chief said, "I can replay that if anyone needs."

"No need!" said the Dar Telku hurriedly.

"I'm good!" said the lab tech.

Silence again.

"Cholley needs an apple!"

Shortly afterward, Teera, Raia, Cholley, Jorgan Rome, and the Dar Telku were sitting on sofas in the more comfortable reception room. The Dar Telku had arranged for tea. A platter of apples was set out for Cholley. Nobody spoke. The only sound came from Cholley dissolving apples.

"Well, you heard it," said Jorgan Rome, finally, to the Dar Telku. "The Allozetts exist,"

"I knew that. I was certain of it," said the Dar Telku.

"You heard what else he said. Never try to contact them."

"We'll just see about that…we'll just see about that, won't we?" said the Dar Telku.

"Not now!" said Jorgan Rome, indicating the wall screen that showed Tokar's squadron.

"All right, fine," said the Dar Telku.

"And not ever," said Jorgan Rome.

"No promises," said the Dar Telku.

Silence again. Everyone looked over at Raia, who pretended to be so caught up in drinking tea that she couldn't notice. "Raia?" said Jorgan Rome, but she didn't respond. "Raia?" said Teera.

"What?" said Raia.

"What did the Dersen Vala tell you?" asked Teera.

"Not much," said Raia. They all waited. Finally, Raia spoke again. "He said he brought something."

"What's that, dear?" asked Teera.

"The Makha Miffin."

The Dar Telku spat out her tea. Spilling the remains of her cup into her lap, she jumped up, while still choking on tea that gone down the wrong way, to brush the hot liquid off of her.

"The MacGuffin," muttered Cholley. "He brought us the MacGuffin."

The Dar Telku coughed. "The Makha Miffin! Impossible!"

"What is it?" asked Jorgan Rome.

"I don't know exactly. The Legends are a little evasive. But I think it's a book. About the Allozetts. By the Allozetts, maybe even their official records. And I think there was only ever supposed to be a single copy."

"Then it's important that we retrieve it?" asked Jorgan Rome.

The Dar Telku fixed him a with a what-do-you-think look.

"OK, if there's no choice, we'll do this." asked Jorgan Rome.

"Why would such a book, that book, be in the possession of a Grand Councillor?" asked the Dar Telku.

"He had a lot of hidden ways," said Jorgan Rome. "Many, many irons in the fire. Let's reconnoiter at the ship in one hour."

An hour later, the whole team met near the Dersen Vala's ship. Word had gotten around. A large crowd of onlookers was milling around. A growing, rhythmic crashing sound announced the marching arrival of the Mettellite chief of security with some sort of armored-up platoon. Heavily-weighted down with body-protectors and high-tech gear, they trudged forward like hoplites with lasers. "We've been drilling for this!" said the Mettellite chief. "Sound off!" yelled the chief. "Fire in the hole!" yelled a platoon member. "Sound off!" yelled the chief, "Fire in the hole!" came the reply.

Cholley nudged Jorgan Rome. "Do we want 'fire in the hole?'"

"No we don't," answered Jorgan Rome, stepping forward. "Uh, Chief, could we have a word?" They conferred out of earshot. Jorgan Rome gestured at the ship. The chief nodded several times, taking it like a soldier. Then he marched away with his troops. He must have developed second thoughts because he returned about five minutes later by himself. He needed to see Jorgan Rome's plan. He needed to know what could be better than his own troops. His jaw dropped when he saw Jorgan Rome giving Raia her final instructions. Raia was, as Jorgan Rome knew, the only one who knew how to use the karamand. She was the only person he would permit to go near the ship.

"At the first sign of trouble, get out of there," said Jorgan Rome. "Find the Makha Miffin and…get out of there!"

"I understand," said Raia. Jorgan Rome took a breath as she began to move towards the ship. He knew that her hand in her pocket was gripping the karamand and that she could do this. Besides, the assignment had come directly from the Dersen Vala.

The crowd swarmed behind Raia. "Clear the path! Clear the path!" shouted Jorgan Rome to little avail. Raia could make her own path but she was jostled around by the crowd. They stopped when she started walking up the ramp. Jorgan Rome pushed forward. Then something on the ground caught his eye. The karamand! He picked it up and dashed for the ramp. He was too late. Raia had entered the ship and the entry door slammed shut behind her. The ramp began to rise. Jorgan Rome was frantic, trying to find some way to get the karamand back in Raia's hands. The engines rumbled and came to life. The ship lifted off the ground. A couple of minutes later, it was in the upper atmosphere. Soon it would be beyond the Earth's orbit and gone.

"Get tracking on that now!" snarled Jorgan Rome to the Dar Telku. She recoiled a bit then turned to confer with an assistant. "We're on it," she said.

"You were right about it being a trap," said Teera. For a moment, Jorgan Rome became so livid, eyes rolling back like the old days before his training, that he almost dashed the karamand against the ground. "I need to go meditate," he said.

14

PERHAPS LADDLO DIDN'T KNOW who Calcha was. But the Ammun Mettell, who paid close attention to even minor political figures, would have known about Calcha. She was the third child of the Sanpegg of Tellapenth. With two brothers ahead of her, she would never come to power. Her fate was to live as a minor royal, her life hemmed by protocol at every turn. She rebelled. With a debauched coterie, she commandeered a royal residence on a faraway continent. There she threw parties that lasted weeks. After one party, bodies strewn about and sleeping everywhere, she dragged herself awake to find the residence surrounded by Royal Lancers, Wandsmen, and Cannoneers. Without looking behind her, she stepped onto the transporter that whisked her back to the Sanpegg's Fortress.

Those were times of great tension between Tellapenth and Naveer. Treaties were signed only to be abrogated again. The former partners, the core of the old Realm, were at loggerheads over everything. Until the Grand Councillor, the Dersen Vala, took over the negotiations personally. An agreement was fashioned. Diplomatic hostages were exchanged. The Sanpegg was thrilled to send his daughter off to Naveer as a diplomatic hostage. But just a few months passed before Calcha began to tear once more through society, this time on Naveer. Only this time she was more cruel. With her expatriate disdain for local ways, she learned to find and exploit weaknesses in the luckless types who would carouse with her. She delighted in lives destroyed through scandal. Until it all came to an end for unexplained reasons. Now she never left the Khadar's Palace. Her only entertainment was whatever came to her door. Like a couple of lost janitors.

She had told them her name was Calcha. "I know," said the Ammun Mettell.

Calcha smiled, nodded a little, made a play of being flattered. "And who are you?" she asked.

"We're janitors. And we're leaving," said the Ammun Mettell, motioning to Laddlo to follow.

"I don't think so," said Calcha.

"Oh, no, we're definitely leaving."

"I don't think you're janitors," said Calcha. "I think you've come here on a mission."

Calcha and the Ammun Mettell locked eyes. Then the Ammun Mettell cocked his head to the right and looked down. "That's it, isn't it?" said Calcha. "Have you come to spy on the Khadar?" Laddlo flinched with indignation—barely—but Calcha noticed. "No, not spying," she said. "You've just come to talk to him." The Ammun Mettell didn't reply. Laddlo shifted his weight from foot to foot.

"You've come to tell the Khadar something he needs to know. That's darling! How sweet of you!"

The Ammun Mettell's face hardened as he moved swiftly to the door.

"What about *me*? Don't I deserve some of your kindness? Isn't there something you could tell me?" asked Calcha with a smirk. "Something *I* need to know?"

The ridicule was too much for the Ammun Mettell. He took the bait. He turned around, looked squarely at her, and said matter-of-factly, "Your plan will not succeed."

"My plan?" laughed Calcha.

"Your plan to terminate your oldest brother's life during his visit to Sahar Pepin. This idea is flawed and cannot succeed."

"Everybody out!" said Calcha to her retinue. "We need to talk," said Calcha to the Ammun Mettell. The room cleared, leaving only the Ammun Mettell, Laddlo, Calcha, and a single confidant of Calcha to even the numbers.

"You had a visitor recently. From your planet," began the Ammun Mettell simply. Calcha waited for him to continue. "He didn't make it home."

"Poor man," said Calcha, her eyes fixed on the Ammun Mettell.

"'Poor man' is right. Halfway home, he's alone in empty space. His ship explodes. Sabotage."

Calcha's confidant dropped his pen and scrambled to retrieve it. The Ammun Mettell smiled. "The trade portfolio of your 'poor man' made him responsible for Sahar Pepin. He went there often. He gave you the idea. But you didn't trust him."

"I've always said that trust should be earned," said Calcha.

"Your father's security apparatus will certainly have figured out most of what I have said. I am, after all, just a janitor here."

"Some janitor!" said Calcha.

"Besides," said the Ammun Mettell, "this is no way to come to power. It's self-limiting. It engenders opposition. The citizens of Tellapenth might never learn the sordid details of how Calcha came to the throne, but they will sense that it was sordid. You can take power in this way, but your rule will be violent, short, and limited to Tellapenth. It's no way, for example, to re-establish the Realm."

Calcha's mouth fell open for a moment before she regained control. "He knows!…" stammered her confidant.

"Tell me what I need to do," said Calcha.

"The key is this: until the Realm is reunited, you must come to power by acclamation."

"Impossible," said Calcha.

"For many people, perhaps. Not for you. In fact, you are perhaps the only one who can make it work."

"How?"

"By going to Gurfann."

Calcha laughed. "And I thought you were serious!"

"Gurfann may be nothing now, but no one forgets that the founding of the Realm happened there. Gurfann, Naveer, and Tellapenth. They're backwards and provincial on Gurfann, so if you show them some love, they will be yours."

"They wear bird feathers and think it's fashion!"

"So will you. As Gurfann's favorite daughter, as a Tellapenth royal, and as one of the Khadar's wives…"

"…you know about that?"

"Your public social…forays…have tapered off noticeably."

"It was to be announced next year."

"As Gurfann's favorite daughter, as a Tellapenth royal, and as one of the Khadar's wives, the Realm will be within reach. Without conquering planets one-by-one."

"It can't be that simple."

"Of course not. There are intermediate steps. Crises to create. A trade war, a patriotic stand-off against the Grand Council, a troubled succession on…" The Ammun Mettell looked around, indicating the Palace with his eyes, "…a certain planet. Simple, really."

"What's the trade war?" asked Calcha and the Ammun Mettell replied and the conversation continued that way into the night. As they spoke, the room and its surroundings faded for them and grew indistinct. An hour passed. Then another. Laddlo watched them, boggle-eyed. Laddlo wanted nothing more than to get out of there.

Finally, the lights dimmed three times—the signal for a Palace Shift in one hour. The Ammun Mettell blinked his eyes and shook his head rapidly to emerge from the world he had been in for the last few hours. "We're leaving," was all he said.

"But you will come back, won't you?" asked Calcha.

The Ammun Mettell looked to his right then down. "Of course," he said, glancing at the floor. Then, with a motion of his head, he gathered Laddlo and went out the door into the hallway.

They walked in silence through the Palace labyrinth. Finally, several hallways distant from where they had been, Laddlo said, "You got a little carried away there."

"No!" said the Ammun Mettell. "Well, maybe."

After a few more minutes, Laddlo ventured to ask, "Are you really going back?"

"Never! She's very, very dangerous."

"What if she acts on your advice?"

"Let's hope that she does."

"You want her to rule the Realm? The galaxy?"

"Of course, not," said the Ammun Mettell. "The first step is…she goes to Gurfann. That's perfect. We'll isolate her there. Contained."

Laddlo nodded as if he agreed. In reality, he was stunned to hear his friend talk as if he, the Ammun Mettell, were already in charge of the planet. Laddlo realized that he had underestimated his friend's aspirations. How far did they extend? The planet? The Realm? Further?

"Details…" muttered the Ammun Mettell. "The detail you overlook is the one that will bite you." Which was something Laddlo's friend had said for years, but now, it seemed, in a much bigger context. That kind of perfectionism was what Laddlo was afraid of now. Because Laddlo had noticed that he was missing one of his eta wave repeater buttons. It had been in his hand when he entered Calcha's chambers. Laddlo knew if he reported the missing repeater button, the Ammun Mettell would make them go back for it. Returning to that room was the last thing that Laddlo wanted. So he kept it to himself.

15

THE DAR TELKU WAS angry, competitive, and in full control. "Oh! Just try *that* again!" she muttered. She made rapid adjustments to keep the Dersen Vala's ship in view. The ship had turned sharply when it was obscured by the Moon, but the Dar Telku had maintained tracking. Now, on the other side of the sun, the ship changed course once more. Her systems spanned the solar system from multiple perspectives. "We're not so stupid here on Earth!" she muttered. As the spaceship settled into its new trajectory and her imaging systems controlled for its motion, she brought up a fuzzy image of the ship. The image sharpened with each additional antenna system she engaged. The Dar Telku felt a pang in her gut when she saw—or thought she saw—Raia looking out the porthole. "You're not alone, Dear," said the Dar Telku. "We're going to get you back." But the Dar Telku had no idea how. After the last course adjustment, the ship with Raia in it was headed in towards the galaxy's central bulge.

The adjacent screen continued to show Counter-Admiral Tokar's command bridge. His entire team seemed focused and efficient. There were maps and diagrams on the walls behind them. The Dar Telku stepped back from her screen. She looked around. No one else was present in the room. She went back to her screen and entered hyper-resolution mode. And got the scare of her life. On the wall behind Tokar was a map of her research compound. And a photo of the Dar Telku.

She decided to look in on Jorgan Rome. Jorgan Rome, the man they were depending on to save the planet from Tokar, was supposed to be meditating in his room. She brought an image up on the screen. There he was, cross-legged in the middle of the floor, but he wasn't meditating. He held the Naveeran Karamand before him and spoke to it. He looked as if he expected the karamand to do something for him. It did nothing. He held the karamand to his fore-head and closed his eyes. Nothing happened. Just pathetic, thought the Dar Telku.

The Dar Telku needed someone who could help. She sent for Teera.

16

A T THE FIRST RUMBLE of the spaceship's engines, Raia had thrown herself forward into the launch seat. Despite the vibration and the g-forces, she managed to buckle herself in and survive the launch uninjured. Once the craft was above the atmosphere, its acceleration diminished. Raia unbuckled the straps and stood up. She reached for the kara-mand and found it was gone. She thought about her predica-ment for only a moment before going over to the spaceship controls. If there was one thing Raia knew particularly well, it was how to fly a spaceship.

The spaceship's controls were locked out.

Around the far side of the moon, the engines began to rumble again so Raia threw herself back into the launch chair in one quick motion. Now she took time to consider her situation. The spacecraft had launched itself automatically and its own controls were locked out. That meant it was likely a trap. Then came the course correction behind the moon, designed to obfuscate its trajectory. So it definitely was a trap. A trap that had misfired. They wanted Jorgan Rome, they got Raia. He would have been the logical one to enter the ship. Someone wanted to curtail Jorgan Rome's activities on Earth. That someone would be Calcha. Raia wondered what Calcha would do when she found out that she had captured the wrong person. Raia wondered what Raia should do at that moment. There was plenty of time to think about that.

Without the karamand, the Rogan-Josh-trap was an effective Raia-trap. There was no way off of this ship. And no way to know where it was headed. Because there would be more course changes.

Cruising around the sun now, on the far side from Earth, Raia guessed that a course change was likely. She sat back in the chair and waited for it. Correction over, she began to look around the ship. She saw dried blood near the door, where the Dersen Vala had been attacked. Behind the launch chair, at floor level, was a suspended animation bed for long-distance trips. Raia hoped she wouldn't have to use it. There was a communications console. If she could send a broadcast of any type, on any wavelength at all, the Dar Telku would pick it up. But the console was locked out. Whoever set this trap had thought of everything.

She rechecked her pockets for the karamand. She tried to recall how she could have lost it. There had been a crowd around the space ship ramp. She was jostled many times. Once, someone had bumped hard into her. Had it been intentional? That would make no sense, as if someone cared to trap little Raia, not Jorgan Rome. One thing was certain: no one had stolen the karamand from her. Only she and Jorgan Rome knew how to handle it safely. It was a very, very unlucky accident. Or maybe it was for the best, thought Raia. At least, this way, it's me stuck on this ship instead of Jorgan Rome. Every one on Earth is depending on him.

She climbed the ladder to the small, upper level. There was not much room there for anything more than a desk for the Dersen Vala to work at during his travels. The desk was covered in papers and notes strewn everywhere. She had met the Dersen Vala before, of course. His office was always filled with papers and actual books. He had an antiquarian attachment to paper documents. There was a small porthole window. She pulled herself up to the window and looked out. Nothing but blackness. She looked down at the suspended animation chamber and wondered how long the journey would be. There was no way to know. And what about water and food? Without water or food, suspended animation might be the only option for survival. Back on the lower level, she opened the door of the chamber—and the smell of a used-but-not-sanitized suspended animation chamber came forth. She closed the chamber quickly and redoubled her efforts to find food and water. She opened every compartment on the ship. She lifted floor panels. There was neither food nor water anywhere. Which meant there were two possibilities. Either the Dersen Vala had used suspended animation during his last trip, or the trap setters cleared away all the food and water, forcing her to choose suspended animation.

Raia was determined to find another way. She began to look for a hiding place. As Jorgan Rome would say, "A ventilation shaft! Find it and use it!" It was difficult to imagine a ventilation shaft on a ship so small as this one. Raia searched carefully and found one behind a grille next to the main computer. The access panel, as always, was easy to remove. The interior of the shaft was just large enough to be comfortable. She found that she could even shimmy up to the upper level of the ship if needed. Halfway up the shaft, she found something that wasn't supposed to be there. A package, bundled in cloth, was tucked into a recess. Raia knew it had to be the Makha Miffin. She pulled it out and exited the ventilation shaft.

Seated in the launch chair, Raia unwrapped the book. The silk bag holding it proved to be a part of the binding. Unknotted, it could be tucked into a pouch on rear cover. The book covers were a pair of intricately-carved sheets of cultured nacre. Its spine was formed from hundreds of brass micro-hinges. This book of legends, itself legendary, was unlike any other book. Only one copy ever existed and here it was in Raia's lap! She opened the book. At the beginning there were about twenty pages of flowery dedications and solemnities from individuals who had possessed the book during its first centuries. Then came a table of contents. It listed many tales of the Allozetts, most familiar to Raia and some she had never encountered. She turned to one of them, the famous tale of Rajmek—and was horrified. Someone had written in the book! It was the rarest old book of all, and here it had someone's opinions in bright blue ink all over the pages. Raia put the book down in disgust. Then she had an idea. She climbed up to the top level of ship and took up some of the Dersen Vala's papers. They were written in the same blue ink with the same handwriting. The Dersen Vala had defaced the Makha Miffin! Curious now, Raia sat back in the launch chair and started to read one of the famous legends—along with the scandalous commentary by the Dersen Vala:

THE BRAVERY OF RAJMEK

There was a single planet orbiting a star, with nothing else anywhere around. This unremarkable solar system was far out in the halo, practically in empty space, beyond the galaxy's central bulge and somewhat above the galactic disk. It was a water planet, or mostly a water planet, having but a single island. It wasn't a very nice place. But it had a vital importance to the Allozetts. The planet's location was on a straight line path between the galactic bulge—the cradle of their civilization—and the barbarian outposts. Travelers from the outposts could take the long way through the disk or the riskier short path through empty space. The water planet, a place for provisions and repairs, made the short route safe and the outposts possible.

From the beginning, the official policy was that no one could own any part of the water planet or settle there. But the official policy became unenforceable. Support crew stationed there either fell in love or brought their families with them. After a few years, there was a resident population. Like anyone else, they wanted comfortable lives and a bit of self-governance. One of these was Rajmek.

Rajmek had been posted there as a Communications Tech. He married, had a family, and eventually became head of the Habitants Association. As head of the Association, he spoke to the Central Government on behalf of the residents. He made requests frequently and demands occasionally. Most were rebuffed. So Rajmek's role was to slink back and tell the residents what they couldn't have. No one thought very much of Rajmek's courage. Until the five ships arrived.

One day five ships appeared out of nowhere in orbit above the planet. They announced that they had kidnapped Rajmek's family. Rajmek was ordered to come aboard the leading captain's ship and negotiate the transfer of the planet and all its resources. But the intruders were in for a surprise if they thought that taking his family would subdue Rajmek. He said he would only meet with all five

"Balderdash!" wrote the Dersen Vala in the margins. "Rajmek was a coward, and worse! The story is all wrong! The first clue, and I wonder what sort of dullard would fail to notice it, must surely be Rajmek's posting as a Comm Tech. Only a Comm Tech would know how to rig the planetary systems so that a ship—let alone five ships—could arrive without anyone noticing. The Allozett's had better technology than that! Rajmek was surely in on the plot, probably as the instigator. I confess a tremendous animus towards the framer of this so-called legend for he surely thinks we're slow-witted. Are we to believe that the intruders really kidnapped Rajmek's family? Who in the entire universe, are we to suppose, knew who comprised Rajmek's family? Nobody, even in the Central Government, would care to know so much about their pathetic 'Habitant's Association!' And then the writer of this legend, (Rajmek himself?) wants us to admire the valor of Rajmek's sons for their part in the attack. I thought they had been kidnapped! But worst of all, those captains. Part of the plot, they end up dead, murdered by Rajmek! And the planet, once held in common, fell into the hands of Rajmek's dynasty!"

Raia had to concede that Dersen Vala made good points. He also appeared to be deeply invested in the old tales. Only a few of the pages were untouched by his blue ink. Near the end of the book were pages that were written entirely in the Dersen Vala's blue ink. He had added new legends to the Makha Miffin! One of them was called "The Fall of the Allozetts." Raia settled in to read.

The Fall of the Allozetts

Was there ever a civilization that collapsed so quickly as did the world of the Allozetts? None come to mind. So ignominious was their downfall, and so needless, that it pains me greatly to record it here. But it must be done. The story of what happened to our people must be reckoned with.

I suppose the seeds of our ultimate end can be detected already in the earliest of our legends. The cruel story of Tal Pitra mocking the outsiders. The paranoia that enabled Rajmek's scheme. Perhaps our civilization was simply ready to go, a rock waiting to be pushed down a hill. Or perhaps not. We had dealt with barbarians and newcomers successfully for eight millennia. We even as-similated the Muro Lawa cult. That changed us, certainly, but we emerged stronger. No, I cannot believe that our final end was pre-destined. It must be said: the era of the

Allozetts was ended forever by the actions of a few individuals. The final trigger may have been the tawdry business of the Urseri Cultural Center, but it was the reaction of a cursed few that put a final end to our eight-thousand year civilization.

The Urseri were merely the latest in a never-ending stream of barbarian cultures that would drift in from the outer reaches of the galaxy. Some were peaceful. Some were hostile. The Urseri were hostile. But when conquest failed to yield a single solar system, they changed their ways. As always with the Allozetts, trade, alliances, and mutual aid were the means to make inroads. The Urseri learned quickly. Many of them made successful lives for themselves at the center of our world. Then they sought permission to construct the Urseri Cultural Center. The Cultural Center became a rallying issue for Allozetts who despised having outsiders live among them. The detestable Kakrennid was the leader of this faction. Kakrennid—curse his name forever—used the fracas over the Cultural Center to gain a seat in the Directorate. "It will only make the Urseri stronger!" cried Kakrennid to his followers. The other members of the Directorate—sensible every one of them— had no time for Kakrennid's xenophobia. As if the Urseri having a cultural center could somehow sap the spirit and strength from the Allozetts! Permission was granted. The Center was built. Which was perhaps unfortunate because it became a place for Kakrennid to rally his mobs. "They're using their so-called Center to exfiltrate our secrets!" yelled Kakrennid. Which was laughable, of course. The stability and well-being of the Allozetts at that time didn't depend on state secrets. But try telling that to Kakrennid and his mobs. Or the Urseri, for they were indeed using their cultural center for espionage. They were caught out in a sting arranged by Kakrennid, who now had the upper hand. Then the Urseri threw fuel on the fire with their absurd claim that the cultural center had diplomatic status rendering Kakrennid's raid illegal. The crisis was on. With Kakrennid calling for the destruction of the Center and mob action against the Urseri, the Directorate acted quickly to restore calm. They closed the Center, ejected a few Urseri leaders, offered secure protection to the rest, and, in a surprise move, released the Urseri communications—including some of the Directorate's own secrets—to the public. Everyone got to see how picayune was the so-called intelligence gathered by the Urseri: proposed changes to sporting rules and details of sewer expansions on the outposts were typical subjects of their urgent dispatches. The Urseri, and Kakrennid, too, became laughingstocks. For instigating violence against the Urseri, Kakrennid lost his seat on the Directorate.

Kakrennid was out. He had lost his standing among the public. But he had become even more dangerous than before. Hateful zealots like Kakrennid never, ever, stop trying to win. No cost is too high. And Kakrennid sought the ultimate victory. He found a willing scientist among his adherents and, together, they planned the unthinkable: a gene drive coupled with an epigenetic power drive that would win the argument forevermore. Long ago, scientists had isolated genes that enhanced stranger-mistrust. It would require a gene drive and several generations to render all of the Allozetts as xenophobic as Kakrennid. But with the help of a simultaneous epigenetic power drive, it could be accomplished in a few years. Kakrennid would win. The outsiders and their enablers would be vanquished. This was the program that Kakrennid put into place.

Kakrennid didn't live to experience the new world that he created. He and his technical friends had initiated the infection at the fringes of our territory. They released their pathogen at transit hubs. They waited and watched for signs. Two years passed without news from the infected planets. So Kakrennid traveled out to the very first planet in order to see for himself the progress of his work. The landing site was derelict. He had to walk to the nearest town. But he didn't make it far. He was soon surrounded by a mob, much like the ones he had attracted in the fight against the Urseri, but this time he was himself the target of their ire. They ripped him to pieces while he was still alive.

Our people ceased traveling. We stopped communicating with other star systems. Birth rates plummeted. In less than a quarter-century, the Allozetts were finished as a force in the Galaxy.

Raia had never heard this story before. Could it be true? Did the Allozetts fall apart so quickly? And the Dersen Vala, himself an Allozett? Was that even possible? There was a lot to think about. But Raia would have plenty of time to think on this spaceship headed to who-knows-where.

Raia looked around. Her eye was drawn to the control console. It occurred to Raia, who had been on many spaceships, that the console was larger than it needed to be. She went over to it and managed to pry it open. Inside it was a hollow space that was filled with emergency food and water. Enough to last maybe a week if she was careful. Relieved, she sat back in the chair and began to read the final chapter as written by the Dersen Vala.

The Legend of the Dersen Vala

The title is sardonic. I'm not so grandiose as to imagine that I have anything legendary about me. I am a criminal. Mine is a story of criminality. But I write it because some things I have done will have lasting consequences for our people.

I was born one hundred and fifty-three years ago. I grew up much as anyone else does among the contemporary Allozetts: in an isolated, self-sustaining clan of extended family on some planet in the corner of nowhere. There were eighty, or maybe a hundred of us, hunkered down on that dismal planet. But I need to tell the story of my first crime. When I was twelve, I stole a rocket. Rockets were never easy to come by. It was a serious crime. I don't recall why I did it. Maybe I just wanted to show that I could. I do recall where I went with it though. I traveled for three days and even managed to land safely on a nearby planet. It was a planet full of Newcomers. I stepped out and saw something I've never forgotten. I saw an enormous crowd of people. They were in their thousands! And yet, they each managed their own business. They were content, happy even, in that staggering density. I'd never seen anything so frightening. I couldn't take off fast enough. Upon my return, my sentence for the crime was my life role selection. We all had roles. Some were in charge of clothing. Others were responsible for food. I got my life's assignment earlier than most: maintaining the rocket engines. I was to learn the hard way how dear a rocket is. When I was sixteen, I was selected to attend the Assembly of the Clan Leaders. It was rare for someone that young to represent the clan. The Assembly was where different clans negotiated business, territory, betrothals, and other serious matters. After a week's journey, our delegation arrived at the Assembly site. We staked out our camp. And I discovered why I had been selected. I've always been big. I was already described as "strapping" at sixteen. That's why I was selected—not for advice, not for negotiating acumen, not so that anyone would listen to me. I was brought along as a clan defender. In clan negotiations better information yields the upper hand. There are spies but spying is very dangerous. A spy might encounter a clan defender. Like me. One evening I encountered an unknown fellow at the perimeter of our camp. Who knows what he was up to? Whatever it was, he didn't manage it. Because he ran into me. I beat that man so hard that he must have carried those injuries for the rest of his life. My hands healed after a couple of months. But I know he didn't. What I had done was applauded by the clan. But I know that it was my second crime.

All this time I never stopped thinking about those crowds, those large crowds, those tranquil crowds, the crowds I'd seen when I was twelve with a stolen rocket.

When I was seventeen I ran away. We had business at a trading outpost run by Newcomers. Once again I came along as a defender. But I ran away instead.

I lied my way into a place at their University. It was the hardest thing I had ever done. When I was challenged by a university official, I wanted to flatten him. I almost did. I was assigned a squalid room in their oldest residence. When the residence overseer showed me my quarters, I I thought I would beat him senseless. Fortunately, I didn't. I spent the most of the first session hiding in that room for fear of what I would do to all of them.

I overcame my instincts by force of will. I learned to converse without looking others in the eye. I would direct my gaze just a little lower, somewhere near their cheekbones.

I studied them as they spoke. And I learned not to listen so closely as I watched their reactions dance across their faces faster than they themselves realized. In this way, I achieved a small measure of power over them. I acquired, too, a dead, leathern face that yields no insight to my own thoughts. I think that my official portrait in the anteroom of the Council Hall shows the price I've paid.

I emerged from my room and managed to study history. Books and lectures occasionally referenced a people called 'Allozetts' (at that time, a phrase unknown to me) and I realized that they were describing my own people. The accounts of the historians resonated too closely with our own oral tradition to be coincidence. The university historians sometimes knew more about my people than I did. And yet all of their accounts ended by lamenting the loss of the Makha Miffin, the legendary history of the Allozetts as recorded by the Allozetts themselves.

Now we come to the story of my third crime. I had never heard of the Makha Miffin. I imagine that few in my clan knew or cared about old books or ancient history. But there were other clans living closer to the center of the old civilization who might. There were also newcomers— barbarians, if you will—who now live in what was the core of our world. These people built museums. Perhaps you know the sort? A provincial museum with a wall full of fossils and a jumble of mislabeled relics. I wanted the Makha Miffin. Instead of searching for it, I would let it come to me. I arranged to curate an exhibit of old books at the University Museum. I invited exchanges with all of those backwater little museums. They were thrilled to cooperate. Fools! One of the items went missing in transit. Apologies were offered. Nominal restitution was made. I had located the Makha Miffin and I stole it.

I wanted all our people to know the stories in the Makha Miffin. I wanted Allozetts to aspire to more. But it wouldn't do to try to broadcast these stories directly to the clans. I had a better idea. I could release these stories among the Newcomers. Spread wide enough, the stories would seep in to the communities of the Allozetts whether they wanted them or not. So I prepared children's books. For "Miss Robinson's True Tales of the Allozetts," I was "Miss Robinson." For "The Old Captain Tells About the Allozetts," I was the "Old Captain." As we know, there has been a resurgence of interest in the Allozetts during the last century. I am responsible for that. And yes, the clans, even the remotest clans, have now heard the stories of how things were.

After leaving their university, this misanthrope, this secret loather of Newcomer society, entered the world of their politics. I became a diplomat, a Councillor, then the Grand Councillor. My first intent was to learn the systems of their world. My later intent was to undermine them as I saw fit. For I understood that the Allozetts could never recover in this galaxy the way it is now. A galaxy with myriad competing planets. Each planet a kingdom! A galaxy enfevered with continual skirmishes and frequent sector-wide wars. I began to tamp down the wars. I replaced hostile governments. That these activities were beyond the remit of a Grand Councillor gave me no disquiet. I have never relinquished my life of crime.

I have intended to smooth the way for the Allozetts to reassume their proper place. But I have committed one serious blunder. Having prepared the path, I failed to see that others might take it. At present writing, a clever and grasping Newcomer—nay, barbarian—named Calcha is

*using my foundation to claim the galaxy for herself. She
must be stopped.*

*Once I harbored the foolish idea that I would help spark
the return of the Allozetts through the example of my own
life as Grand Councillor. In this pathetic fantasy, I would
reveal my identity as an Allozett after years of guiding
galactic policy. Our people would see what was possible.
But I was a fool. Eventually, my researches uncovered
the story of Kakrennid and the genetically hard-coded
misanthropy of modern Allozetts. I had imagined my
own abhorrence of others was a personal issue that I had
overcome through discipline. In fact, it is genetic, the gift
of Kakrennid! So much for my dream of changing my
people by setting an example! They, each of them, possess
a powerful genetic barrier—in every cell nucleus of their
bodies—to engagement with the galaxy. I went into a deep
depression.*

*It became obvious that restoring the Allozetts would re-
quire undoing Kakrennid's work. Which brings me to my
fifth crime, perhaps the most serious of all. It may be my
final crime, in fact. I meddled with a genome. Not my own,
unfortunately. I haven't the technical means that Kakrennid had, that our people once had. I located a fertility
clinic used by Allozetts. A clinic that suited my needs by
having an eminently corruptible chief of staff. I arranged
that a couple, on making a return visit to the clinic, would
give birth to a second child identical to their first but un-
sullied by Kakrennid's poisonous genomic insertions. An
Allozett of the old style would be born. And it happened!
A healthy child came into the world on a day that will
mark the beginning of the turnaround for our people.*

*But there was a setback. The clinic chief, fool that he was,
let slip what he had done. Not widely, perhaps, but enough*

that the Allozetts heard about it. I saw images of what remained of his clinic. It had been obliterated to ashes. Nothing remained but a carbonized crater. The chief was never located. I presume that he died. How could he not know who he was dealing with?

I immediately dispatched one of my agents to find the child. He and his gelatinoid friend found her, I don't know how, on a disabled freighter that had been set on a course to fall into a gas giant. The stunningly brave gelatinoid saved her even though it almost cost him his own life. They are impressive people, this agent of mine and his friend. I am proud to have placed the girl in their care. Traveling the galaxy with them, she will have an education befitting the Allozetts of before. And she will be safe because her parents will not know that she survived.

Then came another setback. A most improbable setback. But it happened nevertheless. How was I to guess that this agent of mine would possess a karamand? He had never mentioned it. I am certain that he has never used it in his life. As a Newcomer, he almost certainly doesn't even know how to use it. But he did indeed have a karamand. And the karamand was used in the most unfortunate fashion. It had come to pass that Calcha had discovered the identity of my agent and cornered him. The karamand fell into the hands of the young girl who used it to rescue them all. News spread throughout the galaxy. For Newcomers, the shocking news was that Calcha had powerful opposition in the form of my adept agent. For certain Allozetts, the shocking news was that the girl was alive. For myself, the unfortunate news is that my life is in danger. For I am traceable now that my agent's identity is known to the Allozetts. That I am connected to the business of the clinic *and the child is incontrovertible. Her family and her clan will be looking for me.*

For my own life I have little concern. But what I have done needs to continue. So I find myself in a small rocket, penning my story, hoping to protect the young girl and wanting a future that will still provide more stories of Allozetts to tell.

Raia put the book down. She looked around. She saw the blood stain by the door where the Dersen Vala had been killed. She suddenly felt very unsafe. She took some food and water from the control console. She took the book and hid herself in the ventilation shaft.

17

THE AMMUN METTELL KNEW all of Laddlo's familiar places. Every few days the Ammun Mettell would find time to make the rounds of Laddlo's cafes, libraries and gadget shops, but Laddlo was nowhere to be seen. The Ammun Mettell wasn't surprised. Laddlo knew his friend well enough to understand that the Ammun Mettell would know how to find him. When Laddlo was not to be found in his usual haunts, it meant that Laddlo wasn't ready to talk yet.

The Ammun Mettell bided his time.

One afternoon after a few weeks had passed, the Ammun Mettell strolled through the Central Plaza and saw Laddlo drinking coffee at an outdoor table. The Ammun Mettell sat down. Laddlo made no response. The Ammun Mettell ordered coffee. They sat in silence.

"I made a discovery," said Laddlo without looking up from the table.

The Ammun Mettell didn't say anything.

"Eta waves," said Laddlo. "They're not uncrackable."

The Ammun Mettell raised his eyebrows. "They're encrypted at creation. Or so I've been told by a reputable source." Laddlo smiled. "That's uncrackable, isn't it?" asked the Ammun Mettell.

"If I make a collection of them, and characterize their higher moments…"

"That's measurement," said the Ammun Mettell. "You're finished."

"No, not at all, what I do is…hey! You're not supposed to know that!"

The Ammun Mettell grinned.

"OK, I'm not really surprised. Anyway, I use the even moments only. I get a differential equation." After a couple of minutes, Laddlo added, "I'll show you. In my workshop, back at the house."

When they arrived at the house, the Ammun Mettell saw that Laddlo lived in a mansion with servants and extensive grounds. Inside the gate, Laddlo paused. "Maybe we'd better go in around back." The Ammun Mettell made a stern look, which Laddlo understood to mean, "I don't do that." Laddlo grimaced. "Look, it's not that my wife disapproves of my friends. It's just that, I mean, things will be easier this way." The Ammun Mettell relented and allowed himself to be guided to a rear basement entrance that opened directly onto the large workshop. All of Laddlo's equipment was huddled in one corner.

"Here's what I meant," said Laddlo. "This is a sender, this is a receiver, and this…is an interceptor. Maybe I can't clone the original waves but I can get arbitrarily close." Laddlo pointed at some waveforms on a display to prove his point but the Ammun Mettell wasn't looking. He was looking at an animated display on the wall behind them.

"What's that?" asked the Ammun Mettell.

"Oh, that," said Laddlo. "That's what you think it is."

"The Palace."

Laddlo nodded. "It's been doing that. Those patterns are the hallways, our little Palace map from the repeater network. It's sped up for the display. I'm showing one day in about ten seconds."

"That's peculiar," said the Ammun Mettell.

"The gap? Yeah, It went blank for about a week. Network failure. The little repeaters didn't sync up. That can happen."

"But then, after, there's this pattern."

"Yup," said Laddlo.

The Ammun Mettell understood that the repeating pattern was really what Laddlo wanted him to see. It was why Laddlo had been drinking coffee in public.

"And this area here, is the Khadar's living quarters," said Laddlo. The Ammun Mettell leaned back in his chair and grinned.

The very next day, in the early evening, Laddlo and the Ammun Mettell were back in the Palace. Dressed once again as maintenance crew working a bit of overtime, no one bothered them as they progressed through the labyrinth of corridors. Halfway down one long hallway, the Ammun Mettell stopped to look through a door. Laddlo paused, too. The door opened on the hallway that had led to Calcha's chambers. The Ammun Mettell shook his head. "Probably doesn't go there, anyway," he muttered.

"No," said Laddlo, "Tonight, that's just a ballroom, I think."

"You think?"

"I know," said Laddlo.

The Ammun Mettell nodded. They went on, through corridor after corridor. Finally, a wide short hallway led to a pair of double doors. In silence, Laddlo gestured toward the doors. The Ammun Mettell stepped out of his maintenance coverall revealing a set of clothes appropriate for meeting the Khadar. The Ammun Mettell took a breath and prepared to enter. He looked over at Laddlo and gestured for him to join. Laddlo thought for a moment, then removed his coverall. He had also dressed to meet the Khadar. They opened the doors and went in.

A swarm of bots appeared suddenly from every direction and pinned them to the wall. The Ammun Mettell reached for his bot-dropper but it had no effect. The bots held Laddlo and the Ammun Mettell fast against the wall. Calcha walked towards them.

"Did you really think that was going to work a second time?" asked Calcha, snatching the bot-dropper away from the Ammun Mettell. Laddlo fumbled in his trouser pocket and the bots fell inactivated to the ground. Laddlo and the Ammun Mettell leapt for the door but they didn't get far. Calcha's human servants grabbed them, manacled their wrists, and sat them down on a sofa in the middle of the room.

Calcha looked at Laddlo. "You must be the smarter one of the two," she said and smirked when she saw the irritation on the Ammun Mettell's face. She began to pace back and forth. "So, I guess we can continue our conversation," said Calcha. "Only this time, I want real ideas, not fabulation. The plan you outlined cannot succeed."

"Of course it can," said the Ammun Mettell, "properly executed."

"Oh, you think you're smart, do you? Smart enough to control a planet? Perhaps even control a galaxy? Do you know why you're sitting here now? Because I wanted to talk. So I summoned you. Do you recognize this..." She gestured to one of her lackeys, who pulled out the eta wave repeater button from his pocket and displayed it on the palm of his hand. "I like to think of it as a little call button. And, conveniently, they're scattered all over this palace."

The Ammun Mettell said nothing.

"There are people like you, and the Khadar, who can control a planet. So if I want to control a planet, all I need is to control…those people. I thought the Khadar would do for me, but you showed me how this planet is far too small. Maybe it's big enough for the Khadar, but not for you. I understood that I need you back in my…sphere. I summoned you."

Again, there was only silence from the Ammun Mettell. Laddlo squirmed a little against his manacles. He had worked his lock pick into his right hand and was trying to free himself until the pick fell away into the depths of the sofa. Laddlo closed his eyes and sank into his seat when his last chance for escape was gone.

"Let's talk now," said Calcha with a smile. "Your plan fails to consider the power of this activist Grand Councillor. He interferes in everything. We need to eliminate him."

The Ammun Mettell made eye contact with her then dropped his face and looked to the side. "That would be a serious mistake."

Calcha made a quizzical look. She said flatly, "I don't believe you."

"The Dersen Vala is preparing the way for galactic control. How can we fail to see that each of his…interventions…has served to weaken federalism and enforce central standards. Notably, in the matter of the Barlundi Secession, he…"

"…The Dersen Vala wants to rule the galaxy!"

"No," said the Ammun Mettell. "He never raises his public profile. He appears to be paving the way for someone else or some other entity. Some entity that is unready to come forward. Until then, we let him do our work for us."

Calcha smiled. "Last time, you mentioned the possibility of violence from the outer galaxy…"

"They must be redirected," said the Ammun Mettell.

"How?" asked Calcha. During the conversation Laddlo thought, "Here they go again. This could last for hours." As indeed it did.

Finally, Calcha stood up, straightened her gown, looked directly at the Ammun Mettell and asked, "Will you join me? Will you help me conquer this galaxy?" Laddlo's skin prickled at the question. He felt a thousand pins and needles while the Ammun Mettell considered his response.

"No," said the Ammun Mettell.

She tried to hide the jolt of pain that went through her body but everyone could see it. She closed her eyes. When she opened them again, she turned to her assistant and said, "Summon the law officials. There are intruders in the Palace. Do not allow the officials entry to these chambers, but hand the two prisoners over at the door."

"I am very sorry," she said to the Ammun Mettell before turning around and leaving the room.

Laddlo and the Ammun Mettell spent a gruesome month in the custody of the law officials. The only job that the law officials had was to find their prisoners guilty. This they did. When it was all over, Laddlo and the Ammun Mettell were brought to a small audience hall with high court officials in attendance. The Khadar himself was there. Calcha sat next to him. When Laddlo saw the Khadar, he felt that his nightmare was over. He would explain everything to the Khadar. The Khadar would listen. Instead Laddlo was thrust into a glass-walled chamber in the center of the room. Laddlo opened his mouth to protest but it was too late when the chamber door was closed and the lightning bolts came at him from all directions. He looked up to see the Khadar but the Khadar had turned away, bored. That was the last thing Laddlo saw before he was disintegrated.

The Ammun Mettell had been less inclined to confess guilt to the law officials. When it was his turn, he was unable to walk. They dragged him and his useless legs into the chamber. When he looked up, he fixed his gaze on Calcha. The lightning bolts came and Calcha gasped.

Part Four

18

IT WAS FORTUNATE that Raia had sequestered herself in the ventilation shaft when she did. Less than an hour later, her sister appeared. As Raia peered through the grille, she saw how Lisseri had aged since she last saw her. Lisseri was only a few years older than Raia, maybe thirteen or fourteen years old. Mostly she looked like an older version of Raia. Lisseri had a larger head and a prominent jaw. She was stocky for a young teenager. She had already developed a haggard look that would be with her for the rest of her life.

Lisseri looked around, perplexed. She went over to the suspended animation chamber, bent down and looked in the glass doors. No Raia. She went up the ladder to the upper level. Still no Raia. Lisseri threw some of the Dersen Vala's papers around in anger. She came down the ladder. She went over to the launch chair. Her nostrils flickered. She calmed down. A grim look settled on her features.

"I know you're here," said Lisseri. "You might as well come out."

Raia opened the hidden grille and stepped out.

"Do you recognize me?" asked Lisseri.

"Of course," said Raia. "You're my sister."

"I'm *not* your sister," snarled Lisseri.

"We used to be sisters," said Raia.

"Well, we're not. You're not my sister, get it straight! You're not anything to me."

"The last time I saw you, we were playing on the cargo deck."

"I used to play, it's true," said Lisseri, "back when I was young." Looking Raia in the eye, she said, "We're not playing anymore."

"OK," said Raia. She took the muster of her sister. Lisseri was all sinewy muscle. If she managed a solid grip on Raia, there would be no escaping it. On a necklace, Lisseri wore a karamand. Lisseri also had a dagger in a sheath at her belt. Lisseri was formidably arrayed. The dagger sheath was more ornately detailed than it needed to be. The dagger itself had been polished and shone brightly in the dim space capsule. If it came to it, thought Raia, the dagger would be the weapon Lisseri would choose.

Lisseri had followed her eyes. After Raia glanced at the dagger, Lisseri asked, "Do you like it? It's new. I had to get a new one. Before coming back here." Raia frowned. Lisseri smiled.

"My assignment isn't really that hard," said Lisseri. "Just come here and dispatch that vile old cretin who made you in a lab. Then bring you back. To home. You're coming home."

"I don't want to go home," said Raia.

"You don't have a choice!" said Lisseri. "Nothing's up to you! It's up to me! Because I, on the other hand, *I* have a choice."

Raia made a questioning look.

"They want your genome. So that you don't happen again. Ever."

Raia nodded, to keep Lisseri talking.

"But I don't see why they need you alive. They can study DNA of dead people, right? That's what I think. So I've got a choice to make." Lisseri looked up and around, making a drama of a person in possession of choices. "I think you'd better start being nice to me," added Lisseri.

"Of course, I'll be nice," said Raia. "I'm your sister."

"You're *not* my sister! You're *not* my sister! You're a growth! You were stolen! Stolen from *me*!" said Lisseri. "And maybe it's finally time for me to take back what belongs to me!"

Raia observed closely and understood that Lisseri was talking herself up to violence. Raia decided to keep her answers short to avoid escalation. Better still, Raia decided that she wanted to manage Lisseri's rising fury, to ride the wave of her anger, maybe even to be in control. Raia decided she would offer a conciliatory "I know" if Lisseri's anger built too fast. If Lisseri lost steam, a mention of "my parents" would stoke things again.

"Where are my parents?"

"*Your* parents! They're not your parents! You don't have parents!" Hand to dagger.

"OK," said Raia, "I understand."

What Raia wanted was time to think, to come up with some way to survive. For the moment, what she needed was a longer sentence, something harder to parse. Something to divert Lisseri's cognition. "I guess I can't really control the circumstances of my birth," she added.

"No," agreed Lisseri, who became sullen, staring at Raia. Lisseri was thinking. But that made her unpredictable again.

"I'm sorry," said Raia.

"You're sorry?' 'Sorry!' 'Sorry' doesn't do it! 'Sorry' doesn't change *anything*!"

"Still, I am sorry," said Raia.

"I don't care if you're sorry! No one cares if you're sorry!"

Lisseri's anger was just about right. Raia could keep Lisseri's fury at this intensity for a long time. But she didn't need to. Raia had formulated the beginnings of a plan. She wanted to control the moment. Since there was no point in waiting, the time had come for Lisseri's anger to explode.

"I want to say this," said Raia. "I have *rights*."

"Oh, you have rights, huh? I'll show you rights!" Out came the dagger in Lisseri's right hand. Raia instantly jumped away to her own right. A chase instinct in the rage-addled Lisseri made her go after Raia without thought. She swept the dagger around and across toward Raia, but this move exposed her hand to a rapid side kick from Raia. The dagger hit the wall and landed on the floor under a console. Raia wanted Lisseri to grab for the dagger so she feinted a move on it herself. Lisseri moved quickly to take up the dagger with one hand while blocking Raia with the other. That was what Raia was waiting for, a raised arm in her direction. Moving quickly, she took the paralysis bracelet that she had from the Dar Telku and slid it up Lisseri's exposed arm. Lisseri fell in a heap to the floor.

"Help me," said Lisseri.

Raia shook her head.

"Turn me over," said Lisseri.

Raia rolled her sister onto her back.

"Are you going to kill me?" asked Lisseri.

"No," said Raia as she began to slide her sister toward the suspended animation chamber. She opened the door to the chamber. First Lisseri's feet were moved into the chamber. Next, her hips, then her upper body and head were wriggled inside. Lisseri made a horrible face as the smell of the chamber overcame her. When Raia activated the chamber, Lisseri's face, nauseated and hate-filled, was frozen onto her for however long her voyage would last.

Raia walked over to the ventilation shaft. She retrieved the Makha Miffin. Using the karamand that she had taken from her sister, Raia left the ship.

19

BARTENG ADJUSTED HIS POSITION in the seat and readied himself for what came next. The Dar Telku started recording video.

"We were talking about the Ammun Mettell," said the Dar Telku.

"OK," said Barteng.

"How did being disintegrated make him feel?"

"Very angry."

"Tell me about that."

"Well," said Barteng, "when they switched him on again, he was furious."

"Switched him on again?"

"That's what they do. That's what they did. There's a projector. When they turn it on, he's back. The disintegrated person is back. Like before. Or mostly. It's not totally the same. Mostly, though."

"So how did it go for the Ammun Mettell?"

"There were two of them. One was adjusting the projector. The other one was in charge. They were right there in the Ammun Mettell's living quarters. They turned it on and the Ammun Mettell appeared. He was there on his sofa, suddenly, thrashing around and saying really tough things about the Khadar."

"Don't do that," said the one in charge.

But the Ammun Mettell wasn't listening. He continued to pound on the sofa. He insulted the Khadar and anyone who would follow the Khadar.

"Don't do that."

The Ammun Mettell looked up, took the measure of the man. The Ammun Mettell started insulting him.

"This is your final warning. Don't do that. As a state criminal, you can be switched off permanently without warning. I can do that. I will do that. I will do that now unless you stop."

The Ammun Mettell said nothing.

"You have been reconstituted and will continue to exist only at the pleasure of our Khadar's government. Do you understand?"

Silence from the Ammun Mettell.

"I need to hear you say that you understand."

"I understand," said the Ammun Mettell.

"This system," said the man in charge, indicating the projector, "teaches state criminals to respect the law. As a disintegrated and reconstituted criminal, you no longer have to worry about fines, prison, or forced labor for infractions against the law. There is only one penalty for state criminals like you. Termination. Permanent. And instant. You might cross the street against the rules someday. And it will be the last thing you do. Do you understand?"

The Ammun Mettell nodded.

"But that's not really a problem—one fewer state criminal out and about, now is it?"

The Ammun Mettell said nothing.

"And I will return to this abode of yours to retrieve the projector unit for the convenience and ease of some other state criminal. As I have done so many times. You are now the fifth…no…sixth…user of this particular projector since I've been doing this. They don't last long, do they? Which is the point. Now please stand up."

The Ammun Mettell tried to stand, fell back, struggled, then made it to his feet.

"Coordination will return rapidly. Some other things, slowly, if at all. You may be sensitive to bright sunlight. That will persist."

The Ammun Mettell tried to take a step but thought the better of it. He sat back on the sofa.

"I need to tell you two other things. The first is curfew. Nighttime curfew is automatic."

"What's the other thing?"

"Never attempt to tamper with the projector unit. Unless you become tired of living. Which is perhaps understandable for a state criminal like yourself. But until you make that commendable decision, keep your hands off the projector unit."

After the two men left, the Ammun Mettell continued to sit where he was. He sat and tried to remember. He wasn't hungry. He wasn't tired. He just wanted to remember who he was. He sat motionless as the light changed outside with with the progression of the afternoon. He recalled falling from a tree once and years of his childhood fell into place. He remembered the feeling of a draft of air, a breezy day, and all his years at the university became accessible to him. The light outside grew dim with evening as the Ammun Mettell sat there, sampling and sorting his life. Quite suddenly, the light became piercingly bright and blue-tinged. He understood that curfew had occurred. The projector had shut down for the night. Projection had resumed in the early morning. Still he sat and arranged his life. After four days he stood up. He was neither hungry nor tired.

The Ammun Mettell might have stayed in his lodgings for another week without moving. Or another month. Or perhaps forever, so he understood that he needed to step out. It would be difficult with his self-confidence shattered. He felt conspicuous. Everyone would know he was projected. They would stare. But he was determined to give it a try at least one time.

Out on the street, the sunlight was bright but it caused him no trouble. He began to walk, and as he did, he remembered his way around. His projector had range enough to cover the city so he had no fear of phasing out by going too far. He walked at first in a self-absorbed daze but gradually began to observe everything the way he always had. He observed that nobody paid him any attention at all. They didn't know that he was projected. Eventually he found himself, by random chance or unconscious habit—if he still possessed unconscious habits—at the plaza where he used to encounter Laddlo. He sat down and ordered coffee. He began to remember about Laddlo. The coffee arrived and he took a drink. He spat it out. There was no taste, no warmth, no feeling at all. Was this also the way it was for Laddlo?

An hour later, the Ammun Mettell was standing outside of Laddlo's family home. He considered what he would say when he announced himself at their front door, realized he had nothing good, and slunk around back to the workshop. The door was unlocked. Once inside, the Ammun Mettell saw that Laddlo's workshop was full of boxes. Equipment was stacked in the middle of the room. The path to Laddlo's main work table was blocked by a crate full of books and gadgets. Underneath the crate was a projector just like the one the Ammun Mettell had at home. It seemed strangely cavalier of Laddlo to treat his projector that way. The Ammun Mettell was looking for a way to reach the work table when he heard someone behind him. A woman had entered the workshop from the house. "Excuse me?" she asked, then quickly said, "you must be Laddlo's friend. Would that be correct?"

"Yes," said the Ammun Mettell, "Are you…"

She shook her head. "I work for the family. My name is Cinda Loi" After a moment she added, "I'm very sorry."

"Well," said the Ammun Mettell, "We'll just try to move forward." When Cinda Loi frowned, the Ammun Mettell added, "That's why I'm here. I'd like to talk with Laddlo if I could."

"Oh, you don't know, do you?"

"What don't I know?"

"Laddlo's gone. His projector failed."

"What?"

"It was just a couple of days ago. He had recovered. Mostly. It was like he was himself again. I was there, too. He was telling a story and he was laughing when it happened. He just disappeared. His projector was in the hall. It had thrown off these tremendous sparks that ignited one of the tapestries. The family was very upset." The Ammun Matter couldn't help but wonder if they were more upset about Laddlo or the tapestry. Cinda Loi must have followed his thoughts because she said quickly, "Don't ask. But I can say this. I won't be with this family much longer. I liked Laddlo."

Neither of them said anything for several minutes. Finally, the Ammun Mettell asked, "What's with all this stuff here?"

"I'm tasked with clearing out his things. Everything."

"Everything?"

"Total erasure, I'm afraid. And I'm angry about it. The marriage will be annulled retroactively. The family does a large amount of business with the State, you see. These sorts of…connections," said Cinda Loi, gesturing towards Laddlo's things, "could harm their interests."

The Ammun Mettell grimaced. Then he added, "Laddlo was doing interesting things with eta waves just before…"

"I wouldn't know about that," said Cinda Loi. "He was inventive, I know. I admired that."

"A shame if it were lost."

"I'll arrange to have his equipment and notebooks sent to you. Would that help?" When the Ammun Mettell made a puzzled face, she added, "Of course I can do that. Nobody cares where they go so long as they're gone."

"Thank you," said the Ammun Mettell.

"May I ask," said Cinda Loi, "are you…projected?"

The Ammun Mettell froze for a moment. He nodded once rapidly.

"Well, best of luck to you then," said Cinda Loi.

20

OVER THE NEXT FEW DAYS, the Ammun Mettell fell again into a listless pattern. He would wander the city. Every day he went a little farther or to somewhere unfamiliar. He saw everything and cared about nothing. His only necessity was returning to his lodging before curfew set in. One day, returning home, he found his place full of things. Cinda Loi's people had let themselves in and delivered Laddlo's stuff. The Ammun Mettell's small place was piled high with equipment, notebooks, boxes, hoses, and cables. The selection of items seemed hasty and indiscriminate. The Ammun Mettell cleared a chair and sat down. This was all a bit much. He had said he would accept some of it. He hadn't wanted all of it. But here was the entirety of Laddlo's avocation. The Ammun Mettell had wanted to preserve some of Laddlo's spark and ended up with a floor-to-ceiling pile of the remnants of Laddlo's life. The Ammun Mettell closed his eyes. Curfew happened.

When the Ammun Mettell reappeared and opened his eyes, he caught a glint of morning light reflected from under the pile of Laddlo's things. From under a stack of meters, draped in dirty lab coats, came a reflection from a familiar shape. It looked like a projector. Had they really delivered Laddlo's defunct projector along with the lab equipment? They had. The Ammun Mettell dug out the projector. Near its rear vent, it was scorched from the fire. There was long-standing corrosion on the housing. The Ammun Mettell went into the back room with his own projector. The Ammun Mettell's projector had visible corrosion, too. It wasn't so bad as Laddlo's projector but neither was it pristine.

He cleared a place on the floor of the main room and placed Laddlo's projector there. He found some of Laddlo's tools and opened it up. What he saw dismayed him. There were scorch marks inside. There were signs of previous repairs, sloppily performed. There were loose components that rattled when the projector was bumped. There was a burnt-out resonator near the rear vent. The Ammun Mettell returned to his own projector. The resonator was warm.

With Laddlo's broken projector open in front of him, the Ammun Mettell extracted the burnt-up resonator. He thought about where he could find another one. He did not want to be seen in public looking for projector parts. He looked again at the piles of Laddlo's stuff. He started to dig through box after box. After a couple of hours, he had found what he needed. He had accumulated enough spare parts to replace everything many times over. He replaced the resonator and switched on Laddlo's projector. He had low expectations. There was, he knew, little hope of see-ing Laddlo spring to life in front of him. Instead, a small blue-gray cube appeared. It was the default projection. He opened the projector again and the blue-gray cube vanished. Or rather it died. The warnings had been true. Opening up an operating projector meant triggering the interlocks and instant death.

The Ammun Mettell set about finding and disabling the interlocks. There were four of them in total. Taking them out of operation, he was able to open and close the projector housing at will, without any interruption in its operation. But could he do that from outside of the projector? He studied carefully. He would need to drill holes, insert insulating rods to particular depths, and bend tabs precisely—all this without being able to see what he was doing. He practiced on Laddlo's projector until he was confident in his ability. Then he went to his own projector.

After drilling the first hole he was still alive. Then the second. He still lived after inserting a small rod to disable the first interlock. And so it went until the last one was disabled. The Ammun Mettell stood there looking at his projector for a moment. Then he lifted the lid.

"I'm still alive," he thought. But what he saw made him shudder. The insides of his projector were in a far worse condition than Laddlo's had been. There were burn marks everywhere, smoke that indicated the final end of some previous state criminal. Essential components of the projector were held by tape. There were careless repairs. There was corrosion from condensation. This projector would not last. It could not be repaired while it was powered up. But shutting it off was not an option. He disabled the interlocks for good, placed the cover back on, and sat down. He sat for nearly an hour before curfew happened.

The Ammun Mettell continued to sit in the same place throughout the next day. He knew how the projectors worked. He had learned how to repair one. What he didn't know was how to repair a projector that was also the source of his life. Hot-swapping the eta wave generator would fry it. In any event, re-patterning a new eta wave generator from an old one was impossible because the waves were naturally encrypted. He was chagrined to understand that his life depended on ancient eta wave technology. Which led him to wonder how long the Khadars had been disintegrating people. He thought about the irony that Laddlo had lived for eta waves as his hobby and then ended up living from them. He thought about what Laddlo had been able to do with them. Then he stood suddenly from his chair.

What had Laddlo said? That eta waves were not uncrackable? The Ammun Mettell needed to find out what Laddlo had achieved. He dug out Laddlo's notebooks. There were five of them. From the very first notebook, it appeared that Laddlo had been intent on gaining control over eta waves. There was discussion of nonlinearities, bifurcations, and second-quantized weak chaos—altogether too much for the Ammun Mettell. But the Ammun Mettell gathered that Laddlo knew what he was doing. In the fourth notebook, Laddlo seemed excited. He had constructed something that could decrypt the waves and then pass them on. He called it an eta-wave repeater. At that moment, a flash of memory burst in on the Ammun Mettell. Those little buttons, the ones they had used in the Palace, Laddlo had said they were eta wave repeaters. Laddlo had not only built repeaters, he had miniaturized them!

The Ammun Mettell engaged in a furious search for the repeater buttons. He scattered Laddlo's things everywhere without finding them. He resorted to taking apart pieces of equipment, one by one. Behind a hidden panel inside of a power supply, he found the little pouch of repeaters.

The next morning after curfew was finished, he set to work with the repeaters. It was just a matter of tuning. He switched on Laddlo's projector. A little blue-gray cube appeared before it. He tuned the resonator to operate at a frequency just below his own. The repeater button had dynamical tuning and would make up the difference if it was small enough. Next it was a matter of tuning the non-linearity of the repeater. As he adjusted the repeater, the Ammun Mettell suddenly felt disoriented. He nearly dropped his tools. "Careful," he thought, "you can die this way." After a few moments he steadied himself and looked up. The little blue-gray cube was coming from his own projector. Without realizing it, he had transferred to Laddlo's projector.

He quickly repaired his own projector. Now he had two projectors. He learned to transfer between them at will. Soon he had projectors sequestered all over the city. And although he could travel between them in the blink of an eye, and although curfew no longer plagued him, he was careful not to make use of his expanded abilities. He was still recognizable to the Khadar's officials.

So he took his time to learn more about the projectors. After three months he figured out how to project a person who looked nothing like his former self. Only then did he feel free to go about the city, or the planet for that matter, because his range now extended to the entire globe. He allowed his original projector to burn up inside and then be sent back to the law officials. As far as they were concerned, he was gone forever.

21

THE AMMUN METTELL'S LIVING and working space had been piled high for a very long time. Organizing Laddlo's things for the last time, he came across a folder that he had seen and ignored on several previous occasions. He opened the folder. In it were papers describing the business dealings of Laddlo's family. Their wealth came from buying foodstuffs off-planet and sending them through the Central Market. The Central Market was where the Khadar took a twenty-percent cut. Why was this folder in his hands? Sending Laddlo's projector along with his lab equipment might have been an oversight. But not this. These documents had never been in Laddlo's laboratory. Why had Cinda Loi slipped this folder into the shipment?

He waited a few more hours. After midnight, switching between projectors, he transported himself into the Central Market. He studied document after document. Now he understood. Different market sectors were divvied among seven leading families, with a bit of overlap to cushion against shocks. After a century of operating this way, the families were extremely wealthy. They were also deeply in debt, but only on paper, to the Khadar. They must have had confidence that the Khadar would never call in those debts.

The Ammun Mettell muttered to himself, "Foolish, foolish Khadar!"

He set himself to work the very next day. What he wanted to achieve would require a large and capable team. He began visiting the debate clubs on their open nights. At the very first club, presented with a sign-in sheet, he thought for a moment. Then he wrote, "Mettell." A name coined on the spot. In the debates, he annihilated all comers. Reducing a debate opponent was nothing for "Mettell," who became a crowd favorite. He developed a small following that never failed to show at his club appearances. So far so good, but he needed more than just followers. He offered coaching in order to observe who could learn and who couldn't. He watched them debate. He identified the fifteen best among them and invited them to his lodgings one evening. He sat them down and announced, "I'm forming a school of philosophy." He watched their reactions. A few had guarded looks. Two of them rolled their eyes. A couple more stared at the floor. "Club debaters, nothing more!" he thought. All the rest became stirred up. The excitement shone in their eyes. They understood what it might mean to become founders of a new school.

"That was me," said Barteng to the Dar Telku. "I knew instantly! But I figured out more than that!"

"What did you figure out?" asked the Dar Telku.

"I knew that he was up to something. That this was going to be about more than philosophy. Here was a guy—I sensed it—who was planning to use the legal protections of a School of Philosophy to do something else. Something big. And I was all in."

"Impressive," said the Dar Telku.

"And I was not disappointed," said Barteng, "Not at all."

One of the eye-rollers asked, "So what's your philosophy?"

"Our philosophy…" said the Ammun Mettell—who now had truly become the Ammun Mettell—"…our philosophy is…" He put his hands on his knees and leaned forward. He fixed each one of the new core members with a look and ignored the rest. "Our philosophy will be…the inviolability of the Self."

"Here's what I've never figured out, though," said Barteng. "I don't know if he just made that up on the spot. I suspect that he did. It would be just like him. I also think it was a private joke."

"A joke?" asked the Dar Telku.

"What had just happened to him?" asked Barteng pointedly

The Dar Telku shook her head.

"He—his entire 'Self'—had been obliterated by the Khadar! I think it was meant as dark humor. I do know that, in private, he never took his own philosophy seriously."

The room went quiet. Most sat and thought about the Self, inviolability and what sort of philosophy that might be.

"This philosophy will have a kind of magnetic attraction for a certain demographic," said the Ammun Mettell. At that point, the savvier ones all understood that the so-called philosophy had no importance in itself and that the Ammun Mettell was up to something.

"And that's how the so-called hundred-and-first school of philosophy was formed," said Barteng. "And how he became the Ammun Mettell."

"I spent the entire next week studying," said Barteng. "I just knew that next week's meeting would be crucial, with the new philosophy and all. I really wanted to come out on top so I crammed my head full of every idea that related to the 'Self.' I showed up prepared to the meeting. I walked up to the Ammun Mettell and said that I was ready."

"Ready?"

"To discuss the Self!" I said.

The Ammun Mettell has this way of looking through you when you say something idiotic. "That's not what we're doing" he muttered. He handed me a folder. Inside was a job application.

"A job application?" asked the Dar Telku. "For working with the Ammun Mettell?"

"No. It was for a job at the Inter-Planetary Mercantile Council! As a trade specialist!" said Barteng.

"Were you qualified for that?"

"Absolutely not! I opened my mouth to say as much. The Ammun Mettell held out his hand to take the folder back. And here's the thing: I knew if I gave the folder back that I was out. I didn't want to be out. I wanted to see where this was going. So I filled it out and turned it in."

"What happened?" asked the Dar Telku.

"I got the job! And so did everyone else. Our little debating club now had a Transport Coordinator, a Tri-Planetary Commission representative, a military analyst, some commerce tribunes, board members and lots of other high-level types!"

"One of us," continued Barteng, "A fellow named Eddlo, was quite upset. All he got was a job called 'Port Concierge.' And he was the smartest of all of us."

"Port Concierge?"

"Yes, that's right. A port concierge spent the day putting stickers on luggage at the main space port. We almost lost him, and he was a good debater, too. But he stuck around. Good thing, too."

The Dar Telku made a quizzical face.

"Because what he did was important. One day, he's applying luggage stickers and he turns around. The Ammun Mettell is standing behind him!"

"Was that surprising?"

"Absolutely. Security was tight. Eddlo never did figure it out."

"He projected himself there?"

"Of course. Which was brave, out in the open like that. But it was important. He told Eddlo that a delegation returning to Rosgurd would be passing through in an hour. They were to be searched."

"'But they will have diplomatic…'"

"'A thorough search. Find it.'"

"Find what?"

"You will know. When I chose you for this job, I knew what I was doing."

Eddlo swallowed a couple of times, then nodded.

"And your report of what you find, escalate it to the Palace."

"OK," said Eddlo.

"And then, disappear. Make sure the report isn't traceable to you. You'll be done here."

Eddlo nodded. He looked down for a moment. When he looked up, the Ammun Mettell was gone.

Nearly an hour later the delegation, just a man and his wife, showed up. Eddlo diverted them to a special room. One that didn't look at all like a search room. It had been tricked out to look like a VIP reception area. But they were locked in all the same and their communications were blocked, they just didn't know it yet.

"That's how smooth Eddlo could operate," said Barteng.

Meanwhile, the couple was being searched, and they didn't know that either. There was no one sharper than Eddlo. There seemed nothing remarkable about them. But Eddlo never missed a trick. He noticed her engagement ring immediately. She hadn't been wearing one when she arrived a few days before.

"Yes, that was Eddlo," said Barteng, "He had already seen the video footage of their arrival."

"That's a lovely ring," said Eddlo. The woman quickly glanced at the man. "May I?" asked Eddlo. But before she could respond he had already produced a scanner and was reading the secret code written in the pattern of diamond NV-centers.

"Oh, dear, dear." said Eddlo, "This doesn't look good. I'm going to have to make a report about this."

"You have no right!" stammered the man.

"I'm afraid I've already done it," said Eddlo. "And I'm taking this," he continued while slipping the ring from her finger.

"You'll not be able to keep us here!" said the man.

"No, I can't. I won't. You're free to leave our planet. I'm just not sure."

"About what?"

"How far you'll get." holding the door open for them.

Then Eddlo prepared and sent his report.

"What was it all about?" asked the Dar Telku.

"A plot to kill the Khadar," said Barteng.

"So the Ammun Mettell saved the Khadar!" said the Dar Telku.

"Sure, the Ammun Mettell didn't want to kill anyone. Besides, there was someone else he was eliminating."

"Calcha!"

"That's right. The Rosgurdians were going to help her kill the Khadar. Some untraceable, disappearing poison only known on Rosgurd. Then they would be the first to recognize Calcha as the new leader of Naveer."

"So how is it that Calcha is still around?" asked the Dar Telku.

"I don't know. The Khadar finds out she plans to kill him and somehow she survives. Never, ever underestimate Calcha, I think that's the point. She got herself exiled to Gurfann, with no chance of return. That was enough, though, for the Ammun Mettell."

22

BARTENG CONTINUED the story of the Ammun Mattar. "After that business with Calcha, Eddlo had an inkling of just how far the Ammun Mettell's plans might go. The rest of them still had no idea. Some were getting impatient for an actual debate because they still imagined it was some kind of debating club, just at a higher level. One night, as we followed the Ammun Mettell through town to our little meeting house—such as it was back in the early days—the situation almost came to mass desertion. The Ammun Mettell stayed calm. 'Then let's have a debate,' he said, opening the door to the meeting house. Inside, it was full of people! Other people! They were all from the school of the Ammun Jorna! Fierce debaters, every one of them! The Ammun Jorna himself had never been bested! You could see the excitement—and fear—in every member of our own little group."

"The debate started. At first, it went well for us. Then something dawned on us. This was a Parlat Pantel! We could lose everything! The Ammun Mettell hadn't told us! We weren't prepared for a Parlat Pantel! We began to stumble, to lose simple arguments. Our intensity was gone. But then the

172

real contest between the Ammuns began. It was fascinating. We could tell that the Ammun Mettell could win whatever point he wanted. When he lost one, he was giving it away. He took the match easily. I still remember the reactions of the two Ammuns when it was over. They were both grinning, clapping each other on the back, acting like the best of friends. I think that they were. In the end, we picked up a few of the Ammun Jorna's people. All of them were scientists. I'm sure that the Ammun Mettell had his eye on those technical people from the very beginning. And some people actually left our school for the Ammun Jorna. They weren't quite part of our program anyway so it worked out best for everyone."

"But," said the Dar Telku, "I thought the Ammun Mettell used the Parlat Pantel to obliterate other schools. No mercy!"

"No, that's not how it was. Not at first. Only near the end, when some other Ammuns saw him turning their world upside down. It was them, they were the ones who decided to take him down," said Barteng. "It didn't work out for them."

"After some time, the Ammun Mettell had his people seeded throughout all the Ministries. They could expedite, or delay, functions of their departments. Which doesn't seem like much, unless it's all coordinated. I mean, a short-term loan could be offered by one agency, while another might delay a shipment that's needed to pay it off. But everything all depended on the technical people. They had learned how to use unprogrammed projectors to put those little blue-gray cubes wherever they wanted. And the little cubes, so small that no one noticed them, were like eyes and ears of the Ammun Mettell. It might go like this, one of us would approach some business, a business we wanted to control, and propose some kind of high-risk, high-return venture. Then we would leave. While they discussed it among themselves, they never noticed the tiny blue-gray cube that appeared on, say, a bookshelf, behind them."

The Dar Telku thought for a moment before muttering, "That sounds…"

"…Nefarious? Yes. It was. But all to a good purpose."

"Are you sure?" asked the Dar Telku, but Barteng offered no response.

"Eventually we controlled some significant parts of the economy. We tried to keep that under wraps but word gets around. People started to understand that the Ammun Mettell could make things happen. They would approach him with pleas for assistance. Usually they wanted to bribe him. The Ammun Mettell was very scrupulous about bribes."

"He doesn't seem like the type to accept a bribe," said the Dar Telku.

"That's where you're wrong. He was always careful to take a bribe every time. If he hadn't, then people would wonder what his angle was. They wouldn't have trusted him. Instead, he would consider their offer, divide it by four, and accept the reduced amount. He made a lot of friends that way."

"At that time, we had great expenses. The technical people were spending way too much money, so the Ammun Mettell had me look into it. What they were doing seemed crazy. The scientists had figured out how to make a giant lens for eta waves, using a star! They had even built a system to do it. They had this underground beam line make a super strong set of eta waves, which they had aimed at Tellapenth's star."

"What were they trying to do to Tellapenth?"

"Nothing! They were trying to project a little blue-gray cube from Naveer to Tellapenth."

"Impossible!" said the Dar Telku.

"No, it works. With help."

"Help?"

"Our scientists found these old robots. They were so old, they had been built with eta-wave capabilities."

"You mean like Teera?"

"Yes, she's one of our robots. Well, she was one of ours. Anyway, these robots can manipulate an input wavefront with sufficient control that star-focusing works."

"And did it work?"

"Yes. But when the Ammun Mettell found out, he was unhappy. He summoned the chief scientist and let her have it. He was tough. He reminded her that we had one planet, the one they were on, that they cared about. But she held her ground. So he backed off and let her do what she wanted."

Meanwhile, little by little, the Ammun Mettell had increased his control over the economy and politics of the planet. Once he felt that he could jettison the Khadar without throwing the planet into chaos, there was no stopping him. The first step was bankrupting the oligarchic families who ran the planet's economy for their own benefit. When the Ammun Mettell had enough control over the banks, be began shifting debt ownership. The seven families had all been in debt to the Khadar, now they owned each other's debt. But they didn't know it. They didn't know yet that they had become a tight little collection of dominos, arranged in a circle. The Ammun Mettell had us start with Laddlo's family. From our separate Ministries, we made a coordinated and sustained attack on their trade shipments. We eliminated their liquidity. Down they went. They pulled down another couple of families with them. The others fought for their share of what remained. Peace among the seven oligarchic families was gone for good. When the Khadar stepped in, each of the families accused him of favoritism and his own position became precarious. The Khadar noticed that his ministers began to spend more of their personal time with him, telling stories, reminiscing, and ingratiating themselves to allay concerns of betrayal. Which meant that betrayal was on their minds.

23

THE AMMUN METTELL knew that he had a strong position. He felt it was time to visit the Khadar in person. The Khadar was in his bed chamber. He sat at a small writing desk with his head in his hands. He was alone. The Ammun Mettell appeared in the middle of the room behind him. The Khadar sensed the extra presence in the room. Without moving, the Khadar said, "I don't know who you are, but leave now. These are private hours." Turning around, he saw the Ammun Mettell. "I know who you are," said the Khadar.

"I'm not so sure about that," said the Ammun Mettell.

"You're that Ammun Mettell," said the Khadar, approaching. The Khadar, who had never in his life shown fear on the sporting grounds, was unafraid now as he came ever closer to the Ammun Mettell. "You're that troublemaker."

The Ammun Mettell said nothing.

"I suppose you have something to say to me before you're arrested, is that right?"

The Ammun Matter smiled bitterly, "It's too late for for that, isn't it?"

The Khadar didn't understand but nodded as if he did. Then, quite suddenly, he charged forward. Anyone but the Ammun Mettell would have been flattened against the wall but instead the Ammun Mettell blinked away and re-appeared behind the Khadar. The Khadar careened at full speed into the wall. When the Khadar turned around, he was dazed, bleeding at the forehead, and fiercely angry. "I don't know how you did that," he said. Then, emphasizing each word: "What. Do. You. Want?"

"I want you to live."

"Well, thank you. Bless you, even. Are you afraid that I'll not?"

"Not afraid. No. Just aware of other possibilities."

"Are you threatening me?"

"No, it's a simple matter of demographic statistics," said the Ammun Mettell, "the average life span of ex-Khadars."

"You are threatening me."

"I want you to resign. To…abdicate. I'll guarantee your safety and comfort. You'll be treated with respect. But you won't be Khadar anymore."

"I'm sorry to disappoint you. But I'm in no mood to resign. I am Khadar for life."

"Which, in present circumstances, is not saying much. I'm offering you protection and a pleasant retirement. Accept."

The Khadar thought for a moment. He shook his head.

"We both know the score," said the Ammun Mettell. "The seven families, who placed you on the throne, are no more. Whoever—whatever emerges from their war, it won't support you. The Palace Guard will support whoever pays them, and that's not you anymore."

"What do you…?"

"You haven't discovered this yet, but I've taken care of your Palace Guard."

"Who are you?" asked the Khadar in disbelief.

"If you persist, someone will take you out. I don't know who it will be," continued the Ammun Mettell. "It could be the Palace Guard, it could be your Minister of the Right, your Minister of the Left, even. Any of the family heads might step up. The point is, someone will. Whether you realize it or not—and you should—you're finished. But there is an easy, dignified way out."

"Am I to declare you the new leader of our planet?"

The Ammun Mettell nodded. The Khadar stared at him. He muttered, "I'll think on it."

The Ammun Mettell said, "Unfortunately, you have a deadline. If you don't resign by tomorrow evening, I will have to put certain things in motion."

"…things in motion," repeated the Khadar. "Perhaps that's what I need. To put things…to put you…in motion."

"Not your best move," said the Ammun Mettell. "Any action against me will cause others—my people—to, as we say, 'put things in motion,' without my help. Choose to resign and you will live a full life."

The Khadar turned to gaze out the window. "I'll let you know," he said. When he wasn't looking, the Ammun Mettell vanished.

At the same time that the Ammun Mettell was with the Khadar, the Mettellites, every last one of them, were assembling at their new meeting hall. The communication had gone out that the meeting was mandatory. All were to attend, without exceptions. Only the leaders close to the Ammun Mettell knew that the purpose of the meeting was to protect their members from being picked-off, one-by-one, by the Khadar's security forces. The meeting hall of a philosophy school was strictly off-limits even to the Khadar. Still, Mettellite security had noticed that each street corner surrounding the Mettellite Meeting Hall, and for a couple of blocks behind that, had members of the Khadar's forces in position. The Khadar's forces wore plainclothes, but were obvious nonetheless.

The Ammun Mettell's closest associates were aware of the imminent change in government. The change in government would put each of them at the very head of their Ministries. The leaders of the Mettellites knew that they were to be the leaders of the planet, but they couldn't talk about that openly. Their assignment was to run a sober, all-night meeting. That they failed to do so was understandable. Their own inner excitement and their swagger radiated to the assembled Mettellites and became the mood of the room. When the Ammun Mettell finally showed up to a distinctly out-of-the-ordinary standing ovation, even he wasn't immune to the feeling in the air. He actually allowed the applause to continue for a couple of minutes before motioning the assembly to sit. Then he spoke. What he had to say was surely extemporized, as it always was with him, but it was unforgettable. He spoke solemnly—at first—like he was trying to tamp down the energy in the room. But at some point he noted that there were a thousand Mettellites present and started playing that word, 'thousand,' saying there were a thousand responsibilities, a thousand ideas, a thousand goals. It became incantatory and riled everyone up again. That kind of energy couldn't be contained, even by the Ammun Mettell.

The Ammun Mettell left the podium and gave the running of the meeting over to others. He spent time conferring with his closest advisors. A few regular soldiers, in uniform, had shown up in the ranks of the Khadar's forces on the streets. "Not a concern," said the Ammun Mettell. "Just intimidation. They can't, and won't, use troops against a school of philosophy." At that moment, the Mettellite security chief interrupted with the news that a visitor had arrived outside of the main entrance.

"Yes…and?" asked the Ammun Mettell.

"The Ammun Ghobar."

"Good," said the Ammun Mettell. "Barteng, come along. We'll step outside and hear what he has to say."

We all understood that the Ammun Ghobar would be a sort of spokesman for the Khadar. His school was venerable, the oldest existing school of philosophy, and throughout history it had been aligned with the Khadars. But the Ammun Ghobar took it to a new level. By drawing himself ever closer to the Khadar, the Ammun Ghobar's school had become the quasi-official school of philosophy for the planet. Their actual philosophy was mutable. The Ammun Ghobar could argue from any stance that supported an initiative of the Khadar's government, imbuing any whim of the Khadar with trappings of learnedness and the tradition of centuries. The political influence of the Ammun Ghobar's school made it attractive to his followers. Donning the blue robes of the Ammun Ghobar's school could make someone a person to be reckoned with. The Ammun Ghobar claimed to protect the purity of his school by never permitting any of his followers to take an official position in the government. What he was really doing was making sure that none of his followers would ever eclipse his own influence over the Khadar. The Ammun Ghobar was a wily old bird.

The Ammun Mettell and Barteng descended to the entry level of the Meeting Hall. The Ammun Mettell walked quickly towards the main entrance before noticing that Barteng was no longer by his side. The Ammun Mettell turned around, puzzled. He smiled darkly. Of course. The Ammun Ghobar wouldn't let himself be seen at the main entrance to the Mettellite Meeting Hall. Looking ten paces back, he saw Barteng pointing in the direction of the side door. "Right," muttered the Ammun Mettell. Reaching the side entrance, the Ammun Mettell paused to collect his thoughts. Then he motioned for Barteng to open the door. The Ammun Ghobar stood there, flanked on each side by his lieutenants. In the distance, members of the Khadar's Security Forces maintained their positions. The Ammun Ghobar's people looked smug. The Ammun Ghobar himself bore the aggressively vacant expression that he cultivated for public meetings. "I bring greetings," said the Ammun Ghobar. The standard formulation was, "I bring greetings from one Ammun to another." In this way, the Ammun Ghobar was signaling that he withheld recognition of the Mettellite school. The Ammun Mettell, for his part, had no time for childishness like this. Did the Ammun Ghobar not understand that they were negotiating the fate of planetary government? The Ammun Mettell simply nodded. He said, "What does the Khadar have to say?" The Ammun Ghobar raised his eyebrows ever so little. "The Khadar?" he asked. As if he didn't know the Khadar. As if he had heard the name. "I have come on my own account. I wish to address your assembly," he said with the barest hint of a smile. The Ammun Mettell stepped back.

"I understand that you are somewhat new to operating a school of philosophy," continued the Ammun Ghobar, "do you perhaps need a reminder that other Ammuns enjoy the prerogative of addressing the assemblies of any properly constituted school?"

"No reminder needed," said the Ammun Mettell.

"And are you, in fact, a properly constituted school of philosophy?" It was a dangerous question.

"Of course we are," said the Ammun Mettell. Any other answer or any attempt to deny the Ammun Ghobar his place at their podium would be admitting that the Mettellites were not a proper school. Without the protections afforded a school of philosophy, nothing would stop the Khadar's security forces—the ones menacing the Meeting Hall—from streaming in and putting a final end to the Mettellites. "I welcome you to our Meeting Hall." The Ammun Ghobar and his lieutenants exchanged glances and moved towards the door. "Not them," said the Ammun Mettell, "Just you."

Barteng and the Ammun Mettell escorted the Ammun Ghobar through the lobby of the Meeting Hall. They walked past display cases, murals, and placards dedicated to Mettellite glory. They passed under banners quoting the Ammun Mettell and along walls with photos of Mettellites doing public service. The installation, intended for motivation and recruitment, had an opposite effect on the Ammun Ghobar. His face grew sour. He walked through the hall giving everything a wide berth as if to avoid getting any of it on his robes.

The Ammun Mettell was lost in thought. The Khadar was not taking the easy path that had been offered to him. Quite aside from the Ammun Ghobar's display of disdain, there had been no negotiation. No offers, no requests. And now the Ammun Ghobar would use an obscure protocol to try and weaken the resolve of the Mettellites. It was clear now to the Ammun Mettell that the Khadar would have to go the hard way. The uncontrolled way. The Mettellites would need to scramble if they were to emerge at the top of a chaotic post-Khadar world.

Attaining the podium, the Ammun Mettell spoke tersely, "We have an honored guest, the Ammun Ghobar. Please show him your best courtesy." But everyone in the room noticed the dark look on the Ammun Mettell's face as he took his seat. The crowd was not inclined towards politeness.

The Ammun Ghobar stood at the podium, not speaking, taking the measure of the room. He could feel the hostility. Someone yelled something rude. Which was what the Ammun Ghobar had been waiting for. "Such bad manners!" exclaimed the Ammun Ghobar. "But all is forgiven. Young people will act up from time to time. For I do see that you are, all of you, quite young. And it is true. I am quite old. And I urge you, I urge you to aspire to, one day perhaps, be as old as I am."

The astute among the Mettellites jolted awake. Was that a threat?

"Youth and age," continued the Ammun Ghobar. "Yours is a young school. Mine is an old one. And in my school, we value the worth of old things. Of tradition. Of continuity. And, as old as we are, sometimes even we need to be reminded of things yet older than ourselves. Older than our memories. Older than our imaginations. Artifacts, for example, from a time before our own civilization. They have a special value for us."

From his robes, the Ammun Ghobar produced the Naveeran Karamand and held it aloft. The crowd went silent. The Naveeran Karamand was the holiest of relics, older than anyone knew. The Ammun Ghobar had made a powerful point. He certainly understood how to capture the attention of a room.

"And we must not lose the meaning of the old words," continued the Ammun Ghobar. "Old words like these," he said, slipping into a language that no one in the room had

heard before. And as he spoke those old words, the Mettellites vanished. The Ammun Ghobar was now addressing an
empty meeting hall. The Mettellite crowd was gone.

Except for the Ammun Mettell. Projected from afar,
he was unaffected by the karamand. The Ammun Ghobar
began to turn towards him when the Ammun Mettell, ever
quick-thinking, chose to vanish. The Ammun Ghobar was
satisfied. He put the karamand in a pocket of his robes.

The Ammun Mettell appeared again as a small blue-
gray cube in the lobby. He watched as the Ammun Ghobar
walked out, humming a tune to himself and running his
finger along the display cases.

Part Five

24

JORGAN ROME WAS BACK in outer space again. Suddenly. And as usual, he didn't have a single weapon with him. He would rely on quick thinking and on luck to survive. He would need both because his survival was very much in doubt. He was floating, unarmed, in a space suit just twenty meters in front of Tokar's enormous, heavily-armed command ship. "You'll end as a splat on Tokar's windshield!" the Dar Telku had said when she heard his intentions.

Only thirty minutes earlier, Jorgan Rome had been meditating in a small dark room. The Dar Telku rushed in and announced, "Tokar's ships will be entering the atmosphere in less than an hour. If they do that…"

"We're finished," said Jorgan Rome, emerging from meditation. He stood and followed the Dar Telku into the main reception room. They watched Tokar's progress on the big screen.

At that very moment, Raia appeared with a karamand in her hand and the Makha Miffin under her arm. Jorgan Rome turned around. Seeing Raia, he grinned. But only for a moment. Turning serious, he said, "Good work, Raia."

"Thank you," said Raia. There was no need to say anything more.

The Dar Telku was thrilled to see Raia, perplexed at Jorgan Rome's curt greeting, and then indignant at his coldness. "Is that all you…I mean…putting this young woman in danger!…in mortal danger even!…brave, brave young Raia!…and then she escapes…somehow…you don't even ask…and all you can say is 'Good work, Raia!'"

Jorgan Rome exchanged glances with Raia. Like Jorgan Rome, Raia understood the space adventurer code. She knew that you didn't talk about adventures unless you had to. Besides, Jorgan Rome had seen the karamand in her hand. Raia knew that he would have noted the missing paralysis bracelet. Jorgan Rome knew in an instant exactly what had transpired. Raia and Jorgan Rome understood each other. There was no use explaining it all to the Dar Telku. "It's OK," said Raia.

"Summon the team," said Jorgan Rome. The team, such as it was, arrived soon enough—four Mettellites in inexpensive, barely-functioning, patched-together space suits. They carried their helmets.

Less than ten minutes later, Jorgan Rome was in space staring down the enormous military ship. Raia had successfully placed him inside of the ship's artillery range—he was too close for them to fire. Jorgan Rome knew that there was little chance of the ship colliding with him. Jorgan Rome had the opposite fear, that they would escape him. He knew that the sudden appearance of an object of his size would trigger automatic evasive maneuvers. They would get away from him. If they got far enough, they would target him and blow him to pieces. That was why Jorgan Rome had strapped himself to a thalden. The thalden would seek out

the ship's nav center, reacting faster than any ship could maneuver. Many a pirate tried to evade a port master's thalden
only to be captured and put on trial.

The ship hove away to his right. Jorgan Rome went into
a tuck. The thalden spun him around and chased down the
nav center. Tokar's ship had no chance at all. Jorgan Rome
unstrapped from the thalden and with magnetic shoes and
gloves, clambered over the exterior surface of Tokar's ship.

At that same moment, the two other ships were under
attack by four Mettellites riding thaldens to their nav centers.
All of them needed to operate fast, before the ship crews
knew what was about to happen. They worked without
communication.

Jorgan Rome scrambled quickly to a place near the bow
of Tokar's ship. Then he made a mistake. He touched his
foot down on a non-magnetic surface. His other foot was un-
attached. Just the light probing touch of boot-on-aluminum-
plate was enough to put Jorgan Rome on a slow trajectory
away from the ship and towards outer space. Jorgan Rome
had insisted on working without tethers. "Tethers will slow
us down!" he had said. "We only have a few minutes at most.
And they'll tangle on all the things that stick up from the
ship's surface." Now Jorgan Rome was paying the price for
working without a tether.

On the planet below, Raia, the Dar Telku, and Teera
watched the team's progress on the Dar Telku's view screen.
The Dar Telku sniffed when she saw Jorgan Rome floating
helpless a couple of meters above Tokar's ship. "As if I didn't
see that coming!" she said. Switching the view, the screen
showed that the Mettellites had all touched down with their
thaldens. They began to unbuckle themselves and move, as
Jorgan Rome had, toward the front of the ships. Except for
one. One of the Mettellites stayed close to his thalden.

"Can you give us a better view of that?" asked Teera.

The Dar Telku made a face.

"It's about saving the planet from invasion, you know," said Teera.

The Dar Telku looked at Teera for a moment, wondering how the robot knew that she had been sandbagging them. The Dar Telku made some adjustments. Suddenly they saw everything. Raia jumped back. They could now see that the Mettellite had a finger of his glove, just the tip, pinned between the thalden and the nav center. He was tugging to free his glove.

"Don't do that," muttered Raia.

"Those suits can't take it, can they?" asked Teera.

Raia shook her head. The Mettellite pulled harder until his hand became free. Then he went into spasms. He had torn a hole in the glove. His face showed the agony and shock of sudden decompression. Raia brought him back to Earth and, with Teera, removed his helmet. "He needs the hyperbaric chamber," said Raia.

Jorgan Rome looked around. He had no tether but he did have a wrench at his belt. He would probably need the wrench for the task at hand. He removed it from his belt and threw it as hard as he could into outer space away from the ship. The recoil sent him into a very slow spin and, just as slowly, on a trajectory back to the ship. It would take a couple of minutes. There was no choice but to wait for a couple of minutes until he could make contact again. And to hope that Tokar's crew made no course alterations in the meantime.

At that moment, a Mettellite moving along the third ship made the same mistake as Jorgan Rome. Except that the Mettellite stepped hard and sent himself flying into space. Raia brought him back to Earth. When he realized where he was, he removed his helmet and said to Raia, "Send me back!"

"She can't," said Teera, "Not to the same ship you came from."

"Why not?"

"Both nav centers are bound tightly to thaldens. There's no way to plant you there safely."

"Then send me to Jorgan Rome's ship, the command ship."

They looked at Raia. Without turning to look at them she said, "If he needs help."

"If?" asked the Dar Telku.

Just at that moment, Jorgan Rome made contact with Tokar's ship. By controlling his tuck and the position of his arms, he landed perfectly on his feet like a gymnast doing a very, very slow dismount. At that instant, he began to move more quickly than anyone imagined possible. With perfect concentration, he released and attached the magnetic actuators on gloves and boots, charging forward like a cat, low-slung and fast towards his goal. He arrived in less than a minute at the ship's Atmospheric Entry Plasma Generator. The AEPG, whose function was to create a magnetic plasma that would deflect heat-ionized atmospheric gases around and away from the ship, was the focus of Jorgan Rome's mission. All he had to do was disable the AEPG. Without a plasma deflector, the ship couldn't enter the atmosphere. The invasion would be cancelled before it even began.

But Jorgan Rome had no time to spare. If they activated the AEPG now, he was a dead man. He made a rapid study of the unit. It was larger than he had imagined. And of course there was no obvious switch to turn it off. But there were a great number of pipes and conduits leading everywhere. One was for magnet power, another for resonator power;

there was a gas source, a starter gas feed, and antenna feeds. One of these, the correct one, had to be severed. From his belt, Jorgan Rome took a handheld plasma torch—one he had taken from the Mettellite workshop—and ignited it. The problem was to choose the correct conduit. If he cut into resonator power, he would be fried. If he cut into magnet power, he would be electrocuted. If he cut into the gas source with a plasma torch, he would ignite an explosion that could damage the ship and cost lives. He had to identify the starter gas feed line. The problem was that all of the conduits and pipes were hardened for deep space travel and looked exactly alike.

Jorgan Rome placed his gloved hand on the unit. He felt each conduit and pipe. Nothing. Trying again, he felt vibration in one of them. The unit was about to be activated. Acting on pure reflex he knelt down and put his torch on the vibrating pipe. It would take only a few seconds to sever the connection. Then Jorgan Rome jumped back. He had nearly made a fatal error. Only the primary supply would rumble like that! The starter feed would be the next one over. And there was no time to lose! Pulling a second plasma torch from his belt, Jorgan Rome went at the starter feed with both torches. A couple of moments later he was done. The crew would realize that their AEPG was out of action. They would abort their landing. They would not be invading Earth today.

Jorgan Rome stood upright to to make himself more visible. He waved his arms to signal that he was finished with his task. As he waved, he took a moment to look around. Tokar's ship, the one he was on, was the lead ship. The two trailing ships, one to the left and one to the right, were following closely at only a kilometer back. Each of those ships, Jorgan Rome knew, had Mettellites on them disabling the atmospheric entry systems. They had still had time available to them. Jorgan Rome did not. When he turned around again, he saw the planet looming large. Tokar's ship would need to make an emergency maneuver very soon. If he was still clinging to the outside hull when they did, he wouldn't survive. His little boot magnets would never hold. Whether from impact against the ship or from rocket exhaust, his death was all but certain if he remained.

He stood and waved again and that's when he saw the explosion. A small fireball erupted from the bow of one of the trailing ships. Grief gripped his heart, a burst of sadness for the Mettellites involved and even for the crew of the invading ship. In all his exploits, over many years, Jorgan Rome had never, ever caused anyone to die. He hoped—he knew—that Raia would be saving as many of them as possible. Maybe they would be lucky. But he needed to put away his grief. Jorgan Rome had to concentrate on making his own luck. With no way of leaving the ship, he had to figure out how to survive the maneuver that might come at any moment.

He scanned the surface of the ship, looking for somewhere, anywhere, to brace himself on all sides. There was no such place. But he did see a hatch. Inside of that hatch would surely be an airlock. He could survive the ship's maneuvers in the airlock. With no time to lose, he scrambled towards the hatch. He didn't give himself any time to consider what would happen when he got inside of that hatch. What would happen when his suit ran out of air and he had to exit the airlock to the inside of the ship? What would he do on his own, an invader in a ship full of hostile soldiers? Would he manage to avoid capture? Would he hide? Would he take over the ship? Would he face Tokar? He would figure all that out later. All he cared about was opening up the hatch and crawling in. If the seal latch didn't release, he still had his plasma torches.

Jorgan Rome made it halfway to the hatch when it suddenly sprung open. He froze. Out stepped Tokar. It was unnerving to see the mostly humanoid robot outside the ship without a space suit. Tokar stood a full head taller than Jorgan Rome, who anyway was crouched down on his hands and feet just to stay attached to the ship. Tokar had any number of weapons available on his belt. Tokar had lightning reflexes. Tokar was unencumbered by a space suit. It wasn't a good circumstance for Jorgan Rome to encounter Tokar.

For his part, Tokar must have understood that Jorgan Rome was already doomed. Tokar didn't waste time. He just smirked at Jorgan Rome before jumping away from the ship. Ten meters away from the ship, he started up some sort of personal rocket and jetted away toward Earth. Two more robots emerged from the hatch and Jorgan Rome braced himself. When they, too, jumped away from the ship, Jorgan Rome jumped after them hurling the ignited plasma torches overhand, one after the other, at the robots. As they spun through space, the little plasma jets tumbled around until they found their targets at the fuel intake of each robot's little rocket. Maybe Tokar was headed to Earth, but these two robots weren't going anywhere.

Jorgan Rome was safe from the quick maneuvers of the ship. He had jumped in the direction of the robots, and whatever course change the ship would undergo would have been planned to keep their own crew members alive. He felt confident of that. Indeed the ship dropped quickly downward, away from them, before accelerating away. Jorgan Rome was alive. But now he faced an a more serious problem. He was in space and nobody knew where he was. He was falling rapidly to Earth. He had maybe an hour's worth of air left, but that was immaterial. Coming toward the earth at high speed, and accelerating every moment, it wouldn't be long before the thin super-heated gases of the upper ionosphere would pile up in front of him. Some small patch of his poor second-hand spacesuit would melt. His suit would depressurize. He would have about ten or twenty seconds of life after that.

He tumbled slowly as he fell. Every minute or so, the Earth rose from below his feet to claim his entire field of view and then passed over his right shoulder and sank behind him again. It was so overwhelmingly beautiful that Jorgan Rome closed his eyes. He couldn't afford distraction. He needed to concentrate on what was truly important. He thought about Raia. He thought about Cholley. But even these he pushed from his mind. For Jorgan Rome, who lived his adventures as they came and never over-prepared a plan, who preferred luck to thought, had always prepared himself for the moment when his luck ran out. He went deeper into his own mind. Images of earlier adventures—of saving Raia, of commandeering an alien convoy, of meeting Cholley—came and went. All good memories but not what he needed now. He remembered his first adventure. The Ammun Ghobar had sent him on a quest for the Karakanth Pasrund. Jorgan Rome indulged this memory. He let it grow. He sensed something in it that befitted this moment of tumbling through space with only minutes to live.

The Ammun Ghobar had given him only two weeks to track down the Karakanth Pasrund. Jorgan Rome had thought it would be an adventure quest, a search for a mystical object, maybe even one that could make a room full of Mettellites disappear. After three days, he was crushed to learn that the Karakanth Pasrund was only a poem. A poem from a thousand years before. Deep in the Library of Antiquities he found a librarian who looked at him sourly and said, "Most people believe that the Karakanth Pasrund has been lost forever." With no way forward on his quest, Jorgan Rome turned away. But not for long. Jorgan Rome, even as a young man, never admitted defeat and so ten nearly-sleepless days later he found himself again confronting that same librarian. "That," said Jorgan Rome, pointing to one of the rare old books in the display case that formed part of the desk, "I'd like to see that." "Very well," muttered the librarian as he produced the book. "Open it for me?" asked Jorgan Rome. When the librarian spread the pages of the book, Jorgan Rome said, "Not that way!" The librarian pursed his lips and took Jorgan Rome's measure. Then he opened the book backwards through a secret fold in the spine. There was the Karakanth Pasrund. "In thirty years," said the librarian, "only one other person has asked." Of course, Jorgan Rome knew exactly who that was. "I need to take this with me," said Jorgan Rome. "I'm afraid you can't," said the librarian, "besides, he'll want you to have it memorized." So with only a few hours to go, Jorgan Rome set to memorizing a long poem in a language he didn't know but with pronunciation assistance from the librarian.

The Ammun Ghobar's door was ajar. Jorgan Rome looked in. The Ammun Ghobar was alone. He didn't see Jorgan Rome slip into the room. The Ammun sat behind a large desk, leaning forward with his hands in his lap. There was turmoil of some sort in the Khadar's Palace, Jorgan Rome had gathered, a turmoil that would necessarily involve the Ammun. Jorgan Rome could see that it wasn't going well. The Ammun noticed Jorgan Rome. "You're a sneaky one, aren't you?" he snapped. "You've come to ask for more time. You want more time on the assignment. Well, here's your first lesson." The Ammun smiled coldly. "Sometimes, time is up. Your time is up. You need to know when your time is up. You need to accept that your time is up." It was probably this last dictum from the Ammun, to accept when your time is up, that brought the memory with such force to Jorgan Rome as he tumbled down into the upper ionosphere.

"I have the poem," Jorgan Rome had said. The Ammun Ghobar was surprised. There was a long silence. "But, can you…" the Ammun started to ask and Jorgan Rome nodded. "Very well, we'll schedule you a fitting for a robe. Welcome," said the Ammun Ghobar turning away. "But," said Jorgan Rome, "It's just that…" Jorgan Rome stopped himself. He didn't want to invite more scorn from the Ammun Ghobar but it was too late. "It's just that you expected more than a poem, is that it?" Jorgan Rome swallowed and nodded. "You are a fool, Jorgan Rome! There may come a day when only a poem, this poem perhaps, will be all that can save you!"

Jorgan Rome, falling to Earth, went into a tuck against the turbulence. He spun around faster in the tuck. He was dizzy and he would burn up very soon. But he still had the poem. He began to say it to himself as he tumbled down. One verse, then another. Who knew how much time he had left?

Everything went white.

25

W HAT WAS IT with all the arches? For a small provincial planet, Gurfann had more ceremonial arches than she could believe. Every couple of months or so, someone found a reason to dedicate a new one. There would be a dinner al fresco under the arch, speeches, and always, always a symphony. As ever, Calcha had no choice but to make an appearance. She loathed everything about Gurfann. She especially disdained their pathetic arches popping up all over. Coming here with this status had been the biggest mistake of her life, or rather, the second biggest mistake if she were honest and counted her failed attempt to kill the Khadar. Now on Gurfann, she mainly regretted the mistake of what she had said at her trial. She had only spoken at the end. She had stood and reminded the court that they couldn't kill her. She was a diplomatic hostage and there would be repercussions. Then she sat down. Through private channels she let the law officials know that she would accept exile to Gurfann, but only on the condition that she had the public cover of being sent as a Special Envoy. Everyone at the Khadar's court was stunned at her nerve. They also understood that it was the easiest way to be rid of her.

So it happened. And now, to keep the fiction going, Calcha was obliged to attend their charity events, salons, openings, closings, and…arch dedications. Tonight it was another arch. She pinned some feathers according to Gurfann fashion onto the shoulder of her gown and prepared to leave.

Calcha always had robots in her retinue. One evening, about a month after arriving on Gurfann, she sent word that she would appear at a charity banquet. She was announced as she entered, "Calcha, Princess of Tellapenth, Queen-Consort of Naveer, Special Envoy to Gurfann!" The effect was electric. She bore grand titles from each constituent planet of the old Realm! It would be a banquet to remember. Everyone present would have a story to tell. She entered to applause. But the applause faded away when she walked in surrounded by five robot companions. Calcha didn't understand and it showed on her face. A young embassy staffer came up behind her. In a low voice, he explained, "This is Gurfann. Very conservative. You can have robot friends, that's fine. But it won't do to try and introduce them to society." Calcha couldn't believe what she was hearing and nearly flew into a rage. She settled for an aloof coldness that saw her through the evening. Her robots, overhearing the embassy staffer, had discreetly withdrawn.

Without her robots, Calcha was more exposed to social interaction. During a cocktail hour at a new museum wing, a gentleman approached. Gray at the temples, he wore an expensive suit, and had genial sympathy on his face. "Ah, well," he said, "The museum has seen better days." He shook his drink. "Time was when it served up the very best." He tried for a wistful expression but when Calcha looked, she only saw social insecurity and miscalculated swagger. These people are so transparent! She thought how easy it would be to lure this man into ruinous scandal or to deliver him into an addiction he would never shake. "I'm sure we'll manage," said Calcha. When Calcha turned around, a young woman exclaimed, "Your Majesty!" and proceeded to curtsy. The curtsy triggered Calcha's mind to think just how this woman could be drawn in and made to do almost anything before the robots disposed of her body. When she said, "Dearest! Do call me Calcha!" the young woman was overcome, feathers aflutter. Encounters like this taught Calcha, finally, late in her life, the skill of maintaining an unreadable face.

When Calcha finally had enough, she petitioned for return to Naveer. She was turned down, of course.

Then came the fall of the Khadar and chaos on Naveer. The Khadar's former Minister of the Right declared himself the new leader. He lasted about ten weeks, ousted by the former Minister of the Guards. The Khadar himself was presumed dead. Calcha sensed that she could make good use of the instability. With the Khadar gone, she decided to lay groundwork for her return. She persuaded two of her newest robots, who were unknown to anyone on Naveer, to go via a circuitous route not traceable back to Gurfann. Once on Naveer, the robots were to scope out the political landscape and find allies for her return. The robots never even made it halfway. Someone had known what they were up to. They were intercepted and told to return to Gurfann. With a message for Calcha. If she tried again, the record of her return requests would be made public on Gurfann. The transcript of her trial transcript would be released.

Calcha was still stranded on that backwater planet. And she apparently had an antagonist on Naveer. Someone who despite the swirling chaos in the government, had put effort into monitoring Calcha on Gurfann. Someone who knew that she was worth monitoring.

Stuck on Gurfann, Calcha had few cards to play. Her only path out of here would be a slow one. Curiously, it was the path that had been described back then by that visitor to her apartments in the Palace. He had come twice. He gave advice unlike any she had heard before, that she, Calcha, could take power by acclamation. By becoming popular, he had said, before she had him disintegrated.

26

R AIA WAS AT the controls. Tireless and focused, she had taken command of the Dar Telku's vast sensor network when the Dar Telku stepped away. Teera stood next to her. Behind her were four of the Mettellites, still half in their spacesuits, some carrying their helmets. Cholley hung from the ceiling. "Maybe that ship flung him into a higher orbit," offered one of the Mettellites. Raia looked at Teera. Teera shook her head. Raia continued searching.

The Dar Telku settled in on the sofa in the middle of the room. She stared silently straight ahead. She looked over at the huddled team all searching for Jorgan Rome. She looked away. She glanced at a side wall where the Makha Miffin, the true history of the Allozetts, the only copy even, lay on a small shelf. She put her hands in her lap. She didn't know how to tell the team the bad news that they had a hundred million cubic kilometers of near space to search. That accounting for his trajectory only reduced the search volume to a staggering hundred thousand cubic kilometers. That she had surreptitiously initiated a rapid, automated foreign-object search of near space. That she had seen the two disabled robots. That she had seen the plasma torches that had put the robots out of action, but not a trace of Jorgan Rome who had surely burned up by now. She looked over at the team. She pursed her lips. She looked again at the Makha Miffin. She walked over and took the book from the shelf. She sat back on the sofa and settled in to read.

A few moments later, Jorgan Rome walked into the room. The Dar Telku jumped from the sofa. "I was just…" Jorgan Rome smiled. "It's OK," he said. At the sound of his voice, everyone turned from the screen. "Daddy!" yelled Raia. Jorgan Rome grinned and put his helmet down on the floor. He scooped Raia up, gave her a hug and put her back down. She collected herself again. She put on her best serious look and said, "Good work!"

"I'm sorry for the delay," said Jorgan Rome. "I guess I'm not as good at piloting this thing as I ought to be," he said, indicating the karamand that dangled from the chain on his neck. The Mettellites came over and clapped him on the back. Teera looked at him. "Your luck…" she said.

"I know," said Jorgan Rome. "But not today, apparently."

Raia was puzzled about how he could "pilot" a karamand at all. There was simply no way that he should have been able to do what he had done. There had been no occasion to teach him how to do it. How could he have known the words— they were in her native language, not his—to operate it? But somehow if anyone could manage, Jorgan Rome could. It had always been that way.

Jorgan Rome went to the center of the room. "Let's gather and take stock of the recent foray." They all formed a rough circle around Jorgan Rome. Cholley rolled over along the ceiling. The Dar Telku reluctantly joined in at the periphery, the Makha Miffin still under her arm. "First, what about our team members involved in the explosion?" Everyone looked down. One of the Mettellites shook his head. "OK," said Jorgan Rome, "Memorial service as soon as practical. Maybe sooner. Next, did we succeed in stopping the invasion?"

Teera said, "Those ships will not be landing on this planet."

"Good, thanks to a first-rate team. That means we've been partially successful."

"Partially?" asked Raia.

"Partially," said Jorgan Rome. "Because of something we didn't anticipate. Tokar. He's a robot of course, we know that he can leave his ship without a spacesuit. What we didn't know, what I didn't think of, is that he can enter the atmosphere and touch down on this planet without a ship. He got away from me. He could be anywhere on this planet in about three hours time."

"Any idea where he's going?" asked Cholley.

"None," said Jorgan Rome.

"Well, take a look at this," said the Dar Telku who had moved over in front of the main screen. She brought up an old image of Tokar and his command crew on the ship. She zoomed in on the diagram hanging on the wall behind Tokar. Everyone could see that the Dar Telku's compound was drawn there.

"Oh," said Cholley.

"Two hours," said Teera.

"That's it!" said the Dar Telku. "You're leaving! He wants you. He wants that karamand. And I want you gone. All of you. Before this place gets destroyed"

"No," said Jorgan Rome.

"No?" asked the Dar Telku, "Did you just say, 'No?'" she asked again with a dangerous smile forming on her face.

"No," said Jorgan Rome, "He may want us, he probably would like the karamand, but he knows we're mobile and it's unlikely he could capture us. Destroying this place, or more likely, taking control of it, is what he really wants. You can imagine how useful this place could be to someone like Calcha who wants to take over the galaxy."

"He's just one robot, right?" asked a Mettellite. "We have weapons. We have a lot of weapons. He shows up, we atomize him. Done."

There was silence. Teera said, "Probably not a good idea." To the Dar Telku she said, "Do you have video from Drappondu?"

The Dar Telku nodded and put it on the screen. In the video, Tokar led a phalanx of six robots across the main square toward the basilica. "What he's doing," said Teera, "is supposed to be ceremonial. He was there to accept their formal surrender. But look here…" The perspective changed, the source of the video was now from a roof on a side street, looking down on Tokar's progress. "In the lower left corner is a gun, then we get a view—right here—of the sniper. Whoever filmed this was part of this particular sniper team. And here…is the moment when Tokar notices them. Now watch Tokar's reaction." Everyone moved in closer to see the video, which now showed Tokar raising his arm. Tokar fired a projectile into the air, about 300 meters high. "Wait for it…" said Teera. The projectile detonated. "And…everyone is dead." The video camera fell to the ground. "All organic life in the capital city was extinguished," said Teera. Nobody spoke. Until Teera said, "He probably won't kill you if you leave him alone."

"Well, okay then…" said one of the Mettellites. "What have we got? We've got…bots. We must have a ton of bots. They could swarm him. Make it impossible for him."

"He can drop all the bots in a millisecond," said Teera. "They're no threat to him."

"What about you, Teera, are you…?" started Jorgan Rome.

"I'm safe. Autonomous, shielded, probably impervious."

"Well, there's that," said the Mettellite. "But what I'm thinking is that you've got that little device, the…"

"The karamand?" said Jorgan Rome, glancing at Raia. "It's not…"

"It's not a weapon," declared Raia.

The room went silent. The Dar Telku said, "I was afraid you two would say that."

"I think that anyone who can leave, or just wants to leave, should get to safety now. Those who stay should help coordinate our response to Tokar," said Jorgan Rome. Nobody got up to leave. "Good," said Jorgan Rome, "But stay close together. At a minimum we should all be in the same room with Raia so that she can evacuate us in a hurry."

"I think we should talk to him," said Teera.

"Who? Tokar?" asked the Mettellite.

"Tokar," said Teera. "Find out what he wants. See what we can do." Jorgan Rome scanned the room. The Mettellites eyes went wide. The Dar Telku was nodding vigorously. Jorgan Rome sensed that the conversation wasn't spontaneous. He looked at Teera but she looked away.

"I have a lab technician who can check your circuit safety," offered the Dar Telku.

"Thank you, I know the way," said Teera, exiting the room into the corridor.

Jorgan Rome stared at the Dar Telku. "Is there something I need to know?"

"No," said the Dar Telku, taking up the Makha Miffin and settling into a chair.

27

THREE QUARTERS of an hour passed without anyone saying a word. The Dar Telku was absorbed in
the book and hadn't left her chair. Raia was at the controls
of the view screen. Jorgan Rome sat motionless at one end
of the sofa.

Barteng wandered in from the laboratory area. He put
his hand to his temple and felt the shaved area. He frowned
and shook his head. He looked around the room and took
in the studied silence. After a moment he walked over to
the view screen. Raia had managed to locate Tokar shoot-
ing down through the atmosphere with a white-hot plasma
stream trailing behind him and an oddly placid look on his
robot face. Barteng gestured toward the screen with raised
eyebrows.

"Tokar," confirmed Raia, silently mouthing the name.

Barteng turned around and walked over to the sofa. He
looked at Jorgan Rome, then the Dar Telku, and back again.
"OK," said Barteng with full voice, "What's the plan?"

"Plan?" said Jorgan Rome.

"For that," said Barteng, gesturing at the screen.

"Well…it's his turn, isn't it? Let's see what move he makes."

Barteng fixed Jorgan Rome with an intent, are-you-serious look that quickly devolved into a sneer.

"Besides," continued Jorgan Rome while glancing over at the Dar Telku, "I'm not exactly in charge, am I?"

The Dar Telku pretended not to listen. She turned away theatrically to indicate that she was definitely, no-doubt-about-it, concentrating on her book.

"Not in charge?" said Barteng. "Have you ever been in charge?" Jorgan Rome thought for a moment, raised his eyebrows, and pursed his lips.

"That's just it!" said Barteng. "Where's the plan—there's never a plan! You have to have a plan. But with you…it's like it's always improvisation with you."

Jorgan Rome took his time before responding. "Since we have a little time, why don't you tell us the rest of the story?"

"The rest? You mean..after…?"

"You know," said Jorgan Rome, "When the Ammun Mettell had to improvise."

Barteng stared at Jorgan Rome, sighed, then dropped heavily onto the sofa. "Well," he said, then bit his lip for a moment. "You're absolutely right about that. But it was bad. Really bad. We had to think fast. We didn't know where we were and neither did the Ammun Mettell."

"It was late when it all happened. The Ministry offices were mostly deserted but that's where the Ammun Mettell went. He had people there. Clandestine people, not obviously affiliated with us, but answering to us all the same. Many of them worked late. He took himself to the Offices of State Security, right to the door of the Deputy Associate

Minister of Laws. That guy was one of ours. The Ammun Mettell opened the door and walked in."

At the sound of the door opening, the Deputy Associate Minister looked up to see the Ammun Mettell standing before his desk.

"Oh, my…!" he said, looking around the room, to see if anyone else was in the room. "You have to leave! Now!"

"Not before we've had a talk," said the Ammun Mettell.

"I thought you were…"

The Ammun Mettell made a quizzical look.

"If anyone sees us…my life will become very unpleasant." He turned quickly to go out a small door behind his desk. Just before closing the door again, he said, "Now get out of here!" But the Ammun Mettell was already on the other side of the door.

"How?…"

"Where are they?" asked the Ammun Mettell.

"Sports stadium. They were trucked over there. To the sports stadium."

"The sports stadium?"

"Yes, and here's a news flash: They're not there to see the game."

"I want full pardons, all of them," said the Ammun Mettell.

"That's not happening. We both know that."

"Exile, then,"

"I'll do what I can."

The Ammun Mettell nodded and turned away. When he was out of sight, he vanished and reappeared as small blue gray cube outside of the sports stadium. There would be time later on to deal with the fragile loyalty of his Deputy Associate Minister. A quarter of an hour passed before he found his people in a holding pen under the stands. They were slumped on the ground, some were leaning against the iron grates, some were just milling around. The Ammun Mettell didn't show himself yet. He continued to look around.

He found an open doorway leading below ground. At the bottom of a damp metal staircase was a big room. There were voices.

"Can we make this happen? We have to be done by morning, every one of them. And then be out of here—no traces." There were three technical types trying to start up a large old military-grade disintegration chamber. It was a five-at-a-go disintegrator that gave no possibility of re-integration.

Barteng looked up. "None of us in the holding pen knew anything about the disintegrator, but you'll understand that we were all pretty scared nonetheless. I'm not sure I can describe the effect it had on us when the Ammun Mettell appeared. He can be very charming when he wants to be. He went around, clapping people on the back, just radiating this aura like he had it all under control. Which he didn't. After he made his rounds, he summoned a few of us to a corner for a quick conference. He told us—it was me, Eddlo, and Parvik—to smile and laugh because everyone was watching. It wasn't easy with what he had to say."

"There's a large disintegration chamber on the floor below us," said the Ammun Mettell. "But it won't be operational tonight. I managed to lure the executioners, all three of them, into the chamber. Then I locked them in." We all tried to laugh.

Eddlo smiled and then said, "The Khadar won't stop." I grinned and looked at the ground. I knew where Eddlo was going, so I added, "He knows who we are. Every one of us. Even if we get out of here…"

Eddlo said, "The best we can do is exile—for now."

"Gurfann," said Parvik.

"Gurfann?"

Parvik continued, "Gurfann's your best bet. I mean, you can't leave when you get there, but you have freedom of movement on the planet when you're…"

The Ammun Mettell interrupted, "Let's stop this right here. I'm not interested in Gurfann. This is the only planet I care about."

"Let me continue," said Parvik. The Ammun Mettell scowled. Parvik went on, "We've built a beam facility there. It works. In fact, it's our only functioning one. The development team on Gurfann made strides so we sent them our best equipment…"

"I have no idea why we did that," said the Ammun Mettell.

"With the beam, you can come and go almost at will."

Ammun Mettell gave him a probing look

"You'll be back here whenever you need."

Ammun Mettell considered.

"And your people will be safe." But the Ammun Mettell knew it wasn't true. The Rubicon was behind them now. The Khadar would never leave them alone. The Ammun Mettell shook his head.

"One other thing you need to consider." said Eddlo. "A few too many of your people know that you're projected."

"So?"

"So any of them can get picked off by the Khadar. Make their own deal, perhaps. The trauma of near-execution can change things, you know. Once the Khadar learns that you're projected, it will be a never-ending race. Can you build projectors faster than the Khadar can find them?"

"OK, point taken," said the Ammun Mettell. "We're all going to Gurfann. Every one of us. We'll all be very happy there." After a pause he added, "That beam line had better work."

As our little conference was ending, Parvik spoke up. "That was very brave of you to get near a disintegration chamber," he said to the Ammun Mettell.

"Well, I don't think I can be disintegrated twice!"

"That's precisely it. You can be. The blast of incoherent eta radiation from a working disintegration chamber, even from outside, just somewhere nearby even, could overwhelm your projection. Just stand near an operating disintegration chamber and it's all over for you. You took a real chance."

The Ammun Mettell raised his eyebrows. "Well, OK, it's done, let's move on."

The Ammun Mettell wanted a private word with Eddlo and me, so Parvik wandered off. "I need to be elsewhere at the moment for…preparations. I'd like you to look in on the people in the execution chamber. Please make sure they're safe. And make sure they can't get out."

Barteng looked over at Jorgan Rome, "I didn't want to go near that thing. But it was an order and it had to be done. Eddlo had to pull me along. We went down some dank stairs and there it was. Even Eddlo shuddered when he saw it. There was a face at the window. Pleading." Eddlo became calm, stood taller, and slowed his walk. They began yelling from inside the chamber,"Open the door!"

Eddlo seemed to consider it for a moment. He nodded absent-mindedly as if struck by a thought, then remembered again the face at the chamber door. He leaned in and said with sympathetic earnestness, "That's complicated…"

"No it's not, you idiot, open the door!"

Eddlo backed away. "No," he said, "It's quite complicated." Waving his arm at the control panel for the disintegrator, Eddlo said, "There are so very many buttons." Leaning his face to the glass and with a wide smile, Eddlo said, "Tell me which one turns it on!"

Barteng looked over at Jorgan Rome. "I was checking around the outside of the chamber when I heard that. I jumped. But I saw Eddlo and it was OK. The corner of his lip was turned down like happens when he's toying with someone. I honestly think that was why the Ammun Mettell send Eddlo down there."

"No worries!" said Eddlo. "We'll have you out of there soon enough." Then a look of concern. "I imagine it's quite cold in there," he suggested, and was answered with emphatic nods. "It's freezing!"

"Well," said Eddlo, "Let's see what we can't do to to provide you some heat…"

28

T HE AMMUN METTELL'S preparations took up the rest of the day and evening. He arranged better accommodations for his people and their transport to Gurfann. He did spot inspections of governmental offices and his people that he had squirreled away in them. He made administrative personnel changes. He was finally satisfied only a few hours before sunrise when there was nothing more that could be done. At that hour everything in the city came to a halt.

Up on the hill, even the Khadar's Palace would settle in for a few hours of sleep. The last recital would have ended long before. The late-night salons had emptied. Even the staunchest of lovers, back-stabbers, functionaries, and hangers-on at the Palace needed to rest at some point so they could stay alert to the next day's changing winds of court life. Which meant that nobody was awake when tragedy struck.

The Palace Shift went very wrong. A council chamber was destroyed when an adjacent corridor came crashing through like a train, then continued through a courtyard and turned a library to rubble. Then another corridor came from another angle, hurtling through the remains of the council chamber until it, too, collapsed. One after another the corridors made war on the structures of the Inner Palace until nothing remained. The outer public palace was untouched, providing an outward-looking facade that covered the ongoing destruction within. Nobody escaped and nobody alive witnessed the final obliteration of the Khadar's Inner Palace. Nobody except the Ammun Mettell who watched it all from a safe distance in the surrounding hills.

Part Six

29

JORGAN ROME GAZED grimly ahead into emptiness while Barteng looked at the floor, and the Dar Telku looked at her book, and Raia looked at her screen. Moments later, Barteng, attuned to the slightest change of mood, looked up to see the Dar Telku staring across the room. Jorgan Rome noticed and followed Barteng's gaze to the Dar Telku, and then hers to Raia. The Dar Telku closed the book. She stood up. Her chair fell backwards. She made no move to right the chair but walked unsteadily to Raia.

"You're an…?"

"An Allozett?" asked Raia.

"Yes," said the Dar Telku.

Raia gave a quick nod. As if a quick nod were enough. As if a quick nod were enough to acknowledge the culmination of the Dar Telku's far-fetched lifelong dream. Unable to speak, the Dar Telku hugged Raia. And she cried.

Raia stole a tentative look at Jorgan Rome. She had never told him. Jorgan Rome smiled because he had suspected as much. It was fine with him if his adopted daughter had her secrets.

Raia didn't notice that the screen behind her showed Tokar's three ships beginning to turn in a wide arc back towards Earth.

30

JORGAN ROME PRODDED Barteng to continue. "So…you were on Gurfann," asked Jorgan Rome. "Yeah," said Barteng, making a sour face. "Have you ever been there?"

"No."

"Well, good for you. First thing they tell you when you arrive is to know where your respirator is. If that alarm goes off, you have maybe a minute or two. That's it. But the crater hasn't burped gas in fifty years so nobody actually has a respirator around."

"Sounds frightening."

"It is. And then there's those flowers. Terrible."

Jorgan Rome was puzzled. "Allergies?"

Barteng snorted, "Yeah, right! Allergies! I'm talking about the Gurfannian Starburst. They're supposed to be super-beautiful or something. People love them, right? Then they go into their second bloom and everyone in the house is dead and so is half the residential quarter."

"I remember hearing that the Starbursts had been eradicated."

"Well, guess again. They may have ruined their agriculture trying, but Starbursts are still around. Collectors, you know. Anyway, Eddlo, I've been telling you about Eddlo. He was renting a room and the guy next door had Starbursts."

"What…"

"Medical evacuation off-planet. I never heard if he lived or died. Either way, we used to say that he was lucky." Barteng paused. "So there we are, stumbling and falling all over the place because the gravity is about twenty percent less and we're not used to it. Banging our heads on their little undersized doorways. But we were free. No one checked on us. We had a big facility. All we had to do was wait for the Ammun Mettell to show up."

"He wasn't with you?"

Barteng gave Jorgan Rome a sidelong glance of amused contempt. "What? Did you think he was going to ride with us on the prisoner transport?"

"Well, maybe, yes."

"Right. They search you. They'd have found the projector. We had to find another way to smuggle him here. It was a big problem. But I knew a way. I knew about a drone ship—no crew, only cargo—called the Demeter. It arrived once a week, usually with a load of potting soil. I figured you could hide a projector in a load of potting soil. And the best part? Drone ships land hard, really hard, like at twelve g's. People can't survive. So they don't search."

"And the projector survives?"

"Well, no, probably not. But we had a network all over the planet, a network of projectors. Anywhere that ship landed, there was going to be a projector nearby. Most likely. He could make a leap before the ship struck ground."

"'Most likely…'"

"Yes, there was some risk. Actually a lot of risk as it turned out. He was on that ship, inside his projector for three whole days. When he felt the ship enter Gurfann's atmosphere he became alert. He scanned for a projector on the planet but he couldn't find one. During a half hour, he's getting closer and closer to the ground, but there's still no projector signal. It was when the ship was only a few hundred meters from impact that he felt a hum. He made the leap just seconds before the Demeter hit hard."

"Shocking," said Jorgan Rome. "An unnecessary risk, too. He could have stayed home."

"But he took it on! And maybe there's something you don't understand here. It's called loyalty!"

Jorgan Rome pursed his lips.

"Okay, maybe you do understand. I guess you have your loyalties. I'll grant that. But the point is that he did it for us."

Jorgan Rome nodded.

"I was watching on a monitor when the ship landed. Less than five minutes later, he was here. When he appeared, he looked at us, looked at the beam apparatus, and said, 'This had better work. Let's go.' Everything was running properly so I nodded and he understood. He closed his eyes and went into a crouch, trying to synchronize with this new kind of projector. He opened his eyes, stood tall, and announced, 'This doesn't work!'"

Ipmayas—he was working the beam control—said, "You need to slow down." That made the Ammun Mettell livid. He was about to tear into Ipmayas, so I stepped in, "He means the resonance."

"It's bigger," said Ipmayas. "It's slower. It's on the scale of a whole planet. You need to go deeper. And you need to slow down."

The Ammun Mettell stared at Ipmayas. Then he smiled. "Thank you," he said. "Thank you all." Then he closed his eyes and began to slow himself. His movements became glacial. His perceptions and probably his thinking, too, came nearly to a stop. And then he vanished. I looked at Ipmayas. He shrugged his shoulders. We waited a little while before shutting off the beam.

"Shutting off the beam?" asked Jorgan Rome.

"Yeah," said Barteng. "For safety, you had to do that. Back there, I mean, not here on Earth. It's different."

The beam stayed off for a few days until everything came into alignment. When it came on again, the Ammun Mettell appeared about ten minutes later. He was just as slowed-down as when he left. When he came back to speed, he said, "We have a lot to talk about." And we did. He wanted us to discuss changes he would make on Naveer. New agencies would be founded, and others eliminated. He wanted currency reform and more. We had all been selected or trained to run ministries on Naveer so we had the expertise that he wanted. It was our job to take all of his ideas and make them concrete. He summoned us to this crazy meeting. The meeting went all night. People wandered in and out, speaking up when the topic touched on their subject area. At the end, I was exhausted. Most of us were. Some were sleeping in their chairs. But it set a pattern. For ever after that, when he returned from the planet, we'd have these marathon meetings. And it was okay to sleep when you weren't needed.

The Ammun Mettell, on the other hand, was alive with energy. "OK, thanks, everyone. I believe I have it all," he would say. "Let's go." Meaning he wanted the beam activated. But when we went to the beam area that morning, it was empty. There were no beam techs anywhere. They had had all gone home during the policy meeting.

"Well, okay," said the Ammun Mettell. "I'll be back when we're ready." He vanished. I contacted Ipmayas and told him to get a team back here as soon as possible. They arrived about 15 minutes later, but without Ipmayas. I gave the team the go-ahead to prepare the beam. But Ipmayas didn't show up until two hours later.

"Two hours?" asked Jorgan Rome.

"Gurfann," said Barteng. "The transport tubes weren't always reliable."

So the beam had already been running for over an hour and a half when Ipmayas came rushing in. He immediately noticed the "Beam is Operating" warning lights. "Goodness!" he muttered. He dashed across the floor without even taking off his coat or stowing his respirator. He powered up his beam monitors, looked at his instruments, and held up his hands to the team to wait until things stabilized. The Ammun Mettell came into the lab area, ready for transit. Ipmayas raised his hands an extended his index fingers. That was his signal to go forward. The Ammun Mettell began to slow himself. Then he stopped. He sped himself back to normal. It had occurred to the Ammun Mettell that he had never taken time to meet the beam techs from Gurfann, who were all new members of his team. He began to introduce himself, shaking hands, and starting to banter with beam techs who were growing ever more uncomfortable. When the Ammun Mettell turned back around, he saw that Ipmayas was beside himself.

"IT'S TIME TO GO! NOW!" said Ipmayas.

"Slow down! Speed up!" said the Ammun Mettell with a less-than-friendly smile. "You get no points for consistency." He slowed himself until he vanished.

"He's arrived there," announced Ipmayas. "Beam off!" he commanded. Then he turned and laid into me for having the beam turned on. I had to take it, too, because the beam floor was his domain.

The Ammun Mettell came back a week later and it was the same scene all over again, but with a twenty-four hour meeting that time. We slept there. We ate there. We tried to stay awake. We were sometimes called to the main table to settle something. I wanted to be a part of every conversation but most people settled for contributing in their subject area. About halfway through the meeting we started talking about reorganizing all the political subdivisions on Naveer. And that's when it dawned on me. We really were running that planet! We had always hoped for that, of course, but it was strange to be running Naveer from Gurfann.

After the meeting wound down, the Ammun Mettell came over to me. "When I left last time…"

"It won't happen again," I said. "I've asked Ipmayas to train some of the beam techs to step in for him if needed."

"Good, but I want to know about that robot I saw working on our team."

I knew that Ammun Mettell wasn't anti-robot. That wasn't like him. So I knew he meant something else. The robot was unfamiliar. I told him, "The robot is a dependable and loyal team member."

"Okay. That's reassuring," he said. But he didn't act reassured.

"You mean why is a two-hundred year old robot on our team?"

The Ammun Mettell nodded.

"Because, as I understand it, this kind of robot, old as it is, has some kind of abilities with eta waves. They used to build them like that back then. Without robots like these, there is no beam control. There is no beam. I'll have one of the tech people explain it better if you like."

"That's OK, no need."

"We have several of these robots, actually."

The Ammun Mettell nodded. He changed the subject. "About Ipmayas and transit," he said, "I want to fix that. I've

arranged assistance from the Interplanetary Friendship Fund
for Gurfann to fix their tubes."

"That's a mistake," I said.

He stared at me for several seconds before shrugging his
shoulders. "Well, it's done," he said, as we walked down to
the beam floor.

Only Ipmayas was there. He was so focused on his instruments, staring down a scope, then making notes, then
holding a straightedge to a graph on his screen, making more
notes, and so forth, that he didn't notice us approaching.

"So…what's this," said the Ammun Mettell, making an
effort to be friendly, pointing at one of the instruments.

"That's a coronagraph," said Ipmayas without looking
up.

"And what's going on here?"

"I'm measuring stellar turbulence using the back-reflected
beam," said Ipmayas.

"Well, OK," said the Ammun Mettell. "Hobby projects
are good. Probably keeps you sharp. Carry on!"

Ipmayas looked up. "It's not a hobby. I don't do hobbies.
This is about safety. About keeping it safe. About keeping
you safe."

The Ammun Mettell frowned. That was the thing about
Ipmayas. It was the way he talked that made people hostile.
I mean, Ipmayas didn't always have the best communication
skills, that's for sure. He could never come to the point fast
enough and that's a big mistake with the Ammun Mettell.
Funny thing is, when Ipmayas sensed hostility, he would dig
in and talk even more technical stuff.

"It's an old star," said Ipmayas. "It only has about a hundred million years left."

The Ammun Mettell laughed but it wasn't friendly. "That
should be enough time, don't you think?"

"No, you don't get it," said Ipmayas, oblivious to the provocation. "Its equation of state has gone…a bit soft for comfort. With this particular star, our beam is resonant at the top of the photosphere."

"So what's the point?" snapped the Ammun Mettell. "Are we talking about a solar flare?"

"If only! A mass ejection event. And…it will follow the beam focus. It will follow you, that is, right to the planet."

The Ammun Mettell dropped the hostility. He was listening now. "This little beam?" he asked.

"This little beam plays off a giant stochastic, parametric resonance. Yes, this little beam."

"And how bad would that be for people on the planet?"

"Not bad at all. But it could take out communications, maybe transit systems. But…your projectors would be the first to go. The real danger is to you. This is all about keeping you safe."

Ammun Mettell paused. "All right, thanks. But if it's only me, then I don't really care. However, I need you to reassure me about one thing. I want you to convince me that there's no danger to the population."

Ipmayas took a big breath which, in turn, set the Ammun Mettell back on edge. "I guess," said Ipmayas finally, "If you ran the beam at full power—like we never do—for a long time—like we never do—then yes, there could be a big enough mass ejection event."

"Big enough?"

"To fry the planet."

"I can tell you," said Barteng to Jorgan Rome, "I was stunned. The Ammun Mettell didn't say anything."

Ipmayas continued, "But we don't operate that way. We watch that star. We keep everything in the linear regime.

We have safety kill switches everywhere and all sorts of interlocks. Everyone on the beam floor understands this. None
of us—not a single person here—will let it happen. Or even
get close."

The Ammun Mettell nodded.

"So, if you'll excuse me," said Ipmayas, "I've got a star to
monitor."

31

H E PAUSED FOR a moment. He looked at Jorgan Rome. "It was unnerving, I admit, about that star instability," said Barteng. "But we did feel comfortable about sending him back to the planet. And when he went back, he had a situation to deal with. The first challenge to our control over the planet."

The head of one of the seven families got the idea to set himself up as a local ruler. You remember the seven families? They used to run things, but not anymore. Anyway, this fellow thought he had enough clout to be independent. He started calling himself the Duke of Ardeppan.

"I remember that," said Jorgan Rome.

"We were ready for him. He didn't see what was coming because he didn't know his position as well as we did. The currency reform had shone a light on his financial shenanigans. His lands had already been divided into smaller jurisdictions. His people, his so-called loyal retainers, were lured away to administer their own far-away jurisdictions. Basically, the guy had nothing but didn't know it yet. And then we had the entertainers and comedians make sport of him. They called him the Duke of Nowhere and Nothing at All."

"I recall it didn't end well," said Jorgan Rome.

"Yeah, he committed suicide," said Barteng. "I didn't expect that. None of us did. Maybe we came at him a bit strong. We over-reacted for sure. But we weren't accustomed to having that much…power. We faced a few other crises in the following months and I'd like to think that we handled them better. It was hard, you know, running one planet from a completely different planet. And without any contact. We didn't even have visitors. It was just us, running the planet through the Ammun Mettell."

"In charge and in isolation," said Jorgan Rome.

"That's right," said Barteng. "But we did eventually get a visitor to our little compound. The Praesial Exquisitur."

Jorgan Rome made a questioning look

"I know," said Barteng. "It's Gurfann. The smaller the place, the more ornate the title. That was their name for the leader of the planet. It was him. He just showed up!"

"He just expected you to be there?"

"Apparently. I mean, it was technically one of the restrictions of our exile, but it had never once been enforced. So there we were, with a lab and a beam line when the head of the whole planet and a couple of councillors show up. We steered them quickly into a conference room. We were lucky that the Ammun Mettell was with us."

"You didn't know he was coming?"

"No."

"But I thought you knew everyone's plans," said Jorgan Rome. "Even before people had fully formulated them."

"We did. Mostly. But it takes resources. And we weren't going to waste those resources on Gurfann. We didn't care about Gurfann. The Praesial Exquisitur was an ebullient sort. He started right in, 'Which of you is the Ammun Mettell?' he asked, giving my shoulder a squeeze. I smiled and shook my head. I pointed out the Ammun Mettell who had managed to appear in the conference room just before we entered."

"Well, well, good to meet you! You seem to have landed on your feet here on Gurfann! Nice place, looks like a nice…facility…out there!"

"Oh, that!" interjected Ipmayas. "The science lab. It's a hobby of mine!"

"Very nice," said the Praesial Exquisitur, "Keep the mind sharp, I suppose! I'm sure you could teach us many things!" Then he turned his attention to the Ammun Mettell, "Welcome! Welcome to Gurfann!"

"Thank you," said the Ammun Mettell.

"I'd like to welcome you in the spirit of inter-planetary friendship! We take the relationship with our sister planet seriously, you know. And we're grateful." I think that was when the Ammun Mettell understood what a mistake it had been to provide funds for the transit tubes on Gurfann. Turning serious, the Praesial Exquisitur said, "Some time, I'd like to show you some plans we have for cooperative ventures. We have a commission—fine people, all of them—and they have good ideas in my opinion. Would you be able to make time to meet with them? See what ideas strike your fancy?"

"Well," began the Ammun Mettell, "I'm nobody to…"

"Oh! Pish-posh!" said the Praesial Exquisitur. "We'll be honored."

"Thank you," said the Ammun Mettell.

"And…" said the Praesial Exquisitur, "I'm inviting you to the Amity Society's annual gala. It'll be a nice event. We're dedicating an arch to Interplanetary Friendship!" When the Ammun Mettell hesitated, the Praesial Exquisitur continued, "I know what you're thinking, that we already have an Arch of Interplanetary Friendship. You're a sharp fellow, but I knew that! It will be arch-on-arch, very proper. And with a symphony!"

The Ammun Mettell accepted the invitations and our visitors left. After they were gone, the Ammun Mettell asked, "How much does he know?"

"Don't underestimate the locals," I said. "They may appear oafish, but don't be fooled."

"Does he know that we're the ones running the sister planet?"

"Doubtful. But their tubes have been broken for a long time. Then they get fixed in our area and soon after we arrive."

"So?"

"I think he has the idea that we have influential friends. Back on the planet."

We laughed at that. Then the Ammun Mettell said, "I don't want to be some kind of personage on Gurfann."

"It's too late for that," I said. "But when you go to the gala, try to be uninteresting."

A month or so later, on the evening of the gala, the Ammun Mettell arrived outside of Festival Hall. From atop a perimeter wall of the central pavilion in the form of a little blue cube, he could see that there was a public reception line. Names of guests were called out as they entered the hall. Since a public introduction was the last thing that the Ammun Mettell wanted, he slipped into the rear of building unnoticed and unannounced. He found his way to the main meeting room and stood against a back wall as if he had always been there. Food and drink was everywhere which was a problem for the Ammun Mettell whose projected form could neither eat nor drink. Sometimes he just held a drink as he watched guests arrive, be announced, and join the crowd.

Calcha was the final guest. She allowed herself to be introduced with an elaborate chain of titles that referenced all of her royal ranks on Tellapenth and also on Naveer, places where everyone knew that she had tried to murder other royals. As she was announced, the Ammun Mettell noticed some eyebrows raise in the crowd. It seemed that notoriety as social currency had only a limited duration on Gurfann. Even from a distance, he could see that Calcha was not thriving in her second exile. She looked drawn. He thought about his own appearance and how it, too, had changed. His own transformation was more drastic. After re-integration he had used Laddlo's technology to craft an entirely new outward form, averting recognition by the Khadar, the Khadar's government, or anyone else who knew him from before. When he had first stepped out of his apartment as the Ammun Mettell, it was as a man without a history. Now of course he had a history, one that had led him to Gurfann. And mastery over a distant home planet.

The Ammun Mettell didn't have to observe Calcha in person to know how unhappy she was. On Naveer, even the lowest-level state employees knew of standing orders to swat down Calcha's transfer requests. Just as they knew to forward them up the hierarchy, eventually catching the Ammun Mettell's attention. So he saw them, already rejected, not long after they came in. The requests were frequent. Some were creative, some frantic, some downright unhinged. Even before seeing her arrival at the gala, the Ammun Mettell knew just how she was faring on Gurfann.

The Ammun Mettell felt conspicuous standing for too long against the back wall. He walked towards the center of room, but he didn't make it far before he felt a hand on his shoulder. "So you are here!" said the Praesial Exquisitur. "I didn't hear you announced!"

The Praesial Exquisitur was in the company of a half dozen of the planet's social prominences. The Ammun Mettell tried to appear bashful. "I hope you'll forgive my unease in unfamiliar circles. It's something I suffer from. I found a back way in."

"Oh, come now! We don't bite!" said the Praesial Exquisitur.

"Speak for yourself!" said the gentleman on his left.

"Well, this one's not for biting! Let me introduce my friend, the Ammun Mettell."

The Ammun Mettell saw their reactions. A slight hesitancy. A missing beat before the resumption of small talk about the pleasures of life on Gurfann. His existence here would be not so different from Calcha's if he permitted it to be that way.

The most difficult part of the evening came with the speeches. They consisted of the usual fare about "our friends, on Gurfann, and interplanetary, too, some old friends, some new friends…" and at that point the Ammun Mettell knew what was coming. The Praesial Exquisitur introduced him and made him stand. The Ammun Mettell did his best to come across as an awkward, modest nobody. He deliberately nodded at the wrong time. He grinned. He sat down too quickly. He wanted everyone there to think, "that guy we've heard about, he's not so much." It worked for the most part. They were all prepared to dismiss him as the non-entity he wanted to be on Gurfann. Except one person, sitting near the front, who was bored to death with the proceedings, and utterly enervated by life on Gurfann. She longed to leave, but barring that, she was simply desperate for novelty. For Calcha, the presence of the Ammun Mettell on Gurfann was at least something new. Rumor had it that this Ammun Mettell character had actually tangled with the Khadar. Some even said that he had tried to topple the Khadar. If that was true, then here was a potential ally. Now the Ammun Mettell was himself exiled to Gurfann. With the Khadar gone, it wasn't a stretch to imagine that the Ammun Mettell wanted to get off this planet. If he wasn't an ally, then he was certainly a kindred spirit. And if he turned out not to be a kindred spirit, he might at least be a bit of entertainment, or a challenge, or a victim. Calcha resolved to meet this Ammun Mettell face to face.

It was time to the dedicate the new arch. The Ammun Mettell prepared to leave, but he was too late. The floodlights came on, and the arch, already missing a few peripheral bricks, was on full display. There were more speeches evincing "…hopes that our planets are ever-aligned…" and introducing a new orchestral movement from "our own Gurfann Planetary Primary Symphonic Assemblage." As the players took their seats, the Ammun Mettell found his time to exit. All he needed was an empty room or hallway from which to vanish. Making excuses, he set his glass down, rose from his chair, and made passage through the crowd. The problem, as he discovered, was that everyone else was trying to get out before the Gurfann Planetary Primary Symphonic Assemblage could get started. He followed them out of the banquet hall, down a staircase, and across a reception hall. He turned through an open doorway into a corridor. There were still people. He walked on. Then he heard a voice behind him. A voice he recognized. The voice of the woman who had arranged for his disintegration.

"So, you are the infamous Ammun Mettell!"

The Ammun Mettell was confident in his projected form. He knew it was unrecognizable. So he turned around, frowning a little at the impertinence of a stranger.

She checked herself. "I'm sorry. Let me introduce my-self," she said, "I'm the infamous Calcha." The Ammun Mettell smiled politely, and as he did, a tiny chill went through Calcha because there was something about his manner, the particular way he smiled. It was like someone she knew before. Someone she hadn't trusted. Someone who came to a bad end. The impression was fleeting and she brushed it off.

"Well," he said, "I imagine that infamy is in the eye of the beholder. It's probably not useful to self-designate."

"Oh, I think it's very useful," she said. "It's served me well. Besides, what are we to say of someone who tried to jettison the Khadar and ended up in exile on Gurfann? By any standard, I think it makes me infamous." She paused for emphasis and then added, "And you, too, Mister Mettell. From what I hear, that standard makes you infamous, too. It's like a club we both belong to."

The Ammun Mettell didn't say anything but he looked her straight in the face. She wore her hair back and high with a large feather stuck in it that bobbed down over her ear.

"You're noticing that damned feather," she said. "One of many accommodations I've had to make to this place."

"Very becoming," he said.

She shook her head. "No," she said. "But about that club, I propose a meeting. And its agenda is getting off of this planet."

The Ammun Mettell, keeping her gaze, took a moment before responding. "Thank you for the…meeting invitation. I am, however, adequately comfortable here. I want nothing more than I have."

She looked at him. Somehow he did seem comfortable, but it made no sense. How could someone who had risen so high, but was now stuck on Gurfann, be content with his situation? "I'm sorry," she said, "I'm not believing you, Mister Mettell. Not for one moment. Let's put it this way, where do you see yourself in twenty years? On Gurfann? For real?"

While he thought of a reply, he looked down and to the right, making a small face. And that's when Calcha knew. It hit her like a bolt of lightning or maybe even a disintegration ray. Suddenly she knew exactly who he was. That visitor to her chambers in the Khadar's Palace, the one who had fed her ideas of galactic conquest, of becoming an Empress, the one who could have made it happen but chose not to. That man. He always made that same face when he was thinking. With no understanding of how he could have survived, or how he could have this unfamiliar appearance, she was certain nevertheless. There was no mistaking his mannerisms and his ideas. To her advantage was the self-control she had learned on Gurfann. Although she was shaken to the core, nothing showed outwardly.

"For real," he said. "And I'm afraid we'll have to postpone that club meeting." He turned to leave.

Calcha made it back to her residence without remembering how she got there. Her robots all saw how agitated she was. They gathered to calm her but she waved them off. She closed the door to her bed chamber. The robots stood a silent vigil outside while her mind churned and she struggled to avoid throwing things.

It was his calmness. That's what bothered her most. It wasn't right for him to be so at ease. When she knew him before, he was hungry. He was hungry for influence and control. He had the kind of hunger that doesn't go away without vanquishing him or giving him what he wants. He didn't seem vanquished. How was that possible? He'd been disintegrated. He came back—somehow—but then he went and got himself exiled. And yet, here he was on Gurfann, but with the odd air of a man who has what he wants.

Could it be? Everyone knew that he had gone up against the Khadar and lost. But then the Khadar's Palace was destroyed that same week. What a coincidence that was! And what if it wasn't? What if the Ammun Mettell hadn't really lost his battle against the Khadar? What if he were…running things? It would account for his demeanor and maybe a few other things, too. Like the treatment she endured from the planetary government of Naveer. With the Khadar dead and gone, why would anyone on Naveer care about Calcha? But someone obviously did. Her transfer requests were denied out-of-hand. Sometimes the responses strayed from official language and were downright flippant. Somehow it was personal. Someone didn't like her there.

He had told her. That visitor to her residence in the Palace had told her that her path to power meant going to Gurfann. That she would unite the Realm from there. Oh, how vile! Like a fool, she had believed him. That's why she accepted exile on Gurfann. First he duped her. Then he trapped her. On Gurfann of all places! She had played into his game and never realized it!

He had told her back then, too, that she would wear a feather just like the provincials do. And there she was at the gala with an oversized feather bouncing against her ear. "Very becoming" he said. He was laughing at her.

Never in her life had Calcha been so angry.

32

BARTENG RUBBED HIS HEAD, shook it from side to side, then stood. He stretched. He looked around for something to divert his attention. The Dar Telku was buried in her book. Jorgan Rome continued to sit on the sofa with that irritating, bland look on his face. Raia was busier than ever. She was adjusting controls and moving images around. Barteng went over to watch. "What's going on?" he asked.

"The ships are back," said Raia.

"You mean Tokar's squadron?"

"Yeah," said Raia. "One after the other, they've gone into these low, fast circumpolar orbits. It's aggressive."

"Can they…?"

"Land? No," said Raia, summoning close-up images of the ships. "Look, see! Those AEPGs are gone. They won't be fixed any time soon and they can't land without them. Our team did what they wanted to do."

"So, what are they up to?"

"It's not clear," said Raia. "They would do this if they were looking for something. Oh…wait…I think we have our answer. Look! They're deploying satellites!" The screen showed a satellite dropping from one of Tokar's ships, igniting its engines, and maneuvering into its own lower, faster orbit.

"That's not good," said Barteng. "That could put us all under some pretty intense surveillance."

"I don't know," said Raia, who was no longer paying much attention to Barteng because she had just seen something more disturbing than the satellites. With a sidelong glance at Jorgan Rome and a curled index finger, she summoned him over to see for himself. As he came forward, the Dar Telku silently closed her book and followed him. Raia pointed down near her feet. Down there was a small portion of the screen showing a video monitoring the activity in one of the Dar Telku's laboratories. Teera was there, partially disassembled, with cables and patch cords attached to her trunk.

"That's enough!" said the Dar Telku as the laboratory video fced went blank. "Not your business!"

Raia discreetly touched the top of her karamand with an index finger and Jorgan Rome nodded. With his hands at his side, Jorgan Rome made a small circle with his index finger, meaning, "all of us." A split-second later, Raia, Jorgan Rome, Cholley, Barteng, and the Dar Telku were in the laboratory.

"This is completely unacceptable!" cried the Dar Telku.

Teera was sitting upright on a table. Her cranial compartment was open. Various of her antennas were scattered on the table. A bulky part of her mid-section had been taken away and was now on a shelf behind the table. Lab techs on either side of Teera stepped back quickly at abrupt appearance of new people in the room.

"I thought she was just going to talk with Tokar," said Jorgan Rome.

"That's right!" said the Dar Telku.

"What's right? That that's what I thought? Or that she's just going to talk?"

The Dar Telku smiled coldly. "Not your concern."

Jorgan Rome went over to Teera. "Are you OK?"

Teera emitted a sudden sharp electronic squawk. Her left arm thrust forward at lightning speed. Jorgan Rome barely jumped away in time to avoid being struck. Teera's hand swept a pile of small tools into the air and across the laboratory.

"We sped her up," said a lab tech.

"What!"

"She's just not used to it yet," continued the lab tech.

"But, that's not…"

"We can't send a human to talk with Tokar. You showed us the video. We get it. Any human between Tokar and what he wants is going to be dead. Teera will do our talking."

"Yeah, but there's no…"

"Teera is a very old robot. Tokar talks faster than she does. He thinks faster. We need her to be at par."

"But you can't do that!" said Jorgan Rome. "Cholley, can they do that?"

"Not what I would call safe…" said Cholley.

"Oh, please enlighten me. Why would that be, Mr. Gelatinoid?" asked the lab tech.

"Race condition," said Raia.

"That's it. You speed them up," said Jorgan Rome, "and some part of their neural circuitry gets out of sync with some other part, thoughts and sensations race each other and never resolve. You get a partial shutdown. Or worse."

"Look at her," said the lab tech. "Doesn't seem to have happened, does it?"

"No, but this is a pretty easy environment," said Jorgan Rome.

"We will put her through her paces," said the Dar Telku with attempted finality.

"And what's that sitting on a shelf?" asked Jorgan Rome.

"That's her eta-wave circuitry. It's partly why these robots are so slow. She won't be needing it today."

33

A WORKING GROUP had been on the schedule for late that next morning, explained Barteng. "I remember it was about the Treasury and some initiatives that the Ammun Mettell wanted us to flesh out. I made sure to be a part of every working group, of course, so I was there early in the conference room. The Treasury stuff was important to the Ammun Mettell so he would be there, too. Usually that meant he would do most of the talking."

The Ammun Mettell arrived early as well. It was just the two of us. He asked me, "Can you handle the meeting without me? I'd really like to get back to Naveer for a bit."

I looked at him like I didn't understand, but of course I did. "That bad?"

"Worse," he said, with a grimace. "It was…it…I've had my fill of Gurfann for a while. I want to get off this planet for a day." He saw the set of my face, so he said, "Sorry, I know that's not an option for you. I know why you're doing this and I'm grateful. But if you could indulge me on this…"

"The working group…" I said.

"Can you handle it?" he asked.

"Of course, but I have to warn you," I said. He looked intently at me. "If you spend too much time on Naveer, the working group might start feeling a bit peripheral. You don't want that."

"Peripheral?" he said. "The working groups are central."

"I know that and you know that, but the teams need tangible reassurance and more often than you might think."

He nodded. "But can you handle it for me just this once?"

We went down to the beam floor. It was cold down there. Ipmayas had taken to turning off the heat at night—I have no idea why. It wasn't usually a problem because Ipmayas was the first to arrive each morning. Everything would be comfortable. But when the Ammun Mettell and I went down there, it was freezing. Ipmayas wasn't around. The beam techs were at their stations. Some of them were wearing double lab coats against the cold.

"Where's Ipmayas?" asked the Ammun Mettell. The response from a group of beam techs was blank stares, raised eyebrows, and shaking heads. "Get those tubes fixed!" he said to me. When I opened my mouth, he continued, "And don't tell me it's a mistake. I already paid for that mistake last night."

We no longer needed Ipmayas to be on the lab floor when we sent the Ammun Mettell on his way. The team had robust backup now, so Ipmayas's absence wasn't an issue. The Ammun Mettell slowed himself as usual and made a smooth transition to Naveer.

His return, almost a day later, wasn't smooth at all. It looked as if he would appear but then he would fade away again. It went like that for several minutes before he managed to attain solid form back in the lab. It was a rough transit.

"Where's Ipmayas?" he said.

"He's around," said Calcha, which amused her robots. Her robots had us pinned to the floor. Some of us were against the wall. There was no escaping, either. Fight back and you were killed. "He's here and there," said Calcha. Her robots thought that was even funnier. "But before he got both here and there, he told me about your little operation. And now I'm going to tell you something. It's over."

The Ammun Mettell didn't move. He just stood there, blinking. He was always a little slow after a transit.

Calcha said, "You don't understand, do you? And you were always so clever! A real fast talker! I know that now. That friend of yours, he didn't figure it out and he got zapped like a bug! You hurt a lot of people but it's over!"

The Ammun Mettell was fully back to speed but didn't say anything.

"You're not listening, are you?" She turned to me. "I know you're his number two. He'll listen to you. Tell him about the state of his little kingdom."

I shook my head.

"Another tough guy. That's too bad," she said.

I gave in. I knew what those robots would do to me if I didn't. I barked out, "Planet's gone! Beam's been going twenty hours…at triple maximum! Rough transit…bad signal lock…means…it's already happening! Planet not…it can't be saved!"

Calcha smiled at me.

"One other thing!" said Calcha. "I want to ask you, are these yours?" She indicated a pile of projectors that had been broken up by her robots. "We found these scattered around the city, the whole region, really. Very inconsiderate of you." Ipmayas had done the original placing of the projectors, so she knew just where to find them.

"You're not going anywhere," said Calcha. "Welcome to Gurfann." Then she turned and walked away with her robots in tow. They left us alive and I knew what that meant.

After the robots released us we stretched and stumbled around. Some of us had been injured pretty badly. I went over to shut the beam off, but the Ammun Mettell stopped me.

"Send me back," he said. I shook my head. "Send me back," he repeated.

"Even if you can, there's no return." I remember look on his face that said "As if that matters at all." But when he spoke, all he said was, "I'll try to come back."

It took more than five minutes for him sync with a transfer signal. All that time, he muttered, "There must be something…there must be something," before finally vanishing. I didn't know if we would ever see him again.

In the meantime, we had an urgent problem on Gurfann. Calcha had walked away and left us alive. We were trapped. She could distance herself from us with confidence that we couldn't get away. We had only a few days left, I figured, before Calcha acquired the means to have us rounded up and put on display. We had to get away from Gurfann.

Normally, leaving Gurfann was impossible. But I always have a backup plan, in case of…in case of I don't know what. And I knew of a ship. It was barely functional, just a relic, but it could fly. But here's the thing that nobody else knew: the ship still had its postal registration intact, so it could take off from Gurfann without triggering alarms. After tending to our injured, I set us to work transferring people and equipment to the ship. We took a few projectors. Some members of the team wanted to disassemble the main parts of the beam generator, but asked them to wait. I wanted to see if the Ammun Mettell would return.

The Ammun Mettell materialized on Gurfann less than an hour after he had left. "There was nothing…there was nothing…" was all he muttered before disappearing into his projector. We loaded the projector on the ship. We took the core parts of the beam generator. We left and didn't look back.

We huddled in that ship until after nightfall when we took off from the planet. We were concerned about the military craft and satellites that circle Gurfann, but they paid us no mind. We made orbit without knowing where we were going. We left the solar system with no better plans in place. We went from system to system trying to leave no trace. We avoided Port Masters like we were pirates. I think we were pirates.

We didn't ourselves see the destruction of Naveer. We were too far away. It happened just after we left Gurfann. Naveer's star belched out a massive plasma stream that took an hour to reach Naveer. But when it did, it burned off the atmosphere and made of our planet a blackened, dead cinder.

34

THE LAB TECH was unhappy. "I just need everyone to back away!" he said. "This is complicated stuff and I need to concentrate."

Teera was still sitting upright on the lab bench with her cranial compartment open. The lab tech faced Teera with his back to the Dar Telku, Jorgan Rome, Barteng, and Cholley. They stepped away as far as they could in the long, narrow laboratory space. Raia had already moved off to a far end of the lab where she found a monitor to keep tabs on Tokar.

"I really can't think with you people practically breathing on me!" said the lab tech. He had been working on Teera without a pause for the last half hour. He would make an adjustment. He would evaluate Teera's response. He would frown and make another adjustment. Now he was slowing down. He stood motionless with his arms out from his body, a tool in each hand, and his head cocked to one side. His posture communicated that he was thinking.

"He's here!" said Raia. She pointed to the screen showing that Tokar had touched down just outside of the Dar Telku's compound. Nobody else said anything. The lab tech held the pose for several more seconds before putting his tools down. "It's fine," he said.

Jorgan Rome summoned Raia back to join the group. "What happens now?" he asked.

"I guess we'll have to talk with him," said the Dar Telku after a pause.

"Is that going to work?" asked Jorgan Rome.

"It's fine," said the lab tech.

Teera closed her own cranial compartment and stepped down from the lab bench. She seemed steady on her feet. Jorgan Rome looked at her questioningly. "I think I'm OK," she said.

The tech walked out of the laboratory and down the hallway. "It's fine," he said, before slamming a door.

The Dar Telku walked Teera to the exit nearest to where Tokar had landed. They conferred for a moment. The Dar Telku handed Teera something small. By the time the Dar Telku had rejoined the group in the laboratory, Teera was outside and ready to confront Tokar. Tokar was a couple of hundred meters away, but he noticed Teera instantly. Being robots, they could see and hear each other with no difficulty at that distance.

"I'd like to ask you to leave," said Teera without raising her voice.

Tokar said nothing.

"I've been authorized to offer you an inducement to leave," said Teera.

Jorgan Rome silently shook his head. Cholley started to say something but Jorgan Rome stopped him. Tokar would be able to hear whatever they said, even from within the building.

"If you leave now, I'm willing to give you this," said Teera, holding a karamand in her hand. After recent events, Tokar would know what a karamand was. Tokar would want a karamand. For his part, Jorgan Rome was stunned. He reached for the karamand that hung from his neck. Raia did the same. They looked at each other, each showing that they still had their karamands. Raia understood. She mouthed the word, "fake!" Jorgan Rome stared at the Dar Telku. Did she really think she could pass a fake karamand off on Tokar? How could she possibly think this was a good idea? The Dar Telku turned quickly away.

Tokar marched forward. He covered the distance between them in five seconds, coming to an abrupt stop only four meters away. Teera didn't flinch. She put the karamand away, tucking it into a compartment in her body cavity.

"I've changed my mind," said Teera. "You don't appear to be a very nice robot at all. I'll need to think about it." Then Teera did something that made Jorgan Rome gasp with surprise. She dropped down into a fighting stance. Cholley stirred, started to yell, but Jorgan Rome waved him into silence.

Even Tokar was taken aback. It was absurd for a two-hundred year old robot to challenge a modern military unit. But in his world, a challenge was a challenge, even a pathetically simple one. It was a nuisance to be sure, but he had to accept. He dropped into the stance. He decided that he would not make the first move.

They held positions for a few seconds. Then Teera twitched. That was Tokar's cue to take her out. He came around with a lazy swing—lazy for him. For an ancient robot like Teera it would hit like a lightning bolt. Teera knew he would go for the head because he would want the karamand intact. She had all the speed she needed to dodge the blow and follow up with a strike that cost Tokar his hand. His right hand hung loose from a cable at his wrist. He pulled the hand off and flung it on the ground. Now he was angry. He was ready to destroy Teera but she dropped into a fighting stance to prepare for round two. Tokar reluctantly but dutifully dropped in to a fighting stance.

This time, Tokar made the first move. He came fast. He struck a fury of blows that no robot of her era could withstand. Teera parried and dodged them all. Tokar stepped back to consider. This robot had been speeded up, that was apparent. He stared at her. He looked at every part of her until he saw it: a fluttering. A vibration at her left ankle. Her timing wasn't perfect. She was teetering on the edge of a race condition. All he had to do was bring that out and the left ankle was the key.

In the third engagement, Tokar also moved first. Instead of striking at Teera, he danced around in ways that made her shift weight on and off of the left foot. He struck at her right and then pulled away as she pushed off on her left. He saw the vibration moved upward, taking over her whole leg and he wasn't going to let her recover. He strobed every light on his body and face. His movements were fast and unpredictable. He overwhelmed her sensory inputs. The jerking moved up from her left leg. It pervaded her every limb. After a few seconds, Teera was a juddering mass of collapsed robot. Her eyes were blank and a low buzz came from her mouth.

Tokar looked at the pathetic spectacle. She had asked for this. But so, too, had the humans who had done this to her. After disposing of Teera once and for all, he would deal harshly with them for what they had done. Tokar leaned over Teera to deliver a final, destroying blow. Just then, Teera, who had only been simulating the race condition, burst up with shocking speed and a precise strike that severed Tokar's head from his body. It flew five meters into the air before landing against a corner of the building.

"She knocked his block off!" yelled Cholley.

"Wait 'til next time," said Tokar's severed head before losing power forever. There would be no next time. Tokar was finished.

Jorgan Rome, Cholley, Raia, and the Dar Telku rushed out to where Teera was standing. She was shaking for real now.

"It's just that…it's just that…it's just that…I don't like…I don't like robots…I don't like people like that," said Teera.

Jorgan Rome nodded. He turned to the Dar Telku and said, "Get her back to normal."

"Certainly," said the Dar Telku with a self-satisfied smile.

35

TEERA WAS SITTING on the lab bench once more. The tech was undoing the modifications and muttering to himself. "It worked," he said to no one but himself. Teera's processors slowed and stabilized. "Of course it worked," said the lab tech, moving probes around her cranial compartment. "I'm not an idiot!"

Jorgan Rome turned to the Dar Telku. "That was a real risk."

"Look who's talking," said the Dar Telku.

"I meant that as a compliment," said Jorgan Rome. The Dar Telku smiled briefly and looked away.

"Are we done here?" asked Barteng.

"I think so," said Jorgan Rome.

"In that case, I have to get back," said Barteng.

Jorgan Rome nodded. Barteng made no motion to leave.

"I have to tell you, though," said Barteng. "I saw some good work done here by, well, all of you," he said, looking at the Dar Telku.

The Dar Telku nodded. "If you can wait just a few moments, I'll help you gather your things," she said. "I can probably find you a hat to cover that." Barteng rubbed the shaved patch of his scalp and grimaced.

The lab tech turned to speak to Jorgan Rome. "Does she still need that?" he asked, gesturing at the eta-wave circuitry package sitting on the shelf. Jorgan Rome pointed at Teera.

"Do you still need the eta-wave circuits?" the lab tech asked Teera.

"Of course," said Teera. But when the lab tech reached for the eta-wave circuitry, he cried out in pain. He threw his tools to the ground and waved his hands around. "It's hot!" he yelled. "I've just burned myself on that lousy circuit!"

"Why would it be hot?" asked Cholley.

"The satellites!" said Raia.

"Eta wave transmitters," said the Dar Telku.

"We need to be at the Mettellite compound! Right now!" said Jorgan Rome. He glanced over at Raia but she was already ahead of him. She had her karamand in her hand. In a blink of an eye, they were transported—Raia, Jorgan Rome, Teera, Cholley, the Dar Telku, and Barteng—to the courtyard of the castle.

The Ammun Mettell was there. Once again, he had a crate of oranges on the ground next to him. He was cutting and sectioning the bitter oranges, adding precise amounts of sugar and vanilla as needed, to oranges that Jorgan Rome now knew that the Ammun Mettell himself could neither taste nor eat. It was nothing more than a kindness for his people. Jorgan Rome noticed that the Ammun Mettell had become a bit slower and less deft with the knife work. The Ammun Mettell looked up.

"This is good luck," said the Ammun Mettell. "I had hoped to see you again."

"The satellites…" said Jorgan Rome.

The Ammun Mettell nodded. "I feel each one as it's deployed," he said. "It's becoming harder and harder to maintain projection."

"But you don't have to take this," said Jorgan Rome. "You can always…"

"…go somewhere?" asked the Ammun Mettell. "I've already come here."

Cholley was becoming agitated. "But you can fight back."

"I've done that, too. Haven't I, Barteng?"

Barteng nodded, his face contorting.

"So sometimes, we just have to take what comes," said the Ammun Mettell.

"You could…", started Jorgan Rome, "…maybe…?"

The Ammun Mettell looked at Jorgan Rome in silence. He had guessed what Jorgan Rome was trying to say, but he wasn't going to make it easy for him.

"Could you…would you…be willing," asked Jorgan Rome, "to show us the way you were before? Before you became the Ammun Mettell?"

"To project again the person I was? I can do that. But I don't like it very much. It's like I've left that person behind," said the Ammun Mettell. "But, if you wish."

The Ammun Mettell's projection became cloudy, dark and turbulent. His whole body swirled around until it formed itself again. When it came together again he was sitting on his chair as an entirely different person. He was Sam.

"Hey, little cousin," said Sam with a sad smile, "These are some hard times, aren't they?"

"Yeah," said Jorgan Rome. "That's right."

"I did my best to keep you away from the Mettellites," said Sam, "but I guess my advice doesn't take, does it?"

"No, I guess it doesn't always," said Jorgan Rome.

"But you knew, right?" asked Sam, "I mean, you knew who I was."

"Not at first," said Jorgan Rome. "But I remember Laddlo. I knew him."

Sam nodded. Then he winced. "Forgive me…another satellite."

"That time," said Jorgan Rome, summoning the nerve to ask what he really wanted to know, "When you went back to the planet. When you went to Naveer. I mean, for the last time. You…"

Sam smiled wanly. He waited for Jorgan Rome to continue.

"You saved me didn't you? You were the one who sent me on that mission. That mission to nowhere. That rendezvous with no one who would ever come. I was just waiting there. But the reason why I survived…it was you, Sam, wasn't it?"

"Of course," said Sam. "At that point, what else did I care about?"

No one said anything for a very long time. Finally, Jorgan Rome spoke up. "We're not done with this, you know."

Sam nodded. "I know. What I expect of you. But I seem to be. Necessarily, I think. What did…you say to me…in that forest clearing? That I had…my whole life…ahead?"

There was another long pause. Jorgan Rome understood. Sam had long known that this end was coming.

Sam said, "If you manage…to work together…all of you…I think……" He winced again. "Forgive me, I need to be the Ammun Mettell…again at this…moment." His projection became cloudy, dark, and turbulent once more. It stayed that way for more than a minute. He had difficulty forming the projection. It finally settled down and the Ammun Mettell was back. He picked up the knife and orange again and went back to work with slow careful cuts.

"We've done some good things…good things…even here …on Earth, under conditions…that…" The Ammun Mettell lost interest in continuing the thought. He picked up a new orange. He held the knife to it. He struggled to focus. The orange fell on the ground, bounced and rolled. The knife clattered to the ground. The Ammun Mettell was gone for-ever.

36 | Epilog

Two months later

JORGAN ROME ADDRESSED Barteng. "Stay close to Raia. Whatever you do, don't get separated." Barteng nodded. He stood next to Raia. Both of them wore full Mettellite uniforms. Barteng had a robe as well, marking him as an Ammun.

"Are you…?"

"I can do this. I probably know their political situation better than they do," said Barteng. Over the previous five years, Barteng had headed up teams of Mettellite specialists who advised the Ammun Mettell. Before he visited a distant planet, the Ammun Mettell knew exactly what to say to keep the local alliance strong and to keep Calcha away. Now the Ammun Mettell was gone but Barteng was even better informed. The Dar Telku's communications and spy network enabled instant updates from inside the top level of the governments on nearby planets. "But…"

"But?" asked Jorgan Rome. "But it doesn't seem like enough?"

"That's right," said Barteng. "I want to do more than just keeping her out of the neighborhood."

"We're going to need the new technology for that. About a month, now?"

The Dar Telku shook her head. "It's ready now. Well, mostly."

"But we need to deploy a deep network of projectors," said Jorgan Rome. "And I need a fast ship."

"I understand," said Barteng. "I think…"

The Dar Telku interrupted. "He's alone now. You've got to go."

Barteng shook his head. He still had a hard time believing that the Dar Telku could see and monitor the leader of a distant planet from here.

"I want to take the fight to Calcha," said Barteng.

"We will," said Jorgan Rome before Barteng and Raia disappeared.

Chapter One of *Falcon, Storm, and Song*

1

JORGAN ROME, Cholley, and Raia had traveled far, so very far, for nothing. Discussions with the Vicenarian League weren't going well. The three of them, but mostly Jorgan Rome, had been talking with twelve members of the Vicenarian delegation. Now Jorgan Rome, Cholley, and Raia had twelve Vicenarian bzzapmasters aimed at their heads.

In the next moment, the Dar Telku appeared in a far corner of the council chamber . She turned to Jorgan Rome and said, "Something's come up that needs your attention."

"Not now," said Jorgan Rome. "This is really not a good time."

The Vicenarians turned their attention to the Dar Telku. "Who are you?" one of them asked. "Are you an accomplice?" asked another of the Vicenarians.

"An accomplice? Hardly!" said the Dar Telku. In response, the Vicenarians, every one of them, let loose with their weapons. She was vaporized in an instant.

"We don't like surprises," said a Vicenarian.

The Dar Telku reappeared. "What was that about?" she asked.

The distraction provided by the Dar Telku was all that Jorgan Rome's side needed. Raia pulled out her karamand and the Vicenarian weapons vanished. Cholley, who had been spinning fiercely, flew out in twelve pieces. Twelve different subCholleys found their targets. The Vicenarians fell to the ground in pain, clutching at their faces.

"Go easy, Cholley," said Jorgan Rome. Cholley re-assembled himself.

"I guess we'll have to agree to disagree," said Jorgan Rome to the Vicenarians writhing on the ground. He nodded at Raia who used the karamand to bring them back to Earth.

"The master negotiator returns!" said the Dar Telku after they appeared in her reception room. Jorgan Rome shook his head.

"Look before you project!" said Raia.

"I did," said the Dar Telku. "And you can thank me for that later, young lady!"

"They were going to come around," said Jorgan Rome. "But that's done. What have you got for me?"

"We've been intercepting messages," said the Dar Telku. "On strange wavelengths, on particle streams, from strange locations all over the galaxy. But they're tagged so that they piece together. It's very strange."

"Okay. Granted. Why do I care?"

"It's peculiar because we—I mean this laboratory—are almost certainly the only people who could detect, let alone assemble all of these messages and put them together."

Jorgan Rome said, "So these messages are private and they're intended for you. That's obvious. What do they say?"

"Do you know someone named Jeri Chette?" asked the Dar Telku.

Jorgan Rome took half a step backwards. With his mouth he made a silent "oh!" He said, "Jeri Chette would know about your capabilities. Everyone knows I'm here, it seems. She would, too. I guess it's natural."

"If she wants to talk to me she could just talk to me. Or you," said the Dar Telku.

"Not if she's onto something. If she's discovered something. Or if she's in danger."

"She gets into danger a lot, then?" asked Teera. Jorgan Rome raised his eyebrows and nodded.

Jorgan Rome said, "Show me what you have."

"There are gaps," said the Dar Telku. "We're still working. Here's what we believe is the first message chronologically."

The floor-to-ceiling monitor in the Dar Telku's reception area came to life with a grainy, yellowish, monochrome image of a young woman. "My name is Jeri Chette," she said. With a hint of a smile, she said, "This message is intended for Jorgan Rome." Then, turning all business, she said "Excerpts of my notebook to follow." That was the end of the message.

Jorgan Rome said, "She's found something and she wants me to know."

"Rubbing it in?" asked Cholley.

"Maybe. But I don't think so. I think she has something that she genuinely wants me to know about." Turning to the Dar Telku, he asked, "What more have you got?"

"We have a jumble of still images. We're still trying to put them together. They're from a notebook," said the Dar Telku. "Is it normal to keep a handwritten notebook?"

"She always has," said Jorgan Rome.

The Dar Telku said, "Here's the first one we managed to assemble. I'd call it encrypted, but that would be an understatement. Bringing it up now."

The monitor showed a single notebook page with crisp handwriting. A notation at the top told them it was page number 253.

Jorgan Rome said, "That's Jeri Chette's writing."

"…luck following that source. The star-hop map I've drawn on page 117 has a gap. Which I only just noticed. Seems important, so I set out. Approached the system. Came under fire. They came out of nowhere behind the smallest outer planet. Didn't expect that but was able to maneuver around them and take them out. (Thanks JR, good ship)."

"Star-hop map? What century are we in?" asked Cholley.

"What millennium, you mean," said Teera.

"Whoever she's looking for, I guess, must still use star-hop maps," said Jorgan Rome.

The rest of the page read:

Dropped probes on the main planet. Looks uninhabited but I don't think so. Only one probe saw anything. A building, big like a ritual site, with this mark carved big on the main plaza

Probe saw a flash of light just before its final transmission. Likely destroyed. Will land and investigate.

The rest of the page was empty.

"Not good," muttered Jorgan Rome.

"What?" asked the Dar Telku.

"Lots of things. For one, the idea of landing just like that. For another, that symbol. That's the star-and-triangle!"

"Old symbol of the Dualists," said Teera.

"That's right. And they were a rough bunch," said Jorgan Rome.

"That was a very long time ago," said Teera.

"Thousands of years. I always heard that their culture collapsed entirely. But you never know. Cholley and I have found some strange, old things thriving in offbeat parts of this galaxy."

"You think that maybe…"

"And I'm hoping not. Maybe I shouldn't say this about an entire culture, but those people wouldn't be missed."

"Who were they?" asked the Dar Telku.

"The star-and-triangle people? Well, you'd want to stay well away from them. They believed in a brutal kind of dualism. A complete merger of opposites. For them, an agent of control was simultaneously an agent of chaos."

"OK, like Yin and Yang?" asked the Dar Telku.

"Early on, maybe. But not at their zenith. Dualism became a rough, dog-eat-dog business. It wasn't long before Yin was out. Baxter was in."

"Yang and Baxter," said Cholley.

"That's right," said Jorgan Rome. "And their principle of Dynamic Tension made them strong."

"I used to hear stories about them. Really dark fairy tales for kids," said Raia.

"Teera, you have the cultural history of Naveer at your fingertips. Anything on the Dualists?"

"Not much. The Dualists never came anywhere near
Naveer. At least when they were alive."

"What are you getting at?"

"Their dead would come to visit. The Dualists had strange
burial practices. They would put bodies into very long, thin,
black rockets. The rocket was a kind of space sarcophagus,
sent on its way for eternity. Most of what is known for sure
about the Dualists comes from the study of captured rockets
and their grave goods. Which are always weapons."

"Remarkable," said Jorgan Rome.

"The rockets are also very difficult to detect. They're
practically invisible."

"Ha!" said the Dar Telku. "I can see them. Those rockets,
they sound like the kind of anomalous derelicts that I find
from time to time in deep space scans."

"Can you show us one?" asked Jorgan Rome.

The Dar Telku nodded. She turned to one of her tech
specialists and said, "Bring up Anomaly…oh..let's try Anomaly Three-Seven."

"Sure," said the lab tech. "It's right…wait…there it is."

But there was nothing on the screen. At first there was
only the gray-blackness of deep space. Until the imaging
system set in to modulate its sources. Only then did the
barest shimmering outline of a long narrow tube come into
view. After a minute or so, the imaging system found its
lock. The tube became a coal-black derelict rocket, over two
hundred meters in length, covered from nose to tail with
hieroglyphs in relief.

"Oh, you mean the 'deadspears,'" said Raia. "That's what
we called them. It was illegal to go anywhere near them."

"Why?"

"People said that some of them were booby-trapped. Like really bad. Bring one of them home, and the explosion could take out half of your planet."

Jorgan Rome turned to the Dar Telku. "So, why do you track them?"

"Oh, no reason, I guess," said the Dar Telku.

"Well, there's the salvage operation we're planning," offered the lab tech. The Dar Telku stared daggers at him. He returned to his work.

The Dar Telku said quickly, "I wasn't really going to do it. I mean, we were just talking about it. That's all."

After a few minutes, the lab tech raised his hand.

"Yes?" said the Dar Telku.

"I've just managed to put together another page. It's marked 'Page 58.' Makes it the earliest one yet."

…story as the other two places. Mostly destroyed. Only a few survivors. Good news is survivors saw the direction of the rocket: went toward the Khar cloud. Now three sightings, all Khar cloud.

Approaching Khar cloud region. Big. Won't find rockets by scanning.

Asked around for rocket repair. All booked. I said it was for the "big guy." Response: "The Falcon?"

Confirmed. Falcon operative. Falcon in Khar cloud region.

"Who's the 'Falcon?'"

"Never heard of him."

Raia said, "I have. In stories anyway. He's kind of a Revenger character. Grownups would tell us scary Falcon stories when we were children. The idea of a Falcon story was to keep you home; otherwise, the Falcon would get you. The Falcon had no mercy. The Falcon was immortal. He came from the People Before. He wandered space to take out our kind."

The Dar Telku said, "There's no mention of a 'Falcon' in the Makha Miffin," referring to the collected mythology of Raia's people.

Raia said, "No. There wouldn't be. Not there. Stories of the Falcon are really dark. And they're just stories anyway, meant to scare you."

Teera said, "Maybe. Maybe not. Do you remember any of the stories?"

"Sure, OK. They're usually about children doing something wrong. Like…OK, I remember one of them. A boy and a girl, brother and sister. They go off somewhere, somewhere they shouldn't go. No…that's right, they find a rocket and fly off in it. They're just having fun. They plan to come right back but something happens. An old guy appears on the ship with them. He just materializes out of nowhere, behind them. They hear him breathing because it's really loud, so they turn around and see him. He has thin, gray hair. Moist eyes. He rasps out the words, 'I am the Falcon. And you are mine!' Then he opens his hand and flings some gray powder at them."

"Fungus attack," said Jorgan Rome.

Raia continued, "The boy gets hit with more of the powder than his sister, maybe because she's sitting forward at the controls or something. Then the old guy disappears. The brother and sister manage to fly home. They don't tell anyone about what they did or what happened. But a couple of days later the boy gets sick. Wait! No…they both get sick and the boy dies but she gets better."

"He's probably not really dead," said Jorgan Rome.

"That's right," said Raia. "The night before the funeral, the girl can't sleep. She feels pulled, like something wants her to go for a walk. So she gets up, dresses, and goes out. Without knowing why, she goes to the outskirts of the settlement. She goes to the Space Defense Battery, which are these guns that protect the settlement. And she sees her brother. He's alive and he's working hard. He has lowered the guns until they point at the settlement. He blasts the settlement into nothingness."

"Horrible!" said Teera.

"It's just a story," said Raia.

"Maybe not," said Jorgan Rome.

"The story's not finished," said Raia. "What happens at the end is a rocket ship lands and the boy walks on to it. And the girl just barely stops herself from climbing aboard and going with him. The rocket ship takes off."

There was a long pause after Raia finished.

"So…space zombies?" asked Cholley.

"After plans one through eight have failed, what do you have left?" asked Teera.

"No," said Jorgan Rome. "This is something serious."

"Be serious. Do you think this Falcon really exists?" asked the Dar Telku.

"Jeri Chette apparently does. And she's usually right about this sort of thing." The Dar Telku snorted.

"But you can't believe that this Falcon is some kind of immortal?"

"No, of course not. But we don't know very much, either."

"But these funerary ships, the…"

"The deadspears," said Raia.

"The deadspears," said the Dar Telku. "If you think this Falcon has anything to do with those things…"

Jorgan Rome turned to the large monitor screen showing the hazy, gray sparkly image of a deadspear. "I didn't say that. That deadspear has been underway for maybe ten thousand years. That's a long time." said Jorgan Rome, settling into a chair to contemplate. The room went silent.

"Wait!" said Jorgan Rome.

"I saw that, too." said Teera.

"What?" asked the Dar Telku.

"It just changed course," said Jorgan Rome. "Just barely, it was just a slight correction, but it happened!"

"I confirm that," said Teera.

"What in the world is going on here?" asked Jorgan Rome.

Nobody said anything for several minutes. The Dar Telku and the lab tech worked furiously at their instruments.

Jorgan Rome said, "Start watching as many of these as you can. If possible, and for every deadspear you can locate, I'd like to know where it's coming from and where it's going." The Dar Telku bridled at taking commands in her own preserve. She started to say something scathing, but thought better of it.

Jorgan Rome said, "I'm going to go take a walk." Everyone knew what that meant. Jorgan Rome needed time to think. And he wanted to consult with Cholley. Nobody said anything. Cholley caught up with Jorgan Rome as he exited the building.

"What has Jeri Chette gotten herself into?" asked Jorgan Rome.

"Something big. Again," said Cholley.

"She really finds these things, doesn't she?" said Jorgan Rome.

"She knows what she's doing."

"Does she?"

Cholley knew better than to answer that. They moved through the landscaped outskirts of the Dar Telku's research compound. Jorgan Rome set a fast pace. Cholley easily kept up, throwing out tendrils before him and rolling them up.

"Well, I owe her one," said Jorgan Rome after a few minutes.

Cholley waited for Jorgan Rome to complete his thought.

"A rescue," said Jorgan Rome.

"Are we going to rescue Jeri Chette?" asked Cholley.

"I think so. Yes."

"She's not going to like it," said Cholley.

That was chapter one of *Falcon, Storm, and Song*.

www.ingramcontent.com/pod-product-compliance
Lightning Source LLC
Chambersburg PA
CBHW061233310726
48971CB00007B/2052